RISE OF THE STRONGEST SOVEREIGN

BOOK 6

RISE OF THE STRONGEST SOVEREIGN

BOOK 6

KAZ HUNTER

Podium

Cover design by Xiaoraini

ISBN: 978-1-0394-5465-1

Published in 2025 by Podium Publishing
www.podiumentertainment.com

RISE OF THE STRONGEST SOVEREIGN

BOOK 6

CHAPTER ONE

[Level: 78]

    [Name: Jason Lee]

[Skills:]

[Monster Trainer: Tame a wild monster of an equal or lower power.]

[. . .]

[Weapons:]

[Beowulf's Dagger]

[Celestial Dagger]

[Ascalon]

[Dagger of Kings]

[Dagger of Doom]

[Dagger of Friendship]

[Incendiary Dagger]

[Dagger of the Ancients]

[. . .]

[Initializing Livestream . . .]

[Connected.]

Portal energy flares around me. This time it's a deep reddish color. The color of blood. Lightning continues to zap at me as I tumble down through the long twisting tunnel, sucked onward toward . . . Well, I honestly don't know where.

A moment earlier, I was minding my own business in the clubhouse of Mr. Wang. Well, preparing for war, I suppose. If you're one of the monsters I'm fighting, I suppose I wasn't *technically* minding my own business, but however you look at it, I wasn't actively trying to kill anyone, which makes this incursion particularly annoying.

[ChaosRider: Ahh!!! Is Jason going to be okay???]

[ShadowDancer: I'm sure he'll be fine! Just stay focused, Jason, and you can do it!]

[ViperQueen: Yeah! Go Jason!!! He's our man! If he can't do it, no one can!]

[DarkCynic: If I'm being honest, ViperQueen, that's sorta my fear. If he can't stop these things, we're all dead.]

I grit my teeth—at least as best as I can; the inside of portals sort of turn you into interdimensional soup—and focus on the chat. It's true. We're dealing with entities that, thousands of years ago, came to Earth and were revered as gods. If I can't stop these things, there's no one else who will be able to do a thing to prevent the slaughter from coming to our world. I have to succeed . . . or everyone else is going to pay the price for my failure.

[GrendleH8tr: You've got this, kid. Just take everything you've learned over the past dungeons and put it into practice.

Keep your head down and don't think too much. Trust your gut and trust your pets. They'll know what to do.]

I breathe a bit easier when I see GrendleH8tr's message. His real name is Beowulf, of course, and he's helped me out a good bit in the past. I do my best to focus, then nod slowly.

I'm ready, or at least as ready as I'll ever be. Now, all that's left is to face—

ZAP!

Another blast of lightning hits me and hits me *good*. I groan as I'm flung out of the portal and land in the dirt. Dust puffs up around me, and I slowly climb to my feet, looking around me. It's dark . . . almost painfully so. Then, with a brilliant flash, spotlights come blazing down.

"Welcome, welcome, one and all!" The high-pitched voice laughs, sounding as if it's projected by some sort of speaker system. "Come and sit down! Sit, and watch the demise of Earth's mightiest hero!"

I squint my eyes against the glare. All around me, lit up like a stage, is a ring of dirt surrounded by a low red-and-white-striped barrier. The ring is probably fifty feet wide, maybe even a bit wider, which gives me a good bit of room. Beyond that, it's hard to tell, but I think I can see . . . bleachers? Overhead, I see what seems to be a striped canopy. I'm in a . . . a circus?

[LunarEclipse: WHAT IS THIS???]

[GoldenShield: Hmm. I have a guess, but I'm not going to say anything in case I'm wrong.]

[IceQueen: This isn't good, for sure. Jason, get out of there if you can!]

I don't say anything as I see dark forms beginning to fill in the bleachers. Most of them are warped and grotesque, with glowing eyes and what seem to be a wide assortment of sharp-looking weapons and claws. I slowly turn, looking around at everything . . . and suddenly, a blast of green smoke rises up from the middle of the ring. When it clears away, I find myself looking at a man in a dapper ringmaster's uniform, a cane behind his back, top hat set squarely upon his head. He has a sinister grin upon his face, and I stalk slowly toward him.

"Ah, none of that!" He holds up a finger, and chains form around my feet, locking me in place. "There are rules to follow here! I think you'll find that this isn't the ordinary sort of dungeon. Nothing will be ordinary from here on out, actually."

"Then start talking," I grind out. "Give me the rules so I know exactly how I can crush you."

"None of that, now." The man begins to twirl his cane around in front of him. "It's quite simple, really. You're Earth's champion. I have three champions here with me. You kill them and I'll come out and face you myself. If you kill me, I'll let you out of this dungeon."

Around me, the crowd begins to laugh, and the man sighs and leans upon his cane. "Of course, the odds of that are . . . low."

"One might even say they're low . . . key," I say and raise an eyebrow. "Loki?"

"That's me!" He cackles and pushes himself upright once more, twirling his cane through his hands. "Oh, this is going to be *fun!* It's been years since Thor let me do anything other than terrorizing small villages."

"You know that if they sent you to face me first, it's because you're the most expendable, right?"

"Silence!" Loki snaps and points the cane at me. A blast of magic erupts from the end, and a metal bracket fits itself around my mouth. I reach up and feel about the edges. I'm fairly certain I could rip it off if I wanted to, but I decide it would be a good idea for him to think I'm slightly weaker than I really am. "Now, more rules. If you step out of the ring, you'll die. You won't be attacked, you'll just die. Same thing will happen if you're thrown out of the ring, or tossed out, or kicked out, or so on. Let's see . . . Nope, that's all the rules! Fight, win or die, and go on with life!" Loki starts to turn away, then pauses. "Oh, and one more thing. You know how everyone sort of vanished from the club, back before I brought you here?"

I nod, desperately wanting to say something.

"Well, I have them right here."

Bodies, wrapped in chains, come tumbling down from above. They all stop with a crash about ten feet above the ground. Some of them are hanging upside down, some sideways, others upright. I can see Mr. Wang, Elrith, John, Ali, and so many others. After I've had a chance to see them, they shoot back up into the darkness above.

"If you beat me, you'll get them all back. If you don't, I'll kill them." Loki starts to back up. "Don't worry, it won't be quick or painless. They'll have plenty of time to contemplate their deeds in life. I might even give them a chance to serve me in the afterlife. We'll just have to see." He shrugs and sighs. "Alright, this talking is getting boring. We'll just free you . . ."

He fires two bursts of magic from his cane. The chains

and the bracket over my mouth both dissolve, and I lunge forward just as fast as I can. He simply laughs and touches the ground with his cane, and a great blast of smoke comes rolling upward.

". . . And I'll bring in my first champion! From the realm of Niflheim, the great ice giant . . . Bah, I don't remember his name. Here we go!"

The smoke becomes thicker, and I draw up short. Suddenly, it clears away, and I find myself staring up at a twenty-foot-tall ice giant.

The thing seems to be made entirely of ice and is proportioned more or less like a human. He holds a large staff set with a head made of ice that glows with an odd blue color. A crown sits upon his head, and he snarls down at me with a fierce glare. Yellow teeth peek out from blue lips, and he slowly swings his staff and advances forward.

Whoosh.

Whoosh.

He's feeling me out, trying to see if I'll attack quickly or hold back. I've taken on bigger monsters before, so I'm not worried, but I do need to be careful. One hit from this fellow could knock me out of the ring, and if *that* happens, I'm dead. I draw out Beowulf's Dagger and the Celestial Dagger, holding both weapons tightly as he advances.

"I've heard much about you," the giant snarls as he swings his staff again. "I expected more."

"I'm not one to be goaded into attacking early," I answer back. "I'll come when I'm good and ready, and you'll know it when I do."

"Then I had best not give you the time."

The giant raises the staff over his head, then slams it down into the ground. A concussive blast of ice and snow erupts outward from the point of impact, and I rush forward with all my might.

I lash out with the Celestial Dagger and hit the wave of ice and snow dead-on. I swing with force, and the dagger cuts through the blast just like a physical object. The ice and snow part and go past me on either side, and with that, I charge forward just as fast as I can. The ice giant snarls and rips his staff back up from the ground, then twirls it around his head and strikes once more.

This time it sweeps horizontally across the ground, drawing a great blast of icy wind along with it. I fall flat on my back and brace myself as it passes by, then jump back to my feet and dart toward the giant again. This time I'm able to shoot straight past his defenses and reach his feet, and I lash outward with all my might.

Beowulf's Dagger hits him in the leg between the knee and the ankle, and a great blast of light explodes through him. Cracks erupt outward from the point of impact, lancing both upward and downward in the same instant, and the giant howls and leaps backward. I move to follow him, but he spins the staff sharply and whacks me in the chest.

The blow is crushing, and I'm lifted off my feet and thrown backward. As my feet leave the ground, I have a moment of panic. Thankfully, I don't go very high, and I slam into the barrier an instant later.

"Would you look at that?" Loki's voice erupts through the

air, and the crowd begins to laugh and cheer. "We have first blood struck! Doesn't look too good for Jacy, eh? The giant has his dander up, that's for sure!"

"My name is Hrungnir!" the giant roars.

"Yeah, no one can pronounce that when speaking modern English," Loki says, dismissing the concern. "Would you just crush him, please?"

The giant snarls and points his staff at me, and I see magic bloom inside. Quickly, I jump to my feet, but the giant is a smidge faster. A great blast of ice erupts outward and flows around me like water. It freezes solid in the blink of an eye, encasing me in a thick layer of ice. I lose almost all my vision, and what I *can* see is distorted and irregular. The giant snarls and starts walking toward me—I can feel that much—and I clench all my muscles.

[ShadowDancer: This is a whole new level of combat! Is this the end of Jason?]

[DarkCynic: Nah. He'll get out. I know how I would do it, but Jason probably has a different plan.]

[GoldenShield: Come on! You can do it!!!]

In all reality, there are probably better ways of breaking free, but I'm in panic mode and brute force seems like the best option. I strain outward, forward, and upward with all my might. Around me, the ice slowly begins to crack.

Pop.

Crick.

Ping!

It's going slowly. I can't breathe, since I'm encased in ice, and my vision starts to darken even more. The giant stops right in front of me, and he raises his staff. He's going to crush me with a single blow, and I'm going to be helpless to stop it. With one final heave, knowing full well that it might be my last, I lunge upward.

CRASH!

Ice explodes around me as I break free of the prison. The staff comes tearing down through the air, and I lash upward with both of my daggers, crossing their blades. They form an X that catches the shaft just beneath the head. I'm driven to my knees and find myself staring up at an icy death.

"You're powerful. That's more of what I was—"

I let out a cry and shove upward, throwing off the staff as hard as I can. The giant staggers backward, just slightly, and I bolt forward before he can stop me. With all my might, I slash my Celestial Dagger across the giant's left knee, then carve Beowulf's Dagger across his right. I then duck between his legs as he comes crashing down to his knees. I'm behind him now and take advantage of that fact.

He lost about five feet of height, maybe seven, when he dropped. I use that fact to my advantage and leap upward as hard as I can, then throw a blow to the back of his skull. It lands perfectly, and he groans and topples forward, then lands face-first on the ground with a resounding crash. He's far from dead, though, and twirls his staff as he rolls over onto his back.

"Death, human!"

A great blast of ice and snow roars off his staff, but I jump into the air, dodging it, and come down on his torso. Before he can stop me, I drive Beowulf's Dagger deep into his gut and slice upward, carving a long path from his navel to his throat. With that, I rip it out, spin, and move to deliver a killing blow to his neck.

He tries feebly to stop me, but it's in vain, and I bring the weapons smashing down. Ice cracks, and his head bounces away from his body. I give it a kick to send it further away, preventing a few sparks of healing energy from saving him at the last instant. Slowly, his body begins to crack, and then the whole thing crumbles into nothing but a pile of slush.

"That's one champion down." I turn and gaze out across the crowd. "Send me the next one. I'd like to get to Loki before lunchtime."

A peal of laughter echoes down, and green smoke begins to slowly swirl about.

"Oh, you do, do you? Well . . . we'll just have to see about that."

The laughter grows louder, and the green smoke billows in a circle, obscuring everything behind the barrier of the circus ring. I keep myself focused, gripping my daggers tightly. I don't know what's coming next . . . but I'm quite certain that Loki isn't going to let me off the hook easily, not if he can at all avoid it.

CHAPTER TWO

When the smoke clears away, I find that the whole landscape has changed. The spotlights are gone. The bleachers are gone. The tent is gone. The circus ring is still there, but it's grown by a fairly substantial amount. Beyond those red and white stripes is nothing but scorched wasteland. Flame. Lava. Death. I can see massive bones poking up here and there and in the distance, several fiery mountains. I'm standing in a volcanic wasteland, and that's the long and the short of it.

"Alright." I toss the Celestial Dagger into the air, then catch it again by the handle. "This is that fire realm, right? Uh, let me see if I can remember those mythology books I read in high school. Hel?"

Loki laughs loudly. "Muspelheim! Land of demons, as your tongue would render them."

"Which means that I'm going to be fighting Surtur."

"Technically, the name is Surtr," Loki's voice snaps.

"So, *his* name you care about," I point out.

[DarkCynic: I don't mean to be a pain, but you probably shouldn't be debating with the god of mischief. He's going to win.]

[ViperQueen: Yeah, but if Jason can antagonize him, it might go in his favor!]

[ChaosRider: Or it might just end in Jason getting squashed.]

[FireStorm: True. Be careful, Jason!]

I keep my head level and focus on the landscape in front of me. With a rumble, a crack breaks open on the opposite side of the arena. There's another loud rumble, and the ground begins to shake.

"It does not matter to you, mortal, what I care about and what I do not!" Loki shrieks. "What you need to know is that you will die! Or I will kill you myself!"

"I do believe that defeating you is an option open to me," I point out. "Just saying."

Loki doesn't say anything more, though I do hear some laughter that makes me think that the audience *is* still around, I just can't see them. In any case, a massive hand shoots up out of the crack and grabs hold of the ground, and Surtr slowly begins to pull himself upward.

Now, in most cases, I consider myself to be somewhat of a gentleman. I'm not going to say that I go out of my way for it, but I'm not going to shoot a man in the back, I'm not going to pick on someone—at least another human—smaller than myself, and I'm not going to engage in battle before the other person is ready. In *this* case, however, I decide to make an exception.

Surtr is just starting to haul himself out of the hole as I come charging up. He looks huge, taller than the ice giant I just fought, and has long black hair that falls down his back. Otherwise, he actually looks fairly human, all things considered. Darkish skin, like he just spent a month or so living on a beach in the Caribbean, and black eyes—other than his size, he looks kind of like a guy that you might sit down and have a beer with. I mean, you'd be keeping a close eye on your wallet while you did it, but he doesn't look terrible.

I suppose that's why I feel a bit bad as I slash my knives across his knuckles.

He lets out a startled scream and drops back down into the depths of the earth. I laugh and twirl my daggers as I look down into the pit after him. The ground trembles, and Loki laughs as well.

That's probably not good.

"Ooooooooooooh, bad choice, mortal! You're going to regret that one. Who here thinks that Jason is about to *severely* regret the decisions he's made in this ring? One, two, twenty, fifty, everyone? Yup, I agree! Hang on, little Jace, here he comes!"

A great blast of fire and smoke rolls up from the crack, and the heat swells to an immense level. I grimace and step backward, and with one final blast of fire, Surtr emerges. The ground closes up beneath him, and he snarls. He's probably twenty-five feet tall and has a glare across his face that could peel paint off a barn. I grit my teeth and stare back up at him, not at all certain that I'm ready for what comes next.

"Filthy human! You come into my realm and challenge me?" Surtr roars and draws out a flaming sword. "You'll pay for that!"

"In fairness, I was brought here against my will." I hold up a hand. "Not that you'll—"

Surtr swings the sword, sending a great gout of flame roaring across the battlefield. I brace myself as flames wash over me, and my health drops by about a quarter. The heat seems to burn straight through my armor and into my bones. It *hurts*—there's no two ways about it—and I try to keep from screaming. As the flames die down, Surtr thunders forward, and I rush forward to meet him.

He swings the sword again, and I narrowly manage to jump over the blow. The giant grunts, not really liking that, and begins to swing wildly. The sword is a good fifteen feet long and sends flames roaring across the area like living things. I'm forced to dodge back and forth, then suddenly see an opening and shoot forward. I've managed to sneak past his guard before he knows what's happening, and with that, I strike.

With all my might, I slash at his legs, then jump upward and land a long slash across his gut. Surtr howls, and I smile and press my attack . . . at least for a moment. Suddenly, a hand reaches down and snatches me up by the waist, and Surtr lifts me above his head.

"Puny human. Survive this."

With that, he flings me to the ground like a toddler throwing a bouncy ball. The only real difference is that I don't bounce. Mostly, I just *splat*. It hurts even worse than the flame, and I groan and slowly climb back to my feet, rubbing my bruised arms and legs as Surtr snarls and stalks toward me.

"Pathetic. I've fought wild animals that have fought better than you do!"

"Well, in all fairness to the animal kingdom, I do believe that humans have learned the vast majority of our fighting techniques from such creatures." I don't really know what to think of the giant in front of me. He's going to be tricky, that's for sure. My health is sitting at around a quarter full, but I have a feeling that he's not going to let me heal. I need to take him down, or at least figure out a way to cripple him. "Try this one out for size!"

[LunarEclipse: OOH! What's Jason going to do now?]

[FireStorm: I bet he's going to do some crazy Kung Fu or something! Like a mantis or a snake!]

[ShadowDancer: Nah, he's going to do something more American! Like a grizzly bear!]

I charge forward, then feint left. Surtr swings his sword in that direction, and I spin around to the right to avoid the immense blast of flame that cloaks the ground. The fire gives me cover, but instead of charging up to challenge Surtr directly, I head through the flames—the milder ones, mind you—to attack the sword itself.

As the flames clear away, Surtr blinks and steps back, trying to find me. He doesn't notice me until it's too late, and I attack his sword hand with every ounce of strength I can muster. My twin daggers cut through his right wrist, and the hand, with his sword, clatters to the ground. Surtr screams and steps back, and I quickly snatch at the sword.

Thankfully, the weapon shrinks down to fit in my own hands, and I tuck my daggers back into my inventory as I take a firm grip on Surtr's sword—which, as a side note, has that exact same name. Surtr snarls down at me, but he knows better than to attack. Slowly, he looks down at the stump of his wrist, then breathes flame across it. The stench of roasting flesh fills the air, and he raises his left hand.

"All you've done is bought yourself a few extra seconds. I hope you enjoy them."

With that, a great ball of liquid flame forms in his left palm. He grunts, then heaves it down at me. I race to the side, and the ball explodes as it strikes, sending boiling lava lapping across the ground. Some of it splashes on me, but I ignore the pain and run toward the monster.

Surtr growls, then forms another ball of fire and throws it at me. This time I brace myself, then raise my sword. Well, *his* sword, but you get the idea. The ball of fire hits the weapon, and I carve it straight in two. Flame burns past on either side of me, but I come through it in one piece. As the fire dies away, Surtr gapes, and he lifts both his arms to the sky.

"Impossible!"

"I'd say that your definition of that word differs slightly from mine." I race forward as fast as my legs will possibly take me. As I come up to the giant, he brings both of his arms crashing down, and long trails of flame fall from the sky. Streaks of fire drawn on immense meteors split the air apart as they tumble down to the planet below. There are dozens, if not hundreds, and I know that my life is about to get a *lot* more difficult.

As the projectiles begin to come crashing down, painful bits of shrapnel sting against my cheeks and hands. I ignore them and slash at Surtr, hitting him on one of the legs. Quickly, I spin and inflict another gash across his calf. He stumbles and falls, and I slash upward, cutting him across his chin. His bottom jaw is smashed up into his top jaw, and he groans before snarling and punching outward.

I'm hit in the gut and knocked backward, where I smash into the barrier once more. This time the barrier bends and cracks, and I start to fall through. I'm only *just* able to catch myself and stagger forward—just in time to be hit by one of the falling meteoroids. This time I'm flattened against the ground, and my health drops to just the barest little sliver you ever did see.

My chat explodes with advice, and I draw in a deep breath. Some people tell me to strike fast and hard, other people tell me that I need to be using my daggers again. After all, I'm really not a swordsman—I've always been a dagger sort of guy. That said, I ignore it all. I know precisely what I'm going to do.

I'm going to call in the cavalry.

"Bjorn," I mutter through clenched lips. "I need you to show this fire monster what it's like to handle a bit of cold."

With a flash, my pocket dimension opens, and a white-furred paw steps out. The air seems to chill as Bjorn emerges, more powerful than ever, and tilts his head back to look up at the giant. I stare up at the beast, snarling softly, and Surtr laughs.

"A little puppy? Did you come to play, puppy? You're nothing more than—"

Bjorn lets out a howl that shakes the ground. The flames trailing off the meteors suddenly fade away as all the heat is sucked out of them. Frost grows across the ground. The flames trailing up from the fissures all vanish. Surtr suddenly clasps himself and shivers, then raises his left hand. Though I can tell that it takes some effort, he forms another fireball in his hand and prepares to launch it down at us.

"Nice try, but—"

I brace myself, then race forward, flashing toward the great beast. At that same moment, Balder steps forth as well and braces himself for a trick that we've done quite a few times. Where Bjorn has the ability to control ice and his wife, Astrid, has the ability to control both fire and seismic activity, Balder has the ability to create shock waves and to exert some sort of telekinetic power over his surroundings. Honestly, it's a little vague, and I don't really understand it, but as long as it's working, I suppose that I don't need to. I jump up into the air, and Balder barks. A shock wave erupts across the landscape and hits my feet, then launches me up into the air toward the giant's face.

Surtr snarls and throws a massive punch at me, but Balder howls as well, and the fist slams into an invisible force field. Surtr grunts, but I flash straight past his fist and slam into his face, where I slash his own sword across his nose.

A chunk of severed flesh drops down to the ground to land with a splat, and I start to fall as well. As I go down, I slash across his neck with the sword, then land one hit on his belly as I go past. When I hit the ground, I see him swaying, but not enough. Fire blossoms in his palm, and I back up.

"Bjorn, freeze him to the core! Balder, be ready!"

Bjorn's howl grows louder and targets Surtr directly. Ice grows across his feet, then up his legs. It pauses there, and Surtr's face becomes more intense. The fire dies out of his palm, and his skin starts to turn more blue. Suddenly, a spike of ice erupts from his chest as his heart freezes, and I nod to Balder.

"Now!"

With one more sharp yelp, a powerful shock wave blasts across the arena and hits him squarely. He explodes into little frozen slivers and comes clattering down all around. I let out a long sigh of relief and slowly sheath his sword as the last of him lands with a splat.

[You have leveled up!]

[Congratulations! You are now Level 79!]

"Getting there, getting there." I slowly turn and look back around as I try to find Loki. He's nowhere to be seen, and I order Bjorn and Balder back into the pocket dimension. "Soon enough we'll get up to level ninety-five, and then onward from there. Until then . . . I reckon we've just got to get to Loki before we're able to do much more."

CHAPTER THREE

Within seconds, green smoke billows up all around me, swirling and churning and raging. Well, around the edge of the ring. It seems to expand a bit more, and I slowly brace myself, wondering what the next champion is going to be.

[IceQueen: Ooh! I bet you're going to have to fight that giant wolf thing!]

[LunarEclipse: Nah. He's going to have to fight a stone giant.]

[RazorEdge: Maybe a giant serpent!]

[ShadowDancer: Or a giant cow!]

[DarkCynic: A giant cow? Really?]

[ShadowDancer: It's a thing. Look it up.]

As the smoke swirls, I open up my inventory and spend a moment scrolling. Within seconds, I manage to find my supply of Pumped! soda. I have very few left, less than ten, and I sigh.

"Alright, everyone. Make sure to remind me to pick up some more Pumped! as soon as I get back to Mr. Wang's club."

A series of supportive cries come back, and I go to crack open the bottle. As I do, though, a putrid smell escapes the lid, and instead of a sharp *pop*, a faint hiss is all that comes out. I frown and glance down at the label, where I find that things have changed.

Instead of holding a bottle of normal Pumped!, I now have a bottle of Pumped! Poison. I take a sniff of the stuff and almost vomit. It smells like . . . Well . . .

"Black licorice." Loki appears with a *pop* in front of me. "Like it?"

"I think I'd rather drink dish soap." I frown down at the stuff. "What did you do to it?"

"I changed it into poison!" Loki grins, then pauses and taps his chin. "Or did I? Tell you what, take this bottle of actual poison, which I've changed into a healing potion!" He throws a small green bottle at me. I catch it and find it to be filled with a sparkling, lovely-looking liquid. "If I actually *did* change the stuff, then drinking from the poison bottle will heal you! If I *haven't* changed anything, but I've only cast an illusion, then drinking the Pumped! will heal you!"

"And if I don't drink anything?" I counter.

Loki shrugs. "We both know you have to heal before your next fight. I'll give you thirty seconds." A timer appears in the air above his head and begins counting down. "Choose wisely! I wouldn't want to be in your shoes if you choose wrong."

He vanishes again with another puff of green smoke, and I stare down at the bottles. If I make no choice, I'll almost certainly die when the next fight begins. If I choose wrong, I'll die. The problem is that I have no clue how powerful Loki's abilities truly happen to be. He *is* a god, after all. One mistake . . .

I sigh as I glance back and forth between the bottles. The timer ticks lower and lower and lower . . .

[DarkCynic: Come on, Jason! Make a choice!]

[IceQueen: Yeah! Drink the sparkly stuff!]

[ViperQueen: It's a classic trick! You can figure this out!]

I sigh, then grit my teeth. I have a feeling I know what's happening and slowly lift the bottle of Pumped! to my mouth. Instead of drinking it, though, I simply let it dribble down the front of my shirt. It would be pretty obvious as a fake-out for anyone watching . . . *except* for people watching my livestream. They only see me chugging the bottle that looks like poison and go crazy. Loki laughs and appears in front of me again.

"You chose wr—ah . . ."

He pauses as I open up my inventory and whip out another Pumped! bottle. Off guard, he doesn't have time to change it into poison before I chug it, and my health slowly starts to rise.

"Age-old tactic. They were both poisoned," I say as I toss all bottles aside. They smash to the ground, shattering into bits, and a small smile cracks across Loki's face.

"A trick. Misdirection. Perhaps we'll get along after all!" Loki laughs. "Alright, alright. Let's see . . . trickster . . . killed two of my warriors . . . Yeah, I reckon it's about time to get rid of you. Bye!"

Loki vanishes with a flash of smoke, and with that, the smoke around the circus ring fades as well. The ring has grown again and now encompasses a good two-hundred-foot radius. I slowly look around and get a sick feeling in the pit of my stomach.

Now I'm standing on a barren island in the middle of a vast, seemingly infinite ocean. Cold waves lap against the shore, just beyond the red and white barrier. The sun shines down from above, rather like a spotlight, and I slowly draw out my daggers and prepare myself for whatever comes next. I still don't remember my mythology perfectly, but I have a pretty good feeling that I know what's about to come.

With a swirl and *swoosh*, the water around the island begins to churn. Great eddies form, spinning rapidly, and I catch a glimpse of dark shapes beneath the waves.

[RazorEdge: I was right!!!]

[IceQueen: It's the world serpent!!!!]

[FireStorm: Uh . . . So, if he kills the world serpent, does that end the world?]

[ShadowDancer: Nah. Only if he kills the magic tree thing.]

[ViperQueen: Right, right.]

I smile slightly at the banter in the chat but don't have time to pay attention to it. Ascalon begins to glow warmly upon my back, and I'm reminded of the assorted buffs that I've been given against serpentine creatures. Suddenly, with a great blast of water, the serpent erupts from the water in front of me, rising up to a truly enormous height.

The bulk of the creature still seems to be in the water, and yet, its head easily arcs a good fifty or a hundred feet from the waves. It slowly looks around, then begins to lower its head as it looks down at me. Lidless eyes stare through my body, piercing my soul, and I shudder. This isn't going to be an easy fight.

"Sssssssssso . . . you are the human who dares to challenge the gods?"

"The way I hear it, I'm not the first, and I probably won't be the last." I shrug. "At the least, I won't be the last unless I manage to kill each and every monster in the entire world. I'll admit that it *is* on my bucket list, but we'll see how feasible that happens to be."

The serpent chuckles, then slowly opens its mouth. I should probably note that the mouth is large enough to swallow me whole with room to spare. Enormous fangs unfold from the roof of the mouth—fangs that glisten with venom.

"I imagine that it will be far less feasible after I'm through with you."

With a sharp hiss, the serpent comes crashing down and bites at me. I know better than to try to strike or parry the monster—it's just coming *so* fast and hard. I jump out of the way, and it hits with force, blasting shards of stone up into the air as it flashes past. I jump backward several paces, and the head of the snake dives back into the water even as the long coil of its body continues to slide across the island, forming a barrier of sorts that cuts the area in half.

Suddenly, the head explodes back out of the water and rushes forward again. It smashes into the ground and races across the island once again, parallel to its original path, but between me and the ocean. I suddenly find myself between *two* stretches of the snake, both of which are uncoiling across the stone so fast that I know the rock-hard scales will tear me to bits. It's penning me in, paring down my movements.

So, it's a smart sort of creature. I'll just have to be smarter.

When it comes up again, it seems to have a smile on its face. I'm trapped between two massive chunks of the snake, and it eyes me fiercely. Slowly, it comes forward, then drops down. Its head fits perfectly between both halves, and it opens its mouth wide.

"Die, Jason!"

With that, it flashes forward at me, and I know I have only seconds to live. Even at full health, one hit from this thing will take me down to nothingness. I think as fast as I can, and then . . . Well, I do something a bit desperate.

"Balder! I need a *really* fast favor."

Balder steps out of the pocket dimension behind me, and I run forward and jump into the air. Balder barks sharply, then dives back into his portal as the snake flashes past. I, meanwhile, go sailing over the head of the serpent and come down on its back. I land about twenty feet back and drive both of my daggers into the gaps between the monster's scales.

It's really, really hard to explain how much that hurts. For starters, as I mentioned, the scales are as hard as rocks. They're also quite sharp, *and* the serpent is moving at a good fifty miles an hour when I hit. I grip my daggers tightly enough, but the sudden sharp jarring is enough to just about rip my arms out of my sockets. Thankfully, the pain is mostly superficial, so I don't actually lose that much health, but I do let out a rather undignified yelp.

In any case, the serpent screams as well and shoots back up into the sky. That, of course, is when I realize the flaw in my plan. I need the snake to stay *inside* the ring or I'll be insta-killed by Loki. Working quickly, I start to climb up the snake, using my daggers as picks. It howls in pain with each strike and starts to thrash around.

"Not expecting this, I reckon," I snarl as I reach the base of its skull. "Let's see . . . There was this old——" I grunt as the snake snaps its head around, which causes my body to bash against the bulk of its head. I grit my teeth, then start to slide my blade around as I peel off one of the scales. "There was this old surgical technique called lobotomy."

"I've heard of it," the serpent hisses. "You have no right to touch me, filth!"

With that, the snake slings around and dives back toward the ground. In that moment, I notice that the serpent *has* cleared itself off the little island, which will give me room again. Of course, the excitement of that discovery is tempered somewhat by the fact that it's about to paste me across the ground like butter, but hey, you have to look for every little victory, right?

As it falls, I stab deep into the hole left by the scale, then leap free. I hit the ground hard, but not as hard as the serpent itself, which spins and grinds against the surface of the island as it tries to crush me beneath. I race out of the way, and it soon flops off and back into the ocean, leaving me alone. The ground now features a long channel carved by the thing, along with a great deal more gravel, but . . . Well, I'm alive, and I can't complain about that fact.

"Burnie, you're up!"

With a flash, my pocket dimension opens again, and my Phoenix shoots out. His pure white feathers almost vanish against the blue of the sky overhead, and he rises up into the air on a thermal plume that he creates himself. All around, the water churns, and far outside the ring—which is getting pulverized, I should note—the serpent rises up.

"Alright, human. If you're going to be tricky, perhaps you should try to survive *this*."

With a hiss, the serpent opens its mouth and spits a great volume of venom across the island. As it lands, rock melts and stone dissolves—it's really quite a sight. It's like watching the world's strongest acid at work, and I take a few steps back to avoid it. There's no need to guess how deadly that stuff is, to be certain.

Of course, there's no need to guess how deadly Burnie has become either.

He comes shooting down from the sky like an arrow and lets loose a great piercing blast of white flame. The purifying blast washes across the serpent's head, and it screams more loudly than I've yet heard a monster cry out. It quickly dives back under the water, and Burnie laughs and flies back up into the air.

That took its health down a good bit, Master.

"Good work, Burnie." I smile. Suddenly, a thought strikes me. "How much fire can you put out these days?"

I imagine that it's quite a bit. I've never really tested myself, to be honest.

"Well, don't kill yourself, but I need you to give yourself a bit of a stress test." I cross my arms in thought. "Heat up the ocean just as much as you can."

You've got it, Master!

With that, Burnie comes down once more and begins flying laps around the island. Gouts of piercing white flame pour across the ocean as he does so, and I hold my breath. One lap . . . two laps . . . three. The water begins to boil, and I hear a distant scream. I don't really know what it's from, but I have to imagine that it's a good thing and that it works in my favor.

Soon, the ocean, at least around the island, has begun boiling fiercely. Great fumes roll upward from the seething tide, gouts of steam and fog pouring up. Suddenly, with a great blast, the serpent reappears. It looks flushed, burned, and is *quite* angry. It stares down at me with dark eyes and opens its mouth wide.

"Die, human!"

A great blast of venom erupts from its mouth, and I move to dodge. Suddenly, I realize that the blast is spreading out far wider than I can possibly move. It was a trap. I grit my teeth and brace myself against the impact . . . but before it can connect, something shoots across my vision.

It's Burnie, white-hot and angry. With a single blast of flame, he vaporizes most of the venom, though I hear him scream in that same moment. I'm forced to watch, in horror, as he falls to the ground and flops over onto his back. A black mark stands out on his chest, a black mark that slowly begins to spread.

"Ha! Now, little human, what will you do? Without your pet, how can you—"

I set my jaw, then bend down and grab hold of a large stone. Once, it would have been a fantasy to even *think* about lifting it. Now, I'm easily able to heft it into the air, then spin and throw it as hard as I can. The projectile punches straight through the bottom of the snake's chin and out the back of its head. The great serpent sways . . . then slowly topples forward and lands on the island with enough force to shake the ground.

I ignore the impact and simply pick up Burnie. His wings and feet twitch, and my jaw sets.

Sorry, Master! I knew you weren't going to be able to weather that venom.

"You should let *me* decide things like that from now on." I draw in a deep breath, then open up my pocket dimension. Astrid bounds out, and I carefully place the downed Phoenix on her back. "Take good care of him."

A laugh, an awful laugh, echoes through the air, and I turn around as the portal to my pocket dimension closes. That was the third champion, which only leaves Loki left.

I just have to make sure that when I face off against him, I'm more careful.

And, of course, that I don't leave him even the slightest bit alive.

CHAPTER FOUR

O h, sorry about that, Jacy." Smoke swirls around the area, only to vanish with a *pop*. I find myself back in the circus tent, surrounded by laughing, jeering audience members. "Looks like you're down a pet! I hope you can hang on to them better than you can hang on to your daggers."

"Come out and face me," I mutter through clenched teeth. "Come out and fight me! I killed your three champions. Come out and face me yourself so I can get back to the business of clearing you people from Earth."

"So touchy." Loki appears in front of me with a puff of smoke. He's still dressed as a ringmaster and gives his cane a twirl around his arm. "Let's see . . . Uh . . ."

"You're not going back on your deal," I snap. "There are rules in the dungeons. You're still subject to the queen, and she sent you to fight me."

"Yes, but if I, say, keep you in prison, that does the same

thing as killing you." Loki points his cane at me. With a flash, I suddenly find myself in a prison cell instead of standing in the circus. Loki stands outside, dressed like an old-time prison guard. His cane has been transformed into a baton, which he rattles against the bars of the cell. "You're out of commission. You can't hurt any of us. I'd say that's a good enough outcome, don't you?"

"I can break out."

"Can you?" Loki laughs.

I march forward, grab hold of the cell door, and pull with all my might. It takes me a few moments, but I *do* manage to rip it away. As I toss it to the floor behind me, Loki goes slightly pale, and he points the baton at me.

"Alright, then." With a flash of smoke, I'm carried out of the cell and into a carnival. Large tents rise all around me interspersed with food vendors, carnival games, and more. Loki *now* is dressed up like a clown and carrying one of those oversized hammers. I have a distinct feeling that getting hit with it isn't going to be nearly as pleasant as the smiley face might indicate. "Here are the new rules. First, no help. My champions are gone, and you can't call your pets. Second, there are no boundaries. Third . . . we try to kill each other."

"That sounds mighty good to me," I snap. "Let's have at it!"

A dagger in each hand, I charge at the annoying god. Loki watches me coming, then swings the hammer as hard as he can. I dodge around it easily, only to suddenly be whacked by it from behind. I'm thrown forward into Loki, though he dissolves into sparks as I hit.

"Yes, let's have at it," Loki mocks me as I climb to my

feet. He's approaching once more, this time from the direction where the hit came from. I don't really understand what just happened there, though I *assume* he used some sort of illusion. This is going to be tricky. "Come at me, boy! Come and play!"

His green curly hair bobs as he charges at me, and I lunge upward. I'm not surprised when my blades cut straight through his body and cause it to dissolve into nothing but sparks, though I *am* a bit annoyed. I hear something scuff behind me, and I spin around, already prepared, and lash out as hard as I can.

Clang!

My steel meets his hammer only a foot from my head, and he snarls at me.

"You're a fast learner."

"Tricks only work once or twice." I shrug. "That's basic combat."

"Then I'll just have to change things up." A cruel smile spreads across his face. "Come and find me!"

With a flash, he vanishes in a puff of smoke. I hear footsteps and spin around, where I see something dart into what looks to be a fun house. I walk forward until I reach the doorway.

Inside, all I can see are mirrors. Little flickers of Loki's clown costume dance about, but they're distorted, as they're meant to be. Slowly, I let out a long breath. This is going to be tricky. If I could use Burnie, I could just burn the whole thing down. Balder could blast it down with a bark, Astrid could drop it into a chasm . . . But me, just me, what can I do?

"Alright, Jason. You've got this." I bounce on the balls of my feet, then nod. "Let's go!"

My chat cheers, and I charge forward just as hard and fast as I can. Loki laughs from within, but I ignore it. Instead, I draw back my fists and prepare myself. The first mirror makes me look huge and muscular, and as such, I feel quite good about myself as I crash straight through it.

Glass shatters around me as I punch forward, taking the shortest route through the fun house. Loki's laugh cuts off in surprise, and with that, I draw out Surtr's sword and take a firm hold on the handle. Flames shoot off the end, and I swing it in a circle.

Fire and smoke explode outward, carrying the force of the swing along with them. All around me, mirrors and windows explode into shrapnel. As it dies down, I find myself standing alone in the middle of the room with Loki nowhere to be seen. Of course, I *do* see the bomb ticking on the floor and nod.

"Not bad, Loki. Not bad."

Before it can explode, I reach down and pick it up, then spin and throw it as hard as I can. It punches through the outer wall and sails into the air, where it explodes violently. The force of the blast knocks the wall inward and flattens a number of nearby tents, and I slowly walk out into the festival once more.

"Come on, Loki! Come and show yourself," I snarl softly. I put away the sword and take out my daggers, ready for anything. "It's just a fight. You're a god. I'm a pathetic human. You're not scared of me, are you?"

The taunt has the desired effect, and Loki appears right

in front of me. He's still wielding the hammer and brings it crashing down on my head. I don't react, don't flinch, don't try to block, and the image dissolves. The real Loki appears not far from me, and I spin and throw the Celestial Dagger as hard as I can. It hits Loki in the chest and knocks him backward, and I spring upon him just as fast as I can.

Beowulf's Dagger burns in my hand as I strike again and again. Loki screams as I manage to stab him twice, then whacks me with the hammer. I'm thrown backward and land on the grass, and he huffs and holds up the weapon. Lightning lances down and, as it hits, transforms it from a hammer back into a staff. He points it at me.

"Dirty little rat!"

Blasts of magic streak from the staff, and I roll as fast as I can, dodging the streaks of red energy. They explode against the ground, showering me with dirt and rubble, and I leap back to my feet just as fast as I can. Before I can move, though, another blast of magic hits me, and living ropes wrap around me in the blink of an eye. My arms are lashed to my sides, my legs are tied together, and Loki laughs.

"Nothing but a pathetic—"

I grit my teeth and snap the ropes, then charge forward. Loki blinks in surprise and fires another blast of magic, but I dodge it and throw myself at him. In doing so, I manage to retrieve my Celestial Dagger, and I attack him with all due force. He vanishes with a puff of smoke, and I frown and glance around frantically. I notice a small trail of blood forming on the grass as a wounded Loki starts to limp away, and I slowly draw in a deep breath.

"Alright, Loki. Where are you?" I start walking more or less perpendicular to the blood trail, making it look like I don't see his path. Loki seems to pause, and I see a small flash of magic from the side. I know he's preparing something, and I brace myself, then jump forward.

A bolt of magic streaks through the space where I was standing, and I spin and throw both of my daggers with all my might. They carve through the air like arrows, straight and firm, and stick in the air like they've slammed into an invisible wall. Blood drips down from the points of impact, golden blood, and Loki shakily appears. He's swaying now and draws in a deep breath.

"Alright, then. No more tricks." He starts to walk forward, and I see magic beginning to flow around him. "No more playing around, I see! No more nice guy! No more fun! No more circuses!"

With that, he breaks into a run, and I turn and ball my hands into fists. He yanks out my daggers and throws them on the ground as he comes, and then, suddenly, he's upon me.

His staff flares with magic, and he swings at me wildly. I dodge once, then twice. Then he punches me in the gut, the blow coming out of nowhere, and grabs me by the collar.

"There's something you should know," Loki bites out. "I. Am. A. God."

With that, he yanks me down, then throws me up into the air. I sail above the height of the tents, and he fires another blast of magic up at me. It hits me squarely in the chest, and a great explosion erupts outward. It's like being punched by a mountain. I fall back through the smoke, losing control, and slam into the ground just in front of him.

I slowly climb back to my feet as he throws another punch, and he hits me in the chest. Before I can fall, he grabs me by my collar. Blood drips down from my lips, and I draw in a shaky breath. That last one *hurt*. "I don't buy it."

"Oh? You don't buy what?" Loki sneers at me.

"That you're a god." I shrug. "A real god . . . wouldn't . . . have to taunt me to prove it."

Loki's face darkens, and I reach out and grab his shirt at the shoulders. With all my might, I pull myself forward and head-butt him in the face. Pain flares through my head. I'm pretty sure that I just gave myself a concussion, but it knocks Loki backward. With that, I reach out and snatch his staff from him. In that instant, his clown outfit fades away leaving him in tattered green robes that hearken back to the Vikings—or at least how they're commonly portrayed in modern television. He snarls, and I point the staff at his chest. A great many options and notifications scroll past my vision, but I ignore the majority of them.

"You don't know how to use that," Loki sneers, though I *do* notice that he freezes solid. He's scared, actually scared.

"I know well enough." I send a mental command to the staff, and it transforms into a pistol, the very same make and model that I used to carry with me. "On your knees."

Loki glares at me but slowly lowers himself to his knees. I take a step back, making sure that there's a good bit of room between myself and the god, and let my finger play across the trigger. "Now, here's the deal. You relinquish your godhood and I'll let you live. Give me your XP, give me your skills and weapons, even your dungeon, and you can come live on Earth."

"You mean like that dragon who betrayed us?" Loki hisses. "Not a chance. I'd rather die."

"I believe you." I shrug. I pull back the hammer, and Loki's face suddenly goes white.

"You'd shoot a defenseless man?"

"I think you've made it very clear that you don't consider yourself a man. You think you're a god."

Loki sneers and starts to rise, and I pull the trigger.

BAM!

The single shot rings out, and a silver bullet punches a hole through his chest. He gasps for air and slowly looks out at me as golden blood drips down the front of his robes.

"I'll give you everything you want, and more."

"The only thing I want is for all of you monsters to die."

I fire the gun a second time, then a third. Loki staggers to his feet and takes a step toward me, and I raise the barrel of the gun. The next two shots go through his forehead. That's finally enough, and he collapses on the ground with a *thud*. I lower the gun slowly and allow it to transform back into a staff.

[You have leveled up!]

[Congratulations! You are now Level 80!]

All around me, the dungeon begins to quake. There's a rumble, and lightning begins to flash about.

And then, with one last blast, I'm carried away.

Back to Earth, where I belong.

CHAPTER FIVE

Lightning explodes through Mr. Wang's club as we all come crashing back. Warriors, attendants, butlers, everyone comes crashing down on tables and couches and chairs and computer consoles. I sway as I stand there, only to gape in horror as I look around.

The attack that sucked everyone away, it hadn't *just* been to kill me. All around, the club looks like it's been ransacked. Computers have been smashed, portal generators are down, the Pumped! machine has been emptied. I gape in horror at all of it, and Mr. Wang slowly staggers up to me. He looks down at the imprints of chains on his wrists and arms, then at my sorry state, then around at the room.

"Do I want to know what just happened?"

"Not a chance," I mutter. "Just . . . Nope. Not at all."

"Then I won't." Mr. Wang sighs. He raises his voice, and everyone in the room, which is rapidly starting to boil over into a panic, drops quiet. "Alright, everyone! We have a lot of work to get done. No questions. Just focus. Do what needs to get done. If you don't have instructions, pick *something* to do. I'm sure you can figure at least a few things out for yourself." The room doesn't move, and he raises his voice again. "I said *get to it!*"

The next several hours are ones of general chaos and confusion. Ali takes Burnie to try and heal him while everyone else throws themselves into the cleanup. It doesn't take long to realize that the computers and portal generators have been smashed beyond repair. Heat weapons have melted the circuits into nothingness, while every screen has been smashed and every wire pulled out. Everything else was given cursory treatment in comparison, just broken up enough to make it hard for us to use.

The sun is just setting on New York as we finish up, casting long shadows from the enormous buildings as it slips beneath the horizon. Sleep tugs at my eyelids, but I ignore it as best I can. Somehow, I have a feeling that it's going to be a long, *long* night before we see the light of day again, and I need to be ready to face that reality.

"Jason." Ali walks up to me, her voice quiet. "Jason, I need you to come here."

I turn and nod, feeling a heaviness in my heart. I follow Ali to one of the bedrooms of the club, where Burnie is laid out across the sheets. He looks sick, with sunken eyes and darkened feathers. I smile and sit down on the edge of the bed, then reach out and stroke the back of his head.

"Hey, Burnie." I smile. "I'm glad you're getting better."

Master, we both know that's not why you were called in here.

My heart sinks, and I sigh. "It's that bad?"

"Jason, if that poison had gotten into *you* . . ." Ali shrugs. "It's dealing an incredible amount of damage every second and has a duration of over a *year*."

"Don't we have antivenom?" I snap. "Don't we have ways of treating it?"

"Stardust *might* be able to treat it, but we don't have access to an Astral Dungeon." Ali shrugs. "We're out of options. I've tried antivenoms, but this stuff is resistant. I've tried . . . I've tried everything."

I sigh and nod. My chat explodes, but I don't have the heart to pay attention to it. Burnie lifts a head, and his eyes flicker.

Master . . . there is one thing I can do.

"What's that?" I ask, turning to him. I don't like the sound of his voice, but I have a feeling that it's going to be the only option.

Phoenixes have an unusual life cycle. I'm sure you're familiar with the fire-rebirth thing?

"Yeah." I nod slowly. "Can you . . . Can you do that?"

Yes. It will take me some time, but I have just enough strength for it. Burnie fluffs up his feathers. *The problem is that it will erase all my memories. It will reset my status to level one. I won't remember you at all, and I won't be any help to you in battle.*

I shrug and shake my head. "That doesn't bother me."

Then I'll begin the preparations. This room will do nicely.

I nod, then stroke the back of Burnie's head again. "I'll stay with you the whole time."

At that very moment, the door clicks open, and John sticks his head inside. He looks apologetic but nods down the hall.

"Jason, I don't mean to interrupt, but we need you."

Go, Master. Burnie puffs himself up again. *I'll be fine. You have work to do.*

I sigh, then nod and stroke him once more. With that, I stand up and slowly make my way to the door. John leads me down the hall and back to the main portion of the club, where the enormous plate glass windows look out across a brightly lit New York City. While the city itself seems to be having a good time, everyone in the room looks as though they'd rather be anywhere else. Mr. Wang alone seems chipper, but I credit that his good mood is one he uses to try and keep people cheered up.

"Alright, everyone! We took a hit today, but we're far from down." Mr. Wang crosses his arms and nods to me. "Jason, glad to see you're up and about. From what I hear, it sounds like you saved us all."

"I just did my job." I shrug. "Any of you would have done the same."

"Yeah, but we would have died in the process!" someone shouts out. I can only laugh quietly at that.

"Allow me to present a status report. It seems that the attack against this club was intended to cripple our movements, our ability to respond to this Ragnarok Protocol." Mr. Wang slowly starts to pace back and forth. "When they hit, they smashed everything in this building, as well as all the stations that we were using to keep tabs on the dungeons. At present, we're running blind, relatively speaking. We can't see any of the dungeons, except for when portals appear. We don't know their movements, and we can't guarantee that the dungeon bosses will follow their orders to stay away. All we know is that there are still dungeons attached to New York and that they're deadly." He pauses, and a smile creeps across his face. "And, if I had to add one other thing, we know that they're scared."

"Here, here!" John calls out. "If they weren't scared, would they be so concerned about knocking us out? Kidnapping us?"

There's a sharp cry of agreement, and Mr. Wang nods.

"Precisely. I don't want to sugarcoat things. We're still in for the fight of our lives, but I do think it's a fight we can win. If I thought we were going to lose, if I thought there was no chance for survival, I'd be running up the white flag and negotiating our surrender." Mr. Wang draws in a deep breath. "But I declare to all of you, here and now, that as long as an ounce of blood still runs through my body, as long as breath remains in a single human lung, I will not give up the fight."

"I second that." I slowly step forward, walking up next to Mr. Wang. "And I'll be fighting right alongside him."

There's a long pause, and Ali slowly raises a hand. "So . . . what now? You're doing a good job motivating us, but I frankly don't know what we're supposed to be *doing*."

Mr. Wang bows his head, then holds out a hand and steps to the side. Elrith and Paul walk up, concern written across their countenances. That said, they hold their heads high enough and nod at the assembled crowd.

"We've spent the last several hours in consultation. News crews from every newspaper and television station are sweeping the city, keeping an eye out for any new activity that might show up. As soon as they see something, they'll let us know. In the meantime, we've put together a map of all known dungeons." Elrith holds up a large notepad, which seems to have a great many names written across it. "This is an assignment sheet. If you're a registered warrior, you're to go to the dungeon assigned to you and clear it out. You'll be working in teams. You're to gather as much XP as possible in preparation for the inevitable conflict. We know Hella is here in town somewhere but can't appear until Jason hits level ninety-five."

"Then tell Jason to sit this one out!" someone calls from the back of the room. A round of nervous laughter flickers around the area, and I smile as well.

"As much as we'd love to do that, I'm afraid that won't be possible. If Loki was able to make an incursion, we have no reason to believe that others of his rank won't do the same thing," Mr. Wang says as he steps forward. "Jason will be tackling the largest threats. He's not going to be actively *trying* to increase his own level, but with the high profile of the monsters he'll be fighting, it's going to happen. Everyone else, you need to be ready whenever he happens to tick over to level ninety-five."

"I'm at level eighty right now," I say.

"That means you've got about three hours." Mr. Wang feigns looking at his watch, then laughs and shakes his head. "I kid, I kid. Probably closer to six. Alright, everyone! You've got your assignments! Get to them!"

Elrith walks forward into the crowd of warriors and

displays the list. Everyone swarms around and begins to look it over while Mr. Wang nods to me. We step over to the plate glass windows looking out across the darkened city. Fire blossoms across the way several blocks over, and Mr. Wang shakes his head.

"All the death and destruction that's been wrought across the world over the centuries, and it all comes down to this." He taps his chin. "What does that say about us as a species? We squabble and bicker over little bits of land when all the time, monsters have been waiting in the wings, just watching and biding their time until they could strike."

I shrug and shake my head. "If you ask me, it isn't quite that bad, but . . ." I sigh. "I get your point."

"You're a good man, Jason." Mr. Wang claps me on the shoulder. "I'll let you know as soon as something crops up. In the meantime, get some rest. You deserve it."

I don't *feel* like I deserve anything, but I nod in agreement. I do need to make sure I'm in top condition if I have to go back into battle. I make my way over to the bar and help myself to a hamburger, then gather up as many Pumped! as the bartender is willing to give me. It's not many, but he hands me five more bottles, which I add to my inventory.

"You wouldn't happen to know where I could get some more, do you?" I ask him.

The bartender, an older bald man, just laughs and shakes his head. "Sorry, bub. I'm not a warrior. I know there are some folks who have been brewing an imitation a few blocks down from here, but I doubt it'll heal you."

"I'll just have to put in an order with Mr. Wang, then.

Maybe his restaurant has a few." I sigh and drum my fingers on the countertop. My body itches with excitement, and I sigh. "Do you ever just want to be doing something, even though you know the thing you're supposed to be doing is insanely dangerous?"

"Can't say that I've ever felt that, no." The bartender snorts, then moves down the bar to start scrubbing the countertop. I get the feeling that I'm not really wanted there, so I push away and go find a chair to sit down on.

I can't rest there either and soon wind up pacing back and forth. The anticipation is *killing* me, but then . . . that might be part of it. Psychological warfare is a horrid thing, and I have a strong feeling that Hella is employing it with a great deal of expertise. It's annoying, but again, there's nothing I can really do about it. Outside, the stars turn, and the night wears on.

And then, finally, something happens.

I feel sort of bad, but my heart gives a leap of excitement as a massive explosion shakes the building. I rush up to the window, where I find a small mushroom cloud rising up from a street half a dozen blocks away. I rush out onto the helipad, all thoughts of sleep forgotten, and look out across the distance as I try to gauge things.

"Jason!" Mr. Wang runs out, a cell phone held to his ear. "Channel Twelve news is on the phone now . . . Looks like a portal just opened up . . . Lots of monsters! This is for you, I'm sure of it."

"Then I'll get right on it." I glance over at the jeticopter, which has several long slash marks across the engine. It's not going anywhere anytime soon.

"Do you need me to call you a ride?" Mr. Wang asks.

"Nah." I shake my head and let out a long breath. "I'll walk. Good exercise."

"Works for me." As I turn away, Mr. Wang holds up a hand, and I pause for a moment.

"Yes?"

"Good luck." Mr. Wang gives me a nod. "We're all going to need it."

CHAPTER SIX

I jump off the edge of the helipad, and for a long moment, I flash downward toward the streets below. Lights whirl past me in a kaleidoscope of color and brilliance, and a moment later, I hit the sidewalk. The concrete cracks under the impact. I'll admit that it hurts my knees a little, but I'm mostly okay. With that, I charge off in the direction of the explosion.

All around me, the streets are *far* more abandoned than usual. A few people are still out and about, but even the drug dealers are glancing around nervously. Another explosion lights up the walls of the buildings ahead of me, and I put on a burst of speed. The few cars still driving on the road quickly turn around and fly in the other direction.

Somehow, even without news of the Ragnarok Protocol being broadcast on civilian airwaves, the city just seems to *know* that something is off. Everyone was getting used to the apocalypse. Everyone was making life work. Now, things are changing. Difficulties are ramping up. The *fun* is being taken out of the destruction.

It's kill or be killed, hide or be found, and most people are choosing to run.

Luckily for our world, I'm not most people.

Ahead of me, I see the flames licking higher and higher, and I come roaring around the corner to find the street ablaze. There are no people anywhere, but buildings on both sides of the street are engulfed in fire and flame. Several dark werewolf-like monsters stalk down the road, snarling and dragging their claws along the walls and concrete. One of them grabs a car and slowly hefts the vehicle into the air, grunts, and throws it through the front of a toy store. A resounding blast shakes the area as the car explodes and flames fill the air.

"Alright, punks." I draw out Beowulf's Dagger, holding it firmly in my right hand as I stalk forward. "Time to come to justice."

One of them sees me and spins in my direction, snarling and growling. Drool drips down from his jaws, and his teeth glint in the light. Slowly, he starts to bound toward me. I should note that he's big, probably a good eight or ten feet tall, and covered in rippling muscle. His claws spark off the concrete as he comes, and as he reaches me, he rears up and slashes his mighty claws at my face.

Crack!

[IceQueen: WHOA!!! Yeah, that's what I'm talking about!]

[LunarEclipse: Did that thing seriously just break its claws on Jason's face?]

[ChaosRider: I wouldn't have believed it if I hadn't seen it.]

I smile as the werewolf staggers backward. Blood trickles from his hand, and he snarls softly and flexes the claws on his other hand. He draws it back to attack, then lunges forward with extraordinary ferocity.

Wham!

He slams into me like a bird hitting a window. A great many bones break in his body, and I grit my teeth and lash out. My dagger cuts through him like a balloon, and he collapses on the ground. With that, I charge forward, and the other werewolves in the area come bounding toward me, howling for blood.

They get blood, alright, but it's not mine that fills the streets. The first one leaps at me, snarling and spinning, and I slash upward. My blow cuts him clean in half, right through the chest, and both halves of the body land on the asphalt with a thunk. A second one comes forward, howling and spitting, and I cut him in half from top to bottom. The next one I punch in the chest so hard that every bone in his body breaks, and he drops with a plop.

That only leaves a single werewolf. He stares down at me, snarls . . . and then turns to run. He bounds down the sidewalk just as fast as he can go, snarling and howling, and I quickly bend down and pick up a penny from the sidewalk.

"I've never been very good with this sort of thing . . ." I put it between my thumb and forefinger, then give a sharp flick of my wrist. The penny zings forward and punches through the back of the werewolf's skull like a bullet. The monster falls flat on his face, dead in the blink of an eye, and I let out a long breath.

"Hey!" John comes running around the corner an instant later. "Those were *ours!* We've been tracking them for the last four blocks!"

"Well, they got away from you." I cross my arms as the rest of his party comes through. A thought hits me an instant later, though, and I frown. "But then . . . I was told that a new portal had just opened."

"Nothing here." John shrugs. "We just cleared one over on Thirty-First Street, but—"

BOOM!

A blast shakes the ground, and I spin around. A *great* deal more fire flickers from several blocks down, and I point toward it.

"That's for me. Got to go!"

John laughs and waves as I go running off, flashing down the sidewalk just as fast as I can move. I can't tell exactly where the flames came from, but I know they're coming from this direction.

[DarkCynic: Come on, Jason! Taking someone else's kills? That's low.]

[IceQueen: He didn't MEAN it!]

[FireStorm: Yeah! Run faster, Jason! You can get . . . whatever's up here!]

[LunarEclipse: I just started watching Channel 12 news, and . . . uh . . . this one's going to be a bit of a beast.]

I frown at that last message. A moment later, I come around a corner and draw up short.

"Beast" is a bit of an understatement.

I find myself looking at a building that I haven't seen since the earliest days of the apocalypse: St. Patrick's Cathedral. The enormous gothic building rises up from the middle of the otherwise modern style of New York City and looks down upon a group of monsters that are snarling and gnashing as they try to break inside. A priest—I think his name is Father Brown, if I remember correctly—stands on the steps calmly sprinkling the crowd with holy water. They all seem quite affected by it and flail back under the blast, only to surge forward a second later. Father Brown sees me and raises a hand in a gesture of greeting, and I draw in a deep breath.

"Alright, then. Let's go get to the bottom of this!"

With that, I charge forward, examining the monsters as I do. Their forms are difficult to make out, but they seem to be entirely arms and legs. As I get closer, I suddenly realize that their bodies aren't really all that solid at all.

They're wraiths.

I really, *really* hate fighting wraiths.

As I come upon the crowd, the first several of them spin toward me, snarling and gnashing their teeth at me. They're sort of human but deformed and twisted, like a ghoul or something from a video game. Several of them lunge at me, reaching out with long spidery hands. I draw out my Celestial Dagger and slash upward, and I'm surprised to actually cut through their wrists. Smoke rises from the stumps of their arms, and they pull back, letting out shrieks. With that, all the wraiths suddenly seem to take a greater interest in me than in the church, and I brace myself for impact.

The wraiths snarl and charge in one great mass, and I throw myself forward, slashing outward just as hard and fast as I possibly can. My Celestial Dagger throws off brilliant beams of light as we come together, and I hack through limbs and necks and torsos. Spectral body parts fall to the ground and dissolve into smoke, and a smile spreads across my face.

Now *this* is how to do things.

I fight my way steadily through the crowd. All the wraiths slash and claw at me, but like the werewolves, I'm a high enough level that they don't affect me all that much. It takes me a few minutes to carve my way through all of them, but as the last one falls, I let out a sigh of relief and turn to find Father Brown still standing there, just on the other side of a salt line sprinkled across the doorway.

"Many thanks." Father Brown dips his head toward me.

"Just doing my—"

A smoky rope wraps around my leg and tightens. Unlike the other wraiths, this actually *hurts*. It pulls so tight that I feel my foot go numb in an instant, and I quickly slash down at the thing. Before I can land a strike, though, the rope pulls taunt and whips me up into the air. I find myself dangling high above the street, swinging back and forth, and glance around as I try to figure out what's going on.

"You think you're something else, don't you?" a dark voice whispers in my ear. "Well . . . I'm here to tell you that you're nothing."

I snarl and slash at the rope once more, but the pressure vanishes. Before I can do a thing, the wraith—or whatever it is—hits me squarely in the back. Loki's hammer hurt just about as much, and it slams me back into the street far below. I actually go crashing straight through the asphalt and into the sewer, and I groan as I slowly pick myself up off the ground.

"You are nothing, and you will die like nothing." The rope wraps around my neck and pulls tight. In an instant, I can't breathe, and it pulls me up into the air. I reach up and try to grab hold, but my fingers simply slip over the smoky appendage without actually being able to grasp it. Desperate, I grab my Celestial Dagger and try to touch the glowing blade to the rope. Thankfully, it vanishes, allowing me to drop back to the ground. I fall into the pit and glance around frantically as I try to determine the source.

Suddenly, I see it: a tiny ball forming in front of me. It can't be more than six inches across, but it very clearly has that *wraith* feel to it. It's made of living smoke, it's just . . . *really* small. I brace myself and raise my dagger, then lunge.

Now . . . I'm fast. Most monsters, and pretty much all people, wouldn't have even seen me coming. This thing darts out of the way, wraps around my wrist, and flashes forward, off into the sewer. I'm dragged along with it, pulled through the darkness.

Wham!

Wham!

Wham!

I bounce off more than a few walls as it yanks me along. Suddenly, I slam into something metal and hear the rush of water. A cold liquid flows over my feet, and I reach up and snatch hold of a metal pipe with my left hand, even as the wraith tries to pull me under the water with my right. I grit my teeth and do my best to pull myself upward, then look down.

In the faint light of the Celestial Dagger, I can see the little wraith. It still has a general ball-shaped form but with a little smokey tail that's wrapped around my arm. I frown as I try to think up a way to get rid of the thing, but unfortunately, nothing comes to mind. It's out of reach of my dagger, and even if it wasn't, I have a fairly solid feeling that it would be able to twist out of harm's way before I had a chance to strike.

[DarkCynic: Hey, Jason! I think that thing is a Ball Wraith!]

[ViperQueen: Yeah, I think so too! I saw them in a guide-book once. They're like . . . Level 92 or something!]

[ChaosRider: 93, actually, but yes. Very powerful! No listed weaknesses.]

"None, eh?" I grit my teeth. The pipe is slimy, and I'm starting to lose my grip. On top of that, I can hear the metal starting to pop and bend. This thing is going to get me in just a moment. It's a fairly certain fact that if I'm pulled under the water, I won't be coming back out again. "Surely it has *something*."

[FireStorm: Wraiths in general don't like light!]

[ViperQueen: Yeah, but Jason knows that already.]

"Don't like light?" I mull over that thought in my head. It doesn't give me many ideas, but it does explain why the Celestial Dagger was able to hurt them when my other weapons have always proven to be less effective. Suddenly, an idea pops into my head. "Gabe! Do you think you might be able to *enlighten* this situation?"

There's a pause, and then my pocket dimension flickers open in front of me. Gabe steps out and shakes his golden fur. It begins to glow, and he draws in a deep breath and howls.

In that instant, light flares throughout the sewer, and I gasp in relief. The wraith howls and lets go before diving into the dark water. I quickly find the ledge and swing up out of the way and stare down after the thing. Slowly, Gabe and I turn away and walk back down through the sewer.

Wham!

The Ball Wraith hits me again only a few seconds after we leave the water behind. It wraps around my neck and drags me down the sewer, then quickly yanks me around a corner as Gabe lets out a blast of light. I can hear his feet pounding on the floor, but I don't know that it's going to be enough. I need to figure something out, and I need to do it fast.

Suddenly, from overhead, I hear a crackling noise.

The sound of fire.

That gives me an idea, and I slash upward with my Celestial Dagger. The weapon grazes the wraith, not killing it by a long shot, but it *does* make the thing let go. It darts off quickly down the hall, vanishing in an instant. I sheath the Celestial Dagger, only to draw out Surtr's sword.

[ShadowDancer: Oh, I know what he's about to do!!!]

[ChaosRider: Good work, Jason! That'll show him!]

[LunarEclipse: This is going to be great!]

I stare off into the darkness, watching and waiting. Behind me, Gabe comes bounding up, but I send him a mental command telling him to stay back. He obeys and slinks back around the corner, but he stays ready to act the instant that I need him. With that, I watch . . . and I wait.

I don't have to wait long. It appears with a whir, shooting out of the inky darkness as a blur, and flashes through the sewer like a dark bullet. I point the sword at the thing . . . and then activate the fire powers that it holds.

A great blast of flame explodes down the sewer hall, crackling off the walls and blazing against the floor and ceiling. In that instant, the whole thing lights up like the Fourth of July. The wraith lets out a piercing scream and comes to a halt just in front of me. It twists this way and that but can't escape from the overwhelming light coming from all around it.

"Now, Gabe!"

Gabe bounds around the corner, eyes glowing, and lets out a howl. In that moment, the sewer fills up with more light than I could have ever previously imagined. My eyes ache from the intensity of it, but it does its job. The wraith explodes into a shower of sparks, and I slowly lower the sword and allow the flames to die down.

[Ball Wraith defeated!]

[XP Awarded: 10,000,000]

[. . .]

[Notice: S-Ranked creature defeated!]

[First Kill of a Ball Wraith from planet Earth!]

[Extra XP Awarded: 5,000,000]

[. . .]

[You have leveled up!]

[Congratulations! You are now Level 81!]

[. . .]

[Extra reward granted for First Kill of a Ball Wraith!]

[Infused Ability: Light]

[Target Item: Surtr's Sword]

I smile as I hold up the sword, which begins to glow softly.

I have a feeling that I'll be able to make it glow a whole lot brighter when I need it to do so, but for now, I'm satisfied with what amounts to a cool-looking flashlight.

"Alright, Gabe." I nod to my pup and start jogging back through the sewer. "Let's get out of here. I've got a dungeon to find, and I'm tired of delays."

CHAPTER SEVEN

It doesn't take me long to find my way out of the sewer. Rather by chance, I wind up climbing through the hole that the wraith made when it smashed me through the street. As I climb up, I find Father Brown still standing on the steps, looking down at me with a worried look on his face. His face softens as I climb up, mostly unharmed, and I wave at him.

"Long time, no see, my friend." Father Brown nods graciously to me as I step over his salt ring. "I've been following your exploits. You've certainly been making quite a mark for yourself."

"We all have our role to play in this apocalypse. I'm just trying to do mine the best I can." I flash a small smile at him. After a moment, though, I scratch the back of my head. "You haven't, by any chance, seen a dungeon entrance open up, have you? I was told that one was over this way, but I've had two false leads so far."

"Yes, I've seen it." Father Brown nods. "I thought it unusual when it appeared, since it seems to have the ability to move. It came right down this street, spat out all those wraiths, and then moved on."

"Interesting." I think for a moment. "In that case, it might be trying to disguise its movements."

"That would be my supposition. Of course, I'm no monster fighter, but it seems to me that if you were going to try to wreak as much havoc as possible, that would be the way to do it. If I might make a suggestion?" Father Brown gestures upward. "*That* might be a good way to narrow down the search."

I follow his gaze. High above, resting on the edge of an apartment building across the street, are two large ravens. They're quite obviously not ordinary ravens, as they're a good three feet long and have glowing red eyes. They don't move. They just stare back at the two of us. I shudder more than a bit. I have a feeling that they're using a skill like Unnerve or Horrify, but knowing it and being able to resist the effects are two very different things.

"Interesting." I frown at them. "Two ravens. That sounds familiar."

"It should." Father Brown gives a small nod. "The wanderer, Odin. His two ravens flew throughout the world, seeing everything, reporting back to him. I imagine that they're quite interested in you right now."

"Then I'd better go have a chat with them." I draw out my

daggers and start toward them. They stare down at me, then spread their wings and fly off.

"You'd better *hurry*," Father Brown calls. "I imagine that they'll lead you straight to your prey, but only if you can catch them."

I nod, then bolt down the street. At a command, Gabe ducks back into the pocket dimension while Lightfax comes charging out. I swing up onto her back, and with that, I shoot down the street as fast as I can upon my noble steed.

Lightfax's hooves pound against the asphalt as we go roaring down the abandoned roads of New York. Overhead, I catch glimpses of the ravens here and there. They swirl between buildings, dart down alleys, pass over apartment complexes, and, in general, do everything they can to lose us. Lightfax is a good horse, though, and we soon go shooting around a corner, where we find a flickering portal in front of us.

In a lot of ways, I feel almost like I've cornered the portal. It sits at the end of a dead-end street, hemmed in by buildings on all sides. The two ravens dart down and flash through the portal, vanishing into its depths, and I smile. Slowly, I climb down from Lightfax and order my steed back into my pocket dimension, then stride forward. My daggers rest heavily in my hands, and I set my jaw.

"Odin!" I cry out. "Will you come out and face me like a man, or am I going to have to come in there and pry you out, just like Loki?"

There's no answer, and I stalk forward. I didn't really expect an answer, though it would have been kind of nice. Suddenly, though, lightning arcs across the portal, and with a *thump*, something emerges.

It takes a moment for my brain to register what I'm looking at. In front of me stands an enormous creature snarling down at me. It looks like a tree, a great oak, and stands a good thirty-five feet tall. Thick bark covers its entire body as well as the many different limbs that seem more than plentiful for whacking me. A fierce face made out of knots and scars in the bark stares out at me, and it walks upon stubby roots. Slowly, it begins to rumble forward, growling and snarling.

"Alright, then." I brace myself. "You know this won't end well for you, right? Throw down your branches right now, and we'll talk about your surrender."

I can't really tell if the tree is a sentient creature or not, and if I'm being honest, that's a good part of the reason why I'm saying anything. I'd sort of like to figure out if it's a giant or a golem or something else entirely. It continues to not answer me, though. The silent treatment. Well, if that's the nature of this dungeon, so be it!

I charge forward, and the tree begins to attack, sweeping its massive arms out across the ground like massive clubs. I don't know the level of the monster, so I pull up short for a moment and let the attacks pass by me without any resistance. As the first round of strikes ends and the monster straightens up, I move in for the attack.

Snip!

A vine shoots down from the canopy of the tree and snaps at my leg. It wraps around my ankle and yanks upward, though only for an instant, and it lets go a breath later. I'm flung a dozen feet or so into the air, and it spins and smashes a massive branch into my torso. I'm slammed back into the ground, and my health drops a rather alarming amount.

[DarkCynic: Ooh! That has to hurt. I wouldn't have gone in quite like that.]

[LunarEclipse: Don't harass Jason like that! He's doing the best that he can! It's not every day you face something like this.]

[RazorEdge: Hey, if it would be helpful at all, my grandpa has some herbicide out on his farm!]

[ChaosRider: RazorEdge, I sorta doubt that that would be helpful. In the slightest.]

As I groan and pick myself off the ground, the tree snarls and rushes forward, then unleashes a rapid-fire series of attacks. It slams branch after branch into the ground. One or two of them hit me, but I do manage to roll out of the way of most of them. Quickly, I leap back to my feet, then rush forward all the way up to the roots of the monster.

Snip!

Another vine shoots down from the canopy, fast as lightning. This time, though, I'm prepared, and I just manage to dodge out of the way. The vine snaps against the ground, and I slash through it with Beowulf's Dagger. The tree howls but doesn't really seem otherwise affected. Quickly, I slash the dagger through one of the roots and sever it quite cleanly. The tree stumbles, and a blood-like sap begins to drip down onto the pavement.

With that, the tree spins and performs a whirlwind attack. The air swirls tightly around it, and I find myself lifted off my feet and blown back. A physical barrier of wind forms around the tree and remains in place as it comes to a stop. The face of the tree continues to glare out at me, and I see magic swirling among the branches. Whatever's about to happen likely isn't good, and I brace myself.

Wham!

The tree slams a branch down into the pavement, and it punches through the asphalt and vanishes. I frown, then leap out of the way as a root suddenly explodes upward from the street. It snaps at me, then retreats.

Blam!

Blam!

Blam!

More roots erupt from the ground, snatching and grasping at me. I slash at a few of them but mostly just avoid the attacks. As they cut off, the wind stops, and the tree rips the limb back up out of the ground.

With that, I attack in full force.

As I run forward, it executes the same attacks again, thundering forward and slashing downward with its branches. This time I see the attack pattern more clearly and dodge the assorted strikes. Two more vines snap down from above, and I dodge them, then dart forward up to the trunk. It's almost too easy. I slam both of my daggers deep into the bark of the tree and drive them in just as hard as I can, then hang on tightly as the tree begins to spin to dislodge me.

Air swirls around me, but I stay strong, and this time the protective barrier forms with me still inside it. The tree comes to a halt and doesn't seem to notice that I'm still there. At least, not until I start climbing it. It howls with pain and anger as I use my daggers like picks to scamper up the side, and it begins to flail as it tries to knock me off.

I brace myself as a particularly large branch hits me. With all my might, I lift Beowulf's Dagger and drive it deep into a knot in the trunk, then twist and push. There's a sharp crack, and a split opens up down the side of the tree. An instant later, the same branch whirls around and whacks me again, and I'm knocked free. The tree takes advantage of that fact and spins, then hits me a dozen times in the span of a second. I'm blasted back through the wind barrier and onto the street, and with that, the tree rumbles forward.

This time it doesn't wait for me to get close and starts shooting the vines at me the moment I climb back to my feet. I manage to dodge twice, but the third one gets my left wrist. I'm lifted into the air as it yanks me back, right into the waiting fist of the monster. I'm slammed to the ground with impossible force, and I groan as it jumps forward and tries to stomp on me. I do manage to roll out of the way just in time, but barely, and as I climb back to my feet, I have a feeling that this fight is taking a lot longer than it should.

"Alright, tree. If that's the way you want it, then that's how you'll have it." I duck a blow. "Burnie!"

Nothing happens, and I remember that Burnie is still back at the club, healing. Or, rather, preparing for—I don't want to think about that. I grit my teeth, then draw out Surtr's sword. The tree doesn't react, except to try to bash me to the ground again. I quickly activate the fire, then step back as the tree lunges at me.

Foooooooom!

Fire explodes from the blade and wraps up around the tree, scorching its bark and burning away its leaves. The monster howls and steps back, trying to avoid it, and I press the attack. Flames rush through the canopy, burning and crackling and raging, and I smile. Now *this* is how I like to fight! I'm going to keep pressing the attack, and I'm going to win, and I'm going to—

Whack!

A branch comes out of nowhere and hits me in the chin. My vision swirls as I'm blasted back across the street and slam into the wall right next to an ATM. As I shake my head and get my bearings, I find the tree slowly stepping out of the flames. It's blackened and scorched, but in some ways, that just seems to have leveled it up, like it's turned from a Tree Giant into a Scorched Tree Giant or something. In any case, it looks angry, and it's coming straight toward me.

"Alright, then. Challenge mode." I groan, then rush forward just as fast as I can go. "Any help would be greatly appreciated! Bjorn! You're up!"

With a flicker, Bjorn steps out of the pocket dimension with what looks like a smile upon his face. As the tree snarls and begins to slash at me, I duck under the razor-sharp branches and attack the trunk with force, hitting it with everything I have. In that same instant, Bjorn howls, his cry echoing off the buildings all around.

Almost instantly, ice grows across the branches and limbs of the tree, stiffening the monster and slowing its movements. I smile and look at it, then lash upward as hard as I can. My daggers meet a large branch crashing down upon my head, and steel connects with frozen wood.

CRACK!

Wood splinters explode through the air, and the branch comes crashing to the ground with a loud thunk. The tree staggers, slightly off-balance, and I hit the thing just as hard as I can. Roots explode under the assault, shattering and sending frozen bits of wood scattering across the area. I slash upward and split the trunk in several long slices, then step out of the way as it slowly topples forward. Dozens of smaller branches shatter into bits as it crashes to the ground, and I rush forward into battle just as hard and fast as I can.

The tree isn't dead, not by a long shot, and it flails about as I attack. That said, with Bjorn continuing to freeze the thing solid, it can't do much. I smile and leap up into the air to hack off the last limb, then come down on the face of the tree itself. It glares up at me, and I lift my daggers and bring them both down right between its eyes.

Crack!

This time the crack explodes up and down the length of the tree—well, it's more like a log at this point, I suppose. It splits clean in two, and the halves slowly fall apart. I drop down to the street once more and nod at Bjorn.

"Many thanks."

Bjorn bows, then slips back into my pocket dimension. I let out a long sigh, then turn toward the crackling portal that Odin controls.

"Alright." I slowly step over the corpse of the tree. "I'm coming for—"

Bzzzzzat!

A blast of red magic shoots down from the portal and hits the ground in front of me. A small portion of the asphalt is melted into goop, and I frown and draw up short. An instant later, one of the ravens flies out, cackling loudly, and begins to swoop back and forth.

"Alright, now. What do *you* want?" I scowl up at the thing.

In answer, it just fires several more blasts of magic down at me. They're not aimed particularly well, and I get the feeling that it's testing me, feeling me out. Suddenly, the raven flies down and lands in front of the portal, just ten or fifteen feet in front of me, and transforms into a woman.

Not a pretty woman, mind you. Some monsters become beautiful maidens with the intent of luring in susceptible men. Not this one. There are warts on her nose, her fingernails look like claws, and her eyes are still glowing. Her hair hangs loosely about her head, and it's long and thin and greasy. Honestly, just picture a witch from a really old movie, and you'll pretty much have it. She leans upon a wooden staff, and I slowly brace myself.

"You're a hag."

"I am a messenger." Her voice is high pitched and shrill, and it makes my ears hurt. "I am here to warn you against setting foot in that portal!"

"Because your boss is scared of me?" I smile and step forward. "He should be."

The hag cackles. "No, not that at all! It would simply be . . . unpleasant for everyone involved."

With that, she transforms back into a raven, spins, and

shoots through the portal. I watch her go, then nod with a smile.

"I imagine it will be. That's sort of my intent."

I stride forward, confident and firm. I'm ready for whatever comes next. Ready to knock the crown off this old buzzard.

CHAPTER EIGHT

Portal energy flickers around me, and I go shooting through the interdimensional realm. As I do, I try to look around to see if I can get a feel for the remaining dungeons in the area, but I find that I can't see a thing. Portals created by artificial means are a lot more transparent—you can get a feel for what's around you—but "natural" portals just shoot you straight from Earth into the dungeons, and that's really that.

When I come shooting out the other side, I panic for a moment. When I land, I find myself on a wide expanse of bark, and as I look up, all I see are leaves and branches. I draw my daggers and prepare for battle, only to realize that I'm not looking at another Tree Giant.

No . . . I'm actually just looking at a giant tree.

[IceQueen: Whoa!!! That's super cool!!!]

[RazorEdge: I'm pretty sure that this is cultural appropriation.]

[LunarEclipse: I mean . . . it's not like Jason *intentionally* put the World Tree in this dungeon, you know.]

I laugh a bit at the comments, then slowly look around. The portal opens onto the limb of a tree, which, as you can tell, is large enough for me to stand on quite easily. It's a good twenty or thirty feet wide and runs for several hundred feet to connect with the trunk of the tree itself. The other end stretches off into space, though the portal blocks me from going that way. Slowly, I walk up to the edge of the branch and glance over, where I find myself looking down at a drop of . . . Well, it's a *long* drop.

The trunk of the tree plunges downward for what seems like miles until it meets a small island surrounded by a vast ocean. I can see the gnarly knobs of roots twisting down into the soil, but nothing more beyond that. On the flip side, as I step back and look upward, I see the tree *rising* for what seems like miles, with hundreds of branches splitting off from the main trunk. The branches all lead to clusters of leaves that seem to me to contain entire worlds, though that's hard to tell for certain. It's quite the thing, in any case, and I whistle softly.

[DarkCynic: I hope you didn't skip leg day, Jason! That's quite a climb!]

[ViperQueen: And you know that Odin is going to be waiting at the *very* top.]

[ChaosRider: Oh . . . Yeah.]

I hear the cackling laughter of the hag, and one of the ravens shoots past the branch, spiraling a few times before rising up higher and higher into the tree. I sigh, then nod and trot down the branch toward the trunk.

As I get closer, I find a long flight of stairs carved into the bark, rising up around the circumference of the trunk. Next to the base of the stairs is an elevator door, and a smile splits my face.

"Yes! Modernization even in the world of mythology!"

I quickly rush up to the doors and push the up button. Maybe this will be the easiest dungeon I've yet had to face!

[Error: Pass card needed.]

"Pass card?" I blink in surprise, then notice a small slot just next to the button. "You've got to be joking me."

[Notice: No joke. Pass cards can be obtained from Sif, realm of Alfheim.]

"Well, I'm not going *there*." I sigh, then turn to the stairs. "Legs, you'd better not fail me now!"

I mount the stairs and start upward just as fast as I can. For the first hundred or so stairs, it's actually not all that bad. The second hundred start to get a bit more difficult, but it's still not bad. I am, after all, a whole lot stronger than the average human.

By the time I pass five hundred stairs, my legs are starting to burn, and I start to wonder if the plan with the stairs is to try and wear out any potential warriors before they ever have a chance to get close enough to do any harm. I don't know that for a fact, but it would sure make sense.

I've topped somewhere around a thousand stairs when I finally come to the next branch. As I arrive, I lean against the trunk of the tree and pause for a breath.

"I think . . . I've earned . . . a bit of a break," I gasp out, then slowly step forward and draw myself upright. "And any-one who—"

Wham!

A large stone falls out of the sky and slams into the trunk right in front of me. No . . . not just a stone. As I stand there, awestruck, cracks spread across the surface, and it slowly unfolds to form a stone giant. The thing isn't actually all that impressively large, but it *is* made of stone, which daggers have a somewhat more difficult time piercing. I slowly put away both of my weapons and ball my hands into fists.

"What is it with you people and giants?" I ask as the giant lumbers forward. It swings a massive fist at me, and I jump backward. The fist cleaves through the air just in front of me, and it follows the attack with a second strike from the other hand. The movements are slow and forceful. I've fought a few other stone monsters in my time in the dungeons, but this one really looks to take the cake. There's just something about it . . . I can't explain it, not really, but it just *looks* like it's ready to smash me into pulp and spit out the bones.

It slowly lumbers forward once again, performing the same attacks. My legs are burning, but I brace myself, and then, as it strikes one last time, I throw myself forward and dash past the thing just as fast as I can move.

That, of course, is when I realize that the stone giant was only pretending to be slow.

Faster than my eyes can follow, it spins and snatches me by the leg, then grunts and flings me high into the air. The whole world spins around me, and I gasp in surprise and shock. I peak a hundred feet or so above the ground and tumble back down, watching as the giant stares up at me with fury in its eyes.

"This is going to hurt," I mutter. As I fall, I ball my hands into fists and draw back my right hand.

Wham!

The stone giant throws a punch up at me at the same moment that I punch down at it. Our two fists meet, and a resounding shock wave explodes outward. The stone giant's hand is blasted into rubble, while I'm knocked backward to slam into the trunk of the tree. I groan and fall to the ground while the stone giant roars in anger. It looks down at the stump of its wrist, then thunders forward. This time it isn't going slow and isn't going to show me an ounce of mercy.

It kicks at me first, trying to smash me flat, and I dodge out of the way. A shock wave that erupts from the point of impact catches me and slides me sideways—right into a blow from its left hand. I don't dodge that one nearly as fast as I might have liked, and the blast knocks me backward into the trunk of the tree once again. I hear something crack in my body, and the stone giant lifts its hand to deliver a final, crushing blow. I brace myself, then launch myself upward with every ounce of strength I have. Once more, my fist meets the stone giant's fist.

Wham!

I don't know if my attack was weaker this time, or if the stone giant was stronger. Whatever the case, the blast knocks me to my knees. I hold the fist above my head as the giant continues to press down, pushing me into the bark of the tree, snarling softly. I grit my teeth as I push upward against it, then slip around to the side. The monster stumbles and cracks its head against the trunk, and I leap behind the thing.

Quickly, I jump upward and try to climb up the knobby back of the giant. The monster is faster, though, and spins around to catch me, wrapping its hand around my torso. It lifts me up into the air, and I quickly try to break free. I'm unable to do so in time, and it smashes me back to the ground with extraordinary force. A great many *more* things pop loudly in my body, and I groan and flop over to the side. With a sense of finality, the stone giant lifts its foot, preparing to stomp me flat.

"Not . . . today," I whisper, then brace myself and lift my hands. The blow is crushing, but I *just* manage to stop the thing from stomping on me. Its foot presses down above me, trying to crush me into dust, and I fight back desperately with everything I have inside of me. The stone giant's face twists into a mask of concentration, and it puts even more weight on my taxed body.

"I said . . . not . . . today!"

With the last of my strength, I twist the foot sharply. Stone cracks and explodes into splinters as I break the ankle cleanly. The stone giant falls forward, off-balance, and hits the trunk with enough force to shake the entire tree. I climb back to my feet, swaying, and the giant snarls and starts to rise up once more. It's missing a hand and a foot, but that's not stopping it.

I can't let a little bit of pain stop me either.

"Stay down!" I charge forward and kick the giant in the face. The force of the blow smashes its head back into the wood, and I follow it up with a blow from my palm to the chin. *That* cracks its head quite loudly, but it doesn't shatter it, and it certainly doesn't kill the thing. Faster than I can react, it sits up and climbs to its feet, swaying a bit as it puts weight on the stump of its leg. It snarls softly, then slowly raises its remaining hand.

I know that gesture. It's about to use magic of some sort, and I charge forward as fast as I can. A blast of gray magic shoots out and roars across the wood where I was just standing, turning the area to stone. Oh! Yeah, that's really not good. I hit the giant a second later, punching it in the gut just as hard as I can. The monster is knocked backward by the blow, and it fires another blast of magic at me. The attack goes wild and flashes upward, and a moment later, several stone leaves fall down and tumble toward the ocean far below.

I leap up onto the chest of the beast and begin to pummel it just as hard as I can, throwing punch after punch. Blood trickles down my knuckles and my bones ache, but I keep up the attack. Suddenly, the giant sits up and headbutts me, knocking me off its body. As I climb back to my feet, it rises and points a finger at me, magic flaring brilliantly at the tip.

Ooooooooooooooooooooooooow!

A howl cuts through the air, and a shock wave hits the giant squarely on the arm. The entire appendage is blasted to gravel, and the magic is discharged harmlessly out into the air. I glance around to see Balder standing there, tall and strong, snarling at the thing.

"Balder! Get back!" I cry out, then charge at the giant once more. It's looking more and more like a crumbling old mountain rather than an actual giant, which I appreciate. Balder either doesn't hear me or, more likely, ignores me. He howls again, and another shock wave hits the giant in the chest, knocking it backward. Stones rattle to the ground, and the whole monster starts to break apart.

I take advantage of that fact and attack the beast with fury. I leap into the air and throw a punch dead center into its chest, and cracks explode across its body. As I fall back to the ground, its entire torso crumbles.

Thunk. The remaining arm slams to the ground just on my left side.

Thunk-thunk. The two legs—what's left of them—fall down just in front of me.

Wham! The head slams to the ground and bounces several times before slowly rolling to the side and falling off the branch. Down it goes, whistling as it falls.

[You have leveled up!]

[Congratulations! You are now Level 82!]

"Nice!" I smile as I watch it go down, then frown. "You know, I don't know that I got a reward for leveling up to eighty. Is *that* gone now too?"

There's no answer except a bit of speculation in the chat, and I slowly turn away. With that, I walk over to Balder, who's standing tall, wagging his tail. I kneel down next to him, and he nuzzles my cheek.

"Balder?" I raise an eyebrow. "I told you to stay back."

Balder's ears droop. *But, Master, you were in danger.*

"So were *you*. That rock magic might have hit you, or . . ." I shrug. "I don't know. I didn't call for help."

Balder looks down at the ground and whimpers. Suddenly, the portal to my pocket dimension flares and Bjorn steps out.

His canine face isn't all that expressive, but he looks somehow grave, and he slowly licks his son's head behind the ears.

Master, I know you're worried because of what happened to Burnie, Bjorn says.

I sigh and slowly nod. "I just . . . I can't . . ."

We're here to help you. We want to drive this blight from the planet just as much as you do. Bjorn seems to smile. *This was where I earned my sanity, where you freed me from the mindless anger and hunger I used to feel. That essentially makes Earth my birthplace. My home.*

"I know, I know, but—"

And, on a more practical note, if you wind up dying, we all get un-summoned into the void.

I bite my lip, then give a nod. "Alright, I get it, but you'd better be careful."

Of course, Master. We all will be.

Bjorn and Balder both retreat back into the pocket dimension, and I climb back to my feet.

I still have a long way to go and a *whole* lot of stairs to climb.

I'd best get to it. After all, the fate of the world is at hand.

CHAPTER NINE

I start up the stairs once more, moving as fast as my aching legs will take me. Let me just say that my legs are *burning* by this point. A thousand stairs will do quite a number on a person, whether or not they have superpowers. I keep climbing, setting my sights on the next limb up.

I lose track of how many stairs I've climbed at the two thousand mark. My chat hangs on for a while longer and tells me when I've hit three thousand, but even they seem to be losing interest.

[DarkCynic: Hey, Jason, can you fight some monsters again? This is getting kind of dull.]

[ViperQueen: Don't pick on him! He's doing the best he can.]

[ShadowDancer: You've got this! Hey, everyone, I'm going to head to the kitchen to eat some lunch. Will someone ping me when things get exciting again?]

Now *that* sounds nice, but I don't have the option of

heading to the kitchen. Instead, I simply press ever upward. The climb is long enough that my natural healing abilities kick in and return my health to a hundred percent, healing up all the wounds on my knuckles, arms, and the rest of my body.

When I finally reach the next branch, I'm a whole lot higher than when I first arrived at the tree. The branch is empty, and I pause to rest while half expecting another monster to appear, but nothing comes. That's a welcome relief, and after taking five minutes or so to recharge, I start upward once more.

I probably climb for about two hours in total before things, as the chat would put it, "get interesting." With a loud caw, one of the ravens shoots down past me, then wheels about suddenly in the air and swoops around. It buzzes past me a second time, and I consider trying to throw something at it. Suddenly, it spreads its wings wide, and I see magic flare from its torso out to its wingtips. That's not good. With a burst of strength, I lunge upward just as it fires.

The hag's cackling laugh echoes loudly through the air as a blast of red magic shoots at me. It hits just behind me, and a great eruption of vines explodes from the trunk of the tree. They snarl about like living things and begin to grow after me. One wraps itself around my ankle and begins trying to pull me off the tree, and I snarl and kick against the stairs. I manage to snap the vine in two, but more vines rumble upward. I grimace and climb ever faster, and the hag cackles.

"Think you can get away from me, eh? We'll see about that!"

The raven flaps its wings and flies ahead just around the curve of the tree. I hear another pulse of magic, and my stomach sinks. As I round the curve, I find more vines uncoiling and snarling all about. A glance over my shoulder reveals that the vines are still coming up from behind, which means that I'm about to be trapped. I don't know the exact capabilities of the vines, but I'm certain that they're not meant to give warm hugs. Quickly, I draw out Surtr's sword and slash it forward.

A great blast of flame explodes off the blade and tears through the vines. They wither and drop off, and I run past, climbing as hard as possible, ignoring the pain building up in my legs. I have to escape, and that's the simple reality.

The hag laughs again, then swoops around and begins firing more magic. It seems rather wanton and hits the trunk of the tree all around me. The effects are varied. Sometimes it explodes, sometimes more vines pop out, and sometimes there are simple flashes of light. It's getting annoying, and I swing my sword outward at the raven. A great blast of flame shoots out at the thing, but it simply flaps out of the way.

[IceQueen: You know, most of the time I'm glad that Jason isn't a ranged warrior, but every now and then it sure would be nice.]

[ChaosRider: Yeah! A bow and arrows might be nice to keep in reserve.]

[DarkCynic: He's proven himself. I'm okay with it if everyone else is!]

I roll my eyes at the chat. I've used one before, and if I want to use a bow, I'll use a bow. Actually, I *am* holding a plan in reserve that could probably kill or knock out the raven, but I want to keep it in reserve. Something tells me that I'm going to need all the tricks I can get once I get up to Odin himself, and I don't want to give any clues.

Of course, if the hag kills me before I can get to him, then it's a moot point, I suppose. I decide not to pull my trump card quite yet and instead bolt upward just a bit faster.

"Ha ha! Die, boy!"

A particularly powerful blast of green magic flashes right past my head and explodes against the bark of the tree. A strange energy wraps around my body, and I find myself lifting slightly into the air. It's as if gravity itself has been turned off. I snarl and snatch for the trunk of the tree, but before I can grab it, claws latch around my left leg. I'm pulled away from the tree and out into the air, and the hag laughs even louder.

"Get out of this one, boy, if you can!"

She lets go, and gravity reasserts itself. Suddenly, I'm tumbling down . . . down . . . down. I see the tree and the ocean and the sky all whirling around me. Carefully, I hold out my arms to stabilize my fall and glance around. I see a particularly large tree branch welling up down below me. Did the raven intend to drop me onto it? Or was it an accident? I don't know, but it's not a branch that I remember walking past. Of course, the stairs don't touch *every* branch, but . . . it's still odd. Whatever the case, I smack onto the tree branch an instant later, which knocks my health down to a fraction of its normal amount. I groan and slowly sit up as I look about for the raven, but I don't see it.

"Well. That was less than pleasant." I climb to my feet and draw out my twin daggers, looking around for any sign of trouble. Something poking up from the cluster of leaves at the end of the branch catches my eye. I should note that these leaves are each as big as a person, maybe larger. Climbing up above them looks like . . . a castle tower? I'm not sure, but I frown and start walking in that direction as I prepare myself for battle.

Snip!

An arrow flashes out of the leaves and hits the branch just in front of me, and I draw up short.

"Who goes there?" a voice demands loudly. "State your name and intentions!"

"Jason Lee," I call back. "I'm here to kill Odin!"

There's a long pause. Suddenly, two leaves are drawn back, and a figure shambles forth. He looks like a wizard and leans upon a staff set with a crystal. Somehow . . . I don't know, but I have the distinct feeling that he's evil, though I can't prove it. I leave my daggers out, in any case.

"You don't kill Odin," the man murmurs. "You might try—I'll grant that—but you don't kill Odin."

"Then count me as someone who doesn't give up easily." I nod to him. "Who are you?"

"My name is Master . . . I don't recall, exactly. Perhaps 'The Master' will do well enough."

"Perhaps you should give me a few more details." I grip my daggers a bit tighter. "I don't like hitting old men, but you wouldn't be the first exception to that rule."

The Master chuckles and sighs as he leans on his staff. "You'd like to know who we are? Well, to answer that, we are the last remaining Focus of Mystical Study. Our world is—was . . . I don't remember that either. It was a world, and it was destroyed by Odin."

"I'm sorry to hear that," I answer. "Help me kill Odin, then."

"I cannot do that." The Master shrugs. "You will fail, and then he'll kill us for being disobedient."

"The alternative is for you to fight me, and then *I'll* kill *you*."

The Master flashes a small smile. "Forgive me if I'm slightly less scared of you than the great Odin." His staff begins to pulse with magic. "Every now and again, the ravens drop off warriors for us to test out. I imagine that they want us to soften you up, and that's just what we're going to do."

"You'll try."

"We'll succeed." The Master turns around and starts to walk back toward the fortress. "A whole lot of people have tried to make it through, and they've all failed. I don't think you'll be the exception."

"Well, forgive me for saying so, but a *lot* of people have tried to put an end to my fight," I answer in kind. "I don't think that *you'll* be the exception. You have one more chance to help me."

The Master pauses, then turns around. For a brief moment, I have a feeling of hope.

And then he shoots a fireball at me.

It's actually a rather impressive fireball, all things considered. Flames crackle and rage as it cuts through the air, and I jump nimbly to the side. It passes me by, doing no harm whatsoever, and I grit my teeth and charge forward. Arrows flash through the air, but most of them don't even come close.

I bear down upon The Master, and his eyes grow wide. I see him mutter something under his breath, and he raises his staff.

Zap!

A bolt of lightning shoots out and forms a dome around him, which I slam into a moment later. It's a force field— and a good one too. I bounce back slightly, and The Master laughs. Still within the force field, he points his staff at me, and yellow energy flares up. I wait for him to drop the field, knowing that he'll have to lower it in order to attack me.

ZZZZZZZZAP!

A blast of brilliant light explodes out from his staff and hits me in the chest. It's like touching a power line. At least, I *assume* it's like touching a power line. It hurts, and I lose every ounce of control in my body. With a loud *plop*, I fall to the ground, whacking my head on the wood, and The Master chuckles.

"The bigger they are, the harder they fall. Well, best get you chained up."

He waves his staff, and blue spectral chains form around my wrists, binding them tightly together. I continue to lie flat and limp as he binds me up, then starts to walk back toward the fortress. The chains drag themselves, and me, along behind him. I bide my time as strength flows back into my body, and I slowly draw in a deep breath.

When I flex my muscles and shatter the chains, a blast of magic leaps back to The Master's staff. He spins, eyes wide, as I jump to my feet. Quickly, he points his staff at me, and a blast of black energy streaks from the crystal.

I jump to the side and let the torrent of deadly magic pass

me by. With that, I charge the old man, my daggers flashing in the air. He gulps, and a bit more lightning flows around him to his shield.

Wham!

I hit the shield with force, making it tremble, and The Master pulls back slightly. A smile spreads across my face, and I ball my hand into a fist and throw several powerful punches at the thing.

Wham!

Wham!

Wham!

The shield flashes brilliantly under each blow. Finally, I draw in a deep breath, draw back, and throw one last punch as hard as I can. The shield explodes under the impact, and lightning arcs back to hit the crystal. The staff is blasted clean out of The Master's hands, and I lunge forward.

The old man isn't done yet, though, and he raises his hands.

Crack!

A blast of lightning explodes from his fingertips and courses across my body. I lose most of my control once more and fall to my knees as I desperately try to get my limbs to work again. The attack lets up after only a moment, but smoke rises up from my body, and my arms and legs still won't work. The Master draws a small knife and marches confidently toward me.

"And now, boy, you'll die. Don't worry, it's no use struggling. You'll only—"

I draw in a deep breath, then throw myself forward. I still have no real control over my body, but I can at *least* fling myself in the right direction. I feel like a bag of wet noodles as I crash into the old man and knock him backward. He slams flat against the wood, and I flop to the side.

Of course, that only makes me start sliding toward the edge of the branch as my legs and waist land on the curve of the bark. Desperate, I force my left hand into motion and latch it around a small outcropping. I come up short, and for a moment I dangle there, swinging back and forth in the wind.

"Impudent lad." The Master climbs to his feet and spits on me. He flashes his knife once more, then slowly walks toward me. He seems wary, but I'm also in a *very* bad position. "Any more tricks you'd like to employ?"

"Several," I manage to bite out. "All I'm going to do, though, is . . . this."

I, of course, don't do a thing. Balder, however, takes that moment to bark sharply, having slipped out of the pocket dimension while The Master was distracted. A shock wave slams into the man and flattens him against the bark, and Balder comes bounding over to help me back up. Limbs still twitching, I scowl down at the old man, then nod to my dog.

"He's all yours if you want him."

Balder snarls, and The Master gulps and leaps to his feet. He runs away, and Balder moves to follow, but I hold up a hand.

"On second thought, let him go." I frown as I watch the old man vanishing into his fortress. "He doesn't like Odin any more than we do. The only difference is that he's scared."

You think he might be useful, Master?

"I don't know," I muse, then shrug and turn away. "What I

do know is that he's not going to follow us if we head closer to Odin. Come on, boy." I pat my leg, and Balder pads up next to me. "We've got a long climb ahead of us, and I'd like to get started as quickly as I can."

CHAPTER TEN

Balder and I walk to the point where this branch meets the trunk of the tree. Staring up at it, I can see the stairs high above, but because of the way they spiral upward around the trunk, they don't actually intersect with this particular branch. I can see some old holes in the bark that make it look like a ladder was once attached here, but it's long gone. I sigh, then draw out my daggers.

"This is starting to get old." I slam the daggers into the bark of the tree and start pulling myself upward. "You'd think there would be a mountain-climber achievement or something that I would get after awhile."

Balder laughs—at least as well as a canine can—and he turns and slips back into the pocket dimension. With that, I'm alone again, and I start on the long climb upward.

It's far from an easy climb, but it's also far from the worst one I've ever experienced. I have to scale around . . . oh, I'd say about two hundred feet before I get to the stairs. As I come to the stairs and haul myself onto the steps, I gasp with relief, then slowly sit up and rub the back of my hands. They ache from the constant grip on the daggers, but that's just life, I suppose. Carefully, I climb to my feet as I glance around for any hags. When none appears, I once more start upward.

I climb the stairs for almost an hour before I come to the place where I was attacked. I recognize the blast marks and the now-withered vines. Fear grips me, and I pause for a moment while I glance around to see if anything else is about to attack. Thankfully, the hags stay well enough away. Satisfied, I start upward once more.

[ShadowDancer: Alright, Jason! Final push! You can do it!]

[ViperQueen: We *hope* it's the final push. It could technically still be a while.]

[ShadowDancer: I'm trying to be optimistic.]

[ChaosRider: I'm optimistic!]

I smile at the chat and say a few words to them here and there, but I mostly just focus on climbing as fast and as steadily as I can. I still have to pause for breaks here and there, but mostly I'm able to make good time.

Half an hour after I pass the place where I was attacked, the stairs become steeper. My legs burn all the more, but I've somehow passed the point of caring. The lower half of my body almost feels robotic, and I simply push myself onward and upward. I climb for another hour, maybe more, before I come to something unusual.

The stairs come to an abrupt stop. A smaller branch, only ten feet wide or so, leads out to a small cluster of leaves. I can't see what's inside the leaves, but I can hear something roaring, growling, pacing. I frown and step out, looking around, but I don't see anything. Very strange. Slowly, I tilt my head backward and look up at the canopy high above. It's a lot closer now than before, but it would be a nigh impossible climb if I were to use my daggers the whole way. The only question, then, is what's located in the cluster of leaves. Is it another way up? A mini-boss? Is the mini-boss protecting another way to ascend to the top? Or . . . is this the actual top? I have many more questions than answers, and my chat isn't helpful in the slightest.

[DarkCynic: Jason, I know this is going to sound crazy, but I think you should jump off. I bet there's a hidden trampoline or something. You know, like in that movie with the archeologist!]

[GoldenShield: Don't do that, please, Jason. I do think you probably have to fight whatever's in there, though. Good luck! We'll be watching the whole time, don't worry!]

[RazorEdge: If you ask me, he ought to just start climbing. I think that'll be the surest and safest path to victory.]

[ViperQueen: Maybe if he looks around, he'll find a bottle of Pumped! that grants flying abilities or something.]

I roll my eyes as the suggestions continue and, if possible, become crazier and wilder. I frown, then slowly start walking toward the cluster of leaves and the monster behind—it really *is* probably the best bet. I find myself standing before a leaf-covered doorway. Carefully, I reach out and push it aside, then step through.

The battle arena isn't large, but that's clearly what I'm

looking at. It's twenty feet on every side . . . No, thirty. Stone walls covered in vines and leaves form the boundaries. The roaring grows louder and louder, and the doors slam shut the moment I'm inside. Then I see something dark beginning to slide around the exterior.

"Welcome, Jason Lee. I'm told that you want to see the boss."

"If your boss is Odin, that's who I'm looking for," I reply as I draw out my daggers. "You can either take me there or I can beat you to a pulp."

The voice chuckles. It's deep, almost impossibly so. Suddenly, a head appears. A *big* head. It's not as big as the world serpent, mind you, but it's probably as big as my entire torso and is clearly reptilian. Long spikes come out of the back of the head and from below the eyes. I'm looking at a dragon.

The only interesting thing is that it's a dragon made out of wood.

Yup, that's right. The dragon is entirely made out of wood, and the spikes are actually topped with leaves and flowers like the branches of a tree. Its eyes are a fiery red, and as it opens its mouth, I see hundreds of sharpened teeth. Wooden or not, it's a dragon, and it looks quite hungry to me.

"My boss is he who sees everything." The dragon chuckles, then slowly lowers its head. "He knows everything. He speaks all languages. He teaches all knowledge. He is the one who—"

"Right now, he's the one threatening my city." I cross my arms. "That makes him a problem. He can either withdraw and forget this whole Ragnarok Protocol, or he can fight me man to man and we can get this over with."

"You are an impudent lad," the dragon snarls. "You will

get your wish, a fight between you and Odin, *if* you can beat me first."

"Then bring it on." I drop into my stance, preparing for combat. "Hit me with your best shot."

Wham!

I should probably keep my mouth shut sometimes. A wooden tail flashes over the edge of the arena and hits me squarely, and I'm flung into the air and slam into the far side. I groan and stagger backward, and it flicks its tail once more, hitting me *again*. I'm tossed up into the air, and it snarls and lunges. I expect teeth to hit me, but . . . no. Claws close around my torso, and I'm lifted up into the air in the blink of an eye.

The dragon spreads its wings and shoots up into the sky like an arrow, flapping toward the crown of the tree. I'm helpless to resist, helpless to fight back, though at this exact moment, fighting back isn't exactly my top priority. Ahead, a large branch looms, and it flies up and throws me down to the bark. I bounce once or twice before coming to a stop, and it spreads its wings and slowly comes down for a landing.

"Here we are, Jason. Your first test. Survive this, if you can."

The dragon takes a few steps back and opens its mouth. Now, it's nothing huge by dragonish standards—maybe fifty feet long, with a wingspan of the same. I know the stance it's taking and prepare myself. It's about to breathe fire on me.

Or, at least, to breathe on me.

Instead of flame, a blast of pollen shoots out, swirling through the air. I catch a single whiff of it and almost pass out. It's a sickly-sweet smell and seems to carry the very essence of pestilence with it. I snarl and brace my body as the pollen washes over me. I'm careful not to breathe in, and as the attack dies down, I race forward.

The dragon simply laughs and swings its tail at me. It comes in low, and I jump clean over the appendage. It flashes beneath me, and I land solidly and keep charging forward. The dragon frowns, then slams both of its wings down. A compressed blast of wind hits me and flings me backward, and I land in the kill zone again.

[Condition: Sick.]

I don't need a list of debuffs to tell me just what's been affected. I sneeze as I stand back up, and my stomach churns. The dragon laughs, then prepares itself once more.

"I would have expected better from you. Now, Jason Lee, it's time to perish!"

It opens its mouth, and I charge forward. Dragons have a single weakness, and it's the fact that when their mouths are open and they're breathing fire—or whatever substance they happen to be able to breathe—they can't actually see what they're doing. As another great blast of pollen explodes out, I drop to the ground, slide under it, and quickly manage to come up underneath the mighty wooden beast.

It's covered in thick scales of bark, but that doesn't stop me from slamming both of my daggers in up to their hilts between the scales, and a thick sap comes pouring out. My stomach revolts from the sickness and I lose my lunch, and the dragon howls and launches itself up into the air.

"Next test, then, boy!"

It flashes around the branch, and as I bend over to vomit once more, it hits me from the side. Once more, claws latch sharply around my body, and I'm pulled higher and higher into the sky.

The air whistles around me as I'm drawn ever higher into the tree. I can see the mighty crowd growing closer and closer, and I set my sights upon that distant target. For a moment, I think that the dragon is heading in that direction, but it veers aside once more and tosses me onto another branch. I land with a *thud* and bounce toward the edge but manage to catch myself. It lands on the branch just a few feet away, then stalks toward me, walking on its wings and claws. Bits of wood burst upward as it slashes its claws across the bark, and it snarls softly.

Quite suddenly, it lunges forward and smashes its body down upon me. It's almost like the dragon is trying to body-slam me, but with the full force of a dragon's body instead of the more modest weight of my own body. I manage to dodge out of the way *just* in time, and it hits the tree with enough force to create a shock wave. I'm lifted off my feet and tossed several feet away, and it rises up and snarls at me, then stalks after me again.

"You're not bad for a human."

"You know what else?" I say, starting to get annoyed. "I don't like being graded by a dragon. By a monster. I'll decide how good of a human I am. Or, at the least, I'll let more competent authorities than *you* tell me."

The dragon snarls, and I bolt forward. The only problem, at least for the dragon, is that I don't intend on attacking straightaway. It roars and lowers itself as it braces for me to try to jump on it, but I don't. Instead, as it lunges upward I duck underneath it and suddenly find myself facing its talons once more.

This time, though, I'm ready.

My daggers flash in my hands, and I cut clean through its legs and drop its talons to the ground. They clatter to the wooden surface, and the dragon howls as it shoots up into the air. Sap dribbles down from the stumps of its legs, and I race forward, up toward the tree trunk. The dragon spins around and shoots down toward me, flashing low, ready to use its body as a battering ram to just smash me clean off the tree.

And that's when I pull out my next trick.

"Skill: Speed!"

I should note that simply as a fact of fighting a dragon, Ascalon has already given me a pretty good boost in speed. I've neglected to make full use of it, however, so with the Speed enhancement, I suddenly blur forward far faster than the dragon was ever expecting. I hit the trunk of the tree full force, then jump upward and push off it as hard as I can. The dragon hardly has a chance to know what's hit it before I land on its back and drive my daggers into its neck, just above the shoulders.

The dragon howls and lets out a blast of pollen that washes over me. *That* makes me quite sick since I wasn't anticipating it and breathed in at that exact moment. That said, I maintain my grip and pull back as hard as I can.

"Alright, dragon, climb!"

I don't know whether it hears me or whether my daggers just do the trick of reins, but the dragon begins flapping its way upward. The air whistles around me as we climb higher and higher, and I see the canopy growing close. A smile breaks across my face, and I call forward once more.

"Alright! If you want a chance to live, head for that gap in the leaves!"

I push the daggers forward, and the dragon obeys. An instant later, we come crashing through the gap onto a broad open platform. It seems to be made of leaves, mostly, and the dragon comes crashing to the ground. I yank out the daggers, and the monster reacts instantly. Its tail flashes forward and whacks me firmly across the torso, and I'm blasted off its back and sent rolling across the ground.

As I climb back to my feet, the dragon snarls and pulls itself upright. Magic begins to flare across its body, and it thunders forward.

"You're going to regret that, boy! Die like the dog you are!"

Ascalon grows warm across my back, and I let my daggers fall to the ground as the dragon throws itself at me. Quickly, I reach up and grab hold of Ascalon's hilt, and a strange strength flows through me. The blade makes a lovely *shing* noise as I pull it free, and with that, I slash downward at the dragon's head.

The dragon hits me with as much force as it can muster. That, of course, only lends more strength to my blade, and the sword chops cleanly through the dragon's neck. The body falls to the ground with a loud *thud*, while the head bounces across the ground. I turn and watch it, keeping an eye on the body, and relax as I realize that neither are going to be moving again anytime soon.

[You have leveled up!]

[Congratulations! You are now Level 83!]

"Good." I sheath Ascalon once more and slowly turn to look at my surroundings. "That's the way I like it. One more dead monster, one more test completed." My eyes harden, and I nod upward. "Odin, I'm coming for you."

CHAPTER ELEVEN

Before I go anywhere, I take a good look at my surroundings. The floor and walls are made of leaves. Have you ever seen those *really* old video games from the '90s and early 2000s? The ones where you're up in a treetop setting and the ground was flat with a leaf pattern on it? That's what I'm looking at here, for sure. The ground is a little uneven with a texture more akin to a rocky landscape, but everything's made of leaves. It's definitely a little odd.

In any case, the platform is broad, running for several hundred feet in any direction. The trunk of the tree is noticeably smaller, about the size of a California Redwood, and is shooting up from the middle of the platform. Above that, there are still a few more platforms I can see, but they're all made of wood and metal, like tree houses built around a tree instead of being made out of the tree itself. I frown as I look it over, then smile as I notice a metal ladder that leads up to the lowest of these buildings. I quickly start walking in that direction and pick up my daggers as I do so.

"Alright, Odin," I murmur. "This looks rather low-tech, if I'm being honest. Well, not *low*-tech exactly, I suppose. More like . . ." It takes me a moment to figure out what I'm trying to say. "Like something you'd see in an apocalypse. It's just cobbled together out of other stuff."

No one answers me except for my chat, but I suppose that a lot of the random stuff I say is for them, anyway. As I get closer to the ladder, though, I feel a tremor run through the area, and I pause.

"You're not doing too bad, you know."

The voice sounds quite a lot like Loki's but is somehow darker—more sinister, less jovial. I take a tighter grip on my daggers and look back and forth.

"Odin."

"You're a sharp lad. Stupid in a lot of ways, but sharp," Odin's voice echoes in my ears. I honestly don't even know if my chat can hear it. It almost sounds as though it's being projected straight into my brain. "Here's the deal. You've made it through a few small challenges, but you're skipping a lot of the challenges I had set in place."

"Not my fault you built your dungeon around a tree instead of in a cave. It's easier to funnel people without freedom of movement," I retort.

"Yes, indeed." Odin chuckles. "It's ironic, really, that you would say something like that."

"Ironic?" I ask, suspicion beginning to churn about in the back of my mind. "Ironic *how*, exactly?"

The only answer is a bit of laughter, which echoes about the area before dying away. My chat explodes with speculation, and I glance at it. Sometimes they have some good insight on what I'm about to face, which could give me a few moments of warning.

[GoldenShield: Hmm. What part of that statement might be taken ironically?]

[ShadowDancer: The tree part, maybe? Maybe Jason will be fighting more tree monsters?]

[FireStorm: That doesn't seem right. I bet it has to do with the open-air bit.]

[ChaosRider: Nah. I think it'll be something to do with the freedom of movement line. I don't know why, but it just sticks out to me.]

[RazorEdge: Plus, if you comment on something that someone just said, it's usually on the *very* last thing they said.]

I have to agree with the chat, but . . . what does that mean? Freedom of movement? What exactly does—

Grrrrrrrrrrrarlarlarl.

The growl is soft but powerful. It seems to come from all around me, and I spin around, looking for the source. Suddenly, I notice a black head rising up from the leaves.

A *dead* black head.

A few arms shoot up from the ground as well and grab hold of the ground to pull themselves free. As they emerge, I find myself looking at dozens of zombie-like creatures, though they're clearly different in several key ways. For starters, their eyes are glowing. Sure, I've seen a few zombies with glowing yellow eyes, but the vast majority of them just have milky dead eyes. Secondly, their bodies are covered in runes. They look like Viking runes, which fits rather well with everything else that I've been seeing as of late. The runes seem to be glowing as well, though it's a bit harder to tell for sure. If they *are*, it's pretty softly, like a glow stick brought into the daylight. Oh, and of course there's the fact that they just passed through a solid floor. Either this floor isn't as solid as I would like to think, or I'm looking at—

[DarkCynic: DRAUGR!]

I nod slowly as I take my stance. The first of the draugr snarls and staggers toward me. It still has the same halting steps that most zombies sport, but this one is a bit more steady than some of the ones I've seen. It certainly doesn't reach out to try to grab me. Instead, it draws an obsidian knife off its belt and lunges, flashing forward at what seems to be the speed of light.

Thankfully, I'm just a *bit* faster.

My Celestial Dagger flashes through the air and hacks off the hand at the wrist, and the knife clatters to the ground. My victory is short-lived, however, as the draugr snarls and snatches a second knife off its belt with its left hand. This time I'm not quick enough to block it, and the thing stabs me in the side.

"Get away from me," I snarl, then headbutt the thing. It's knocked backward slightly, and I slash Beowulf's Dagger through its neck. The head falls off and bounces on the ground, and the body sways before collapsing. Suddenly, the other draugr around me surge forward, and I dive through the small gap left by the dying monster.

There are a lot of them, and more of them start to emerge

from the ground as I back up, keeping my eye on them all. About thirty of them that have emerged from the ground so far, and more of them are coming. Suddenly, I feel a hand grasp my heel and glance down to see one of the draugr snarling up at me from below. It bites at my foot—thankfully breaking several teeth on my boot—and I kick it as hard as I can before ripping my foot away from its grasp. More hands begin to pop up around me, and I grit my teeth.

"Alright, everyone, this is getting hairy." I think as fast as I can, running through a wide assortment of options. There are a handful of promising ones, but I don't know what's going to be best. "Watch my back, will you?"

[ChaosRider: We will!]

[ViperQueen: Yeah! You've got this, and we've got you!]

I nod, then leap over the ring of hands and charge into the body of monsters. As they surge at me, I spin as fast and as hard as I can, hacking and slashing with all the force I can possibly muster. My blades are sharp, and my aim is true. I hack through a dozen arms and legs, sending the draugr sprawling, before I suddenly realize that a *lot* of them are pressing around me, harder and faster than I anticipated. I grit my teeth and lunge forward, but hands suddenly grab me and pull me back. I quickly stab one of them in the skull, and it drops, but another just steps forward to take its place.

None of the draugr is hard to kill, but they're not water balloons either. Each one takes a couple of seconds to hack through, and with so many, that's putting me into quite the pinch—one I really wasn't prepared for. My mind races as I try to come up with a way out of the situation. I could try to call one of my pups, but I'm not sure it would help. Since I'm in the middle of the pack, their area-of-effect attacks aren't going to work without also hitting me. Burnie would be able to use more concentrated attacks, but he's not here. Blub might be able to . . .

Blub!

The thought springs into my mind. I always forget about him since he's so weird, but he's really quite useful in a pinch. I open up my pocket dimension and hold out my hand as I call out as loudly as I can, "Blub! I could use you right about now!"

There's a pause, and then my Living Bomb shoots out of the portal and lands in my hands. A draugr bites down on my arm, and I punch it in the face with my other fist. The thing's skull is crushed under the blow, and I spin as I attack just as hard and fast as I can. Blub floats up into the air and begins to inflate, and I spin again as I try to break free. I know I'll take some collateral damage from the blast, but that's just something I have to accept. A few moments later, Blub calls out, *Blub-blub! Blub! BLUB!*

"I'll assume that you mean you're ready!" I call back up to him. "Anytime!"

Blub suddenly drops like a rock and lands in the middle of the draugr about ten feet from me. At first, I honestly wonder why he decided to hit so far away.

And then . . . he explodes.

A brilliant white light shines straight through my eyes and seems to bore through the back of my skull. Looking down at my body, I find that I can see each and every one of my bones.

When the shock wave hits an instant later, it rattles me to the core, and I stumble backward as smoke pours around me. I shouldn't have to describe what happens to the draugr. Any and all of them close to me are utterly obliterated, turned to ash, and I frantically stumble out of the ash cloud.

My health has fallen to about 10 percent. I turn around and find a small mushroom cloud rising up from the point of impact. A few other draugr around the edge of the area have suddenly drawn up short, and I cross my arms.

"Well, it certainly seems like *he's* gotten a few more levels."

[GoldenShield: Your pets *do* level up as you do, and it's been a while since you've used him.]

"Yeah, that's about to change." I hold out my hand, and Blub bounces out of the smoke and lands in my palm. I place him back in my pocket dimension, then turn to the last of the draugr. "Let's end this."

The last of the draugr don't really stand a chance, but they're sort of fun to kill. I charge forward at the closest one. It draws a large sword, and I block it with Beowulf's Dagger while stabbing it with the Celestial Dagger. It slumps and falls, and I spin as another one comes charging up, jaws agape. That one loses its entire head, and I nod in satisfaction as the thing collapses in a heap.

With that, I charge forward into battle. The draugr try to form up into a larger crowd, like the others had done previously, but they're too scattered and I'm too fast. I charge forward as fast as possible and pick them off like deer, and the last one soon collapses. I wipe my blades off on my pants and give a sharp whistle.

"Now that's how you take care of business!" I smile as I start walking toward the ladder once more. "Alright, let's get on with—"

Thump.

Another rumble shakes the area, and I turn around. One last draugr rises up from the ground, snarling softly. As it takes its stance, it begins to grow and soon transforms into a ten-foot-tall draugr beast. The monster snarls softly, then slowly marches forward as it draws out a *massive* sword that's almost as long as my entire body.

"Hey! I don't suppose we could come to an agreement?" I drop into my stance. "You seem like a fellow who's going to be quite painful to kill, and I'm a fellow who doesn't really like pain."

The draugr snarls and runs forward as it slashes at me. I jump backward, and the blade tears straight through the ladder. Bits and pieces of the metal fall to the ground, and before the monster can do anything, I charge forward at it. It slashes, trying to block me, but I'm too fast and hit it in the legs with immense force. My blades slash through them, and it staggers but remains standing.

I decide to remedy that fact.

As fast as I can, I spin around, slashing several more times, and cut through the tendons in the draugr's knees. It groans and falls, landing upon said knees, only to snarl at me menacingly. It begins to crawl forward, and I run backward as I draw Blub out of my pocket dimension.

"You ready for one more?"

BLUB!

Blub begins to inflate, and the draugr draws up short. It suddenly begins to grow again, inflating as well, and I watch it rising up. When Blub reaches his full size, he gives me a small nod—at least as much of a nod as an inflatable bomb can give—and I throw him at the monster with all my might.

Blub slams into the draugr's chest and explodes with extraordinary force. A horizontal blast rips through the monster's torso and bisects it while an immense outpouring of heat explodes upward and wraps around its head. Bones, bits and pieces of the skull, come crashing down, while the main body of the thing slowly topples over backward and lands on the ground with a resounding *thud*. Blub hits the ground and bounces back to me, and I catch him and carefully place him in my pocket dimension.

"Not too bad, boy." Odin's voice returns once more. "Not too shabby at that."

"I'm here to protect the Earth." I glare around, looking for the source. "You can either surrender or you can face me as well. Stop hiding behind your generals and come out like a man!"

"I am no man, at least not a mortal one." Odin chuckles deeply. "You have nothing on me, boy, and I would appreciate it if you would stop taunting me. I will face you in due time, but I will not be goaded. For the time being, there is one more test you must face. For your sake, boy . . . I hope you fail miserably."

CHAPTER TWELVE

I glance around as the bodies of the draugr all suddenly fade into nothingness, leaving the battle arena as if nothing has happened. I frown, then once again walk toward the ladder. This time no one stops me, and I climb up to the lowest of the buildings.

Now, these buildings . . . Like I said earlier, they're like something you might find in an apocalypse. They're made out of tin stretched over frames made out of square pipes. I mean, I could probably build something better without a lick of construction experience to my name. I whistle as I look it over and try to find the purpose of it.

Strangely, there doesn't seem to be one. There are no computers, no wires, nothing to indicate that it's anything more than a very simple room. The other side has another ladder going up through a hole in the roof, so I climb on upward, being careful not to cut myself on the tin.

The ladder goes up another twenty feet or so, where another building has been situated carefully on the crook of two more branches. Climbing up inside, I find it to be abandoned as well. Upward I go, looking in each of the buildings, becoming more and more bewildered with each passing structure. Finally, I reach the very top one, two hundred feet or so above the battle arena, where I find . . . Well, it's more than *nothing*, but not by much.

This last structure is built rather like a children's tree house. There's a small table with several sheets of paper, some crayons, and a few crude drawings. I smile despite myself as I look them over. There's a picture of a boy playing with a hammer that shoots lightning. And a picture of a boy dressed up as a clown. And a picture of a man hanging upside down from a tree branch like a bat—it's an odd one to say the least, and I slide it to the side. But I don't find anything else, and I start to wonder if maybe I've come to the wrong area. I *thought* this was the best place to send the dragon, but maybe this is just some sort of bonus area for the intrepid explorer. Or, more likely, maybe this is a secret clubhouse that Odin built for his sons and has nothing to do with the dungeon overall.

"Having fun snooping around?" one of the hags says in my ear with a cackle.

"I am, yes," I murmur, not acknowledging her otherwise. Anytime someone sneaks up on you like that, they're expecting a reaction. More than expecting it, they're *preparing* for it, so if you spin around suddenly, they'll be ready.

So, instead, I take hold of the table as I lean forward over the drawings and *then* spin around. The table is ripped cleanly from the floor and smashes the two hags flat as they're slammed against the back wall.

At least, that's my goal. The reality is that the wall, being made of tin, simply crumples under the blow, and both hags are knocked clean out of the clubhouse altogether. They transform into ravens and flash upward, out of my sight. I hear them charging up their magic, and horror shoots through me.

I have seconds to get free or I'm going to be blasted to bits.

Ignoring the pain, I dive through one of the windows in the hut. The tin cuts me a bit, but not as badly as it might have, and I find myself plummeting toward the ground far below. Above me, a powerful explosion rocks the air, and I glance back upward to see the top of the tree wrapped in flames and smoke.

When I hit the ground, it hurts—but not as badly as it might have. I come up in a roll and grip my daggers tightly, looking for any opening. These hags are Odin's top generals, which means that they're not going to go down easily.

Thankfully, I won't go down easily either.

The first one shoots down out of the smoke, wings folded, eyes glowing. Lasers explode down from her eyes, scorching the ground. I narrowly dive out of the way, and she shoots by, leaving a trail of smoking lines behind her. As she flies upward, the second one comes down and fires blast after blast of magic from her wings.

The magic explodes all around me. This magic is mostly red and erupts into small mushroom clouds with each blast. I'm battered back and forth with each explosion, but none of them really knocks my health down all *that* much. I grit my teeth and do my best to stay strong, but I can tell that they're in this for the long game. They want to wear me down, and right now, it looks like they can probably do it.

Peeeeeeeeeeeeeeeew!

The first one shoots down again, making another run at me. I jump out of the way once more, but in doing so, I stagger right into one of the explosions. I'm lifted off my feet and thrown backward across the arena to land, stunned, with a splat. As I slowly sit up, the ravens land and transform back into hags. Leaning heavily upon their staffs, they walk toward me, smiles across their crinkly faces.

"And now, boy, you—"

"Please don't tell me that I'm about to die," I say as I climb back to my feet. "I've heard it, thank you very—*ahhhhhh!*"

The first hag fires a blast of red magic from her staff, but instead of streaking through the air and exploding, it forms a tendril of energy that connects me to the staff. There's no dodging—it simply connects to my body just as easily as I might tie a knot in a rope. In that moment, energy begins to siphon out of my body and into the hag, and I find myself growing weaker.

"I was going to say that you'll join us!" The hags both cackle. "We'll just suck out your soul, nice and tidy, and then you'll be ready to help Odin on his conquest of blood and glory!"

[IceQueen: OH NO!!!! THIS IS TERRIBLE!!!]

[DarkCynic: If he manages to get Jason, our world is doomed!]

[RazorEdge: Jason, you have to fight it!]

"Guys!" I bite out. "They're not controlling my mind. They're . . . just . . ." I have to pause as I become weaker. "They're sucking the life out of my body and will then just stick in a wraith or something in my stead. It won't be *me*."

[FireStorm: Whew! That's a relief!]

[IceQueen: Okay! I feel better now!]

"You guys are full of heart," I mutter, then turn my attention back to the hags. My grip loosens around my daggers, and they fall from my hands. I take a step forward, mustering every bit of energy I have, and the second hag fires a blast of magic that hits me in the chin. I'm lifted off my feet and knocked backward onto the ground, where I groan as I slowly try to stand back up.

"Hey!" the first hag scolds the second. "You broke the spell!"

As I climb back to my feet, I find that I actually *do* have a bit more strength than before. The red rope seems to have died away, which is fortunate. As the first hag points her staff at me again, I snatch my Celestial Dagger off the ground and throw it at her as hard as I can.

Thwack!

The dagger slams into her staff and sticks tightly, and she utters a handful of swear words that make me hope no children are watching the livestream. I quickly scoop up Beowulf's Dagger as well and charge at her, but she raises her staff.

FOOOOOM!

A great blast of fire explodes from the end of the staff. Thankfully, a great deal *also* explodes out through the small nick that the dagger made, which sets her robes on fire. She screams and jumps away, and I cross my arms in front of my face to weather the blast. As it clears away, I charge at the second hag.

That one cackles and raises her staff. Magic flares around the thing, and she swings it at me. I simply reach out and catch it—at least, I try to. It turns out that the magic actually made it a much stronger weapon than before, and I find myself quite surprised to be knocked to my knees by the force of it. I groan as she cackles and steps backward, then swings at me again.

"Didn't expect this, did you?"

The staff catches me in the chest and smashes me backward to the ground. She suddenly seems to be standing above me and raises the staff to deliver a final, crushing blow to the skull. I raise my hand and catch hold of the staff as it falls, but that only makes my arm crack loudly and knocks my hand back against my skull.

All things considered, it's not looking good for me.

"Hey! He's mine!"

The first hag, having apparently gotten control over her fire, launches a blast of magic that hits the second one and sends her flying across the arena. Before I can move, vines explode around me and hold me in place, and I see red magic flickering through the air. She's going to drain me again, and I can't say I really like that idea. Quickly, I flex my muscles and sit up, rip the vines from the ground, and climb to my feet.

"None of that!" The first hag laughs. She's removed the Celestial Dagger from the staff, and I notice it lying on the ground not too far away. Quickly, she points her staff at me, and that same blast of red energy streaks out at me, ready to drain my energy.

This time, though, I'm ready.

I'm already in motion by the time it hits me, and before any substantial strength can be drained, I have my hands on the staff. The hag screams and tries to draw back, but with her magic focused on draining me instead of enhancing herself, it doesn't work. My strength starts to wane, but I grit my teeth, grab hold of the staff just below the nick, and squeeze as hard as I can.

Light explodes through the air as I break the staff, and the red magic surges all about. It flows through the air like a living thing, and my stomach churns. Having the life sucked out of you doesn't mix particularly well with dragon pollen, I can assure you of that. In any case, the hag lets out a few more curses, but I ignore them and instead jab the broken end of the staff down into her foot.

Suddenly given focus once more, the magic begins to drain the hag instead of me. I push down harder, making sure that the staff is stuck good and solid, then step back. There, I find the hag frozen in place, mouth agape, as the deadly magic sucks her dry before channeling the energy back through her staff and into her once more. It's a deadly loop, one that I've seen in the real world plenty of times—at least in science fiction books. The hag opens her mouth in a silent scream, and I back up.

BOOOM!

The old crone explodes violently. There's no gore—she simply vanishes in a great plume of ash and smoke and fire and energy. I smile as the last bits of her staff come clattering down, then turn around.

BAM!

A blast of red energy hits me in the chest. This one is the exploding type, and I'm lifted off my feet by the blast and flung across the clearing. I almost hit the tree trunk, but instead, I simply whack my head on the ladder as I go past. As I hit the wall on the far side, I groan and sink down to the ground. My health is at 60 percent, which isn't terrible but isn't good either.

"My sister was greedy," the hag says with a cackle as she approaches. "Me? I just want you dead. I'm willing to do whatever it takes to get you there."

I sigh and climb back to my feet, then charge at her. She flips her staff around, holding it like a gun, and begins shooting at me. Magic flashes and explodes on both sides of me as I dodge frantically through the arena. Ascalon glows brightly upon my back as it decides that this situation can be counted as peril, and I smile. The hag's face twists into one of confusion and anger, and she starts shooting faster and faster, but I only dodge faster and faster. Of course, I'm getting closer and her shots are getting more and more accurate.

"I'm not going down like this!" she screams. Suddenly, she flips her staff around and plants the end on the ground. Magic begins to flare around her, and the sky darkens. "Behold the power of the gods! Behold the true strength that can be channeled through me!" Her eyes begin to glow. "Behold—"

I snatch up my Celestial Dagger and throw it at her as hard as I can. It hits the magical barrier and dissolves in an instant.

Great. I'm down *another* dagger. I grit my teeth, and lightning begins to flash all around. The hair rises on the back of my neck, and I know I don't have many options left.

"Behold my trump card." I sheath Beowulf's Dagger, then open up my inventory. "I was hoping to save this for Odin. I suppose you should feel flattered."

Now, if the hag had continued her spell and unleashed whatever attack she was planning on bringing against me, I might have fallen. Instead . . . Curiosity flickers through her eyes, and for the briefest moment, the storm calms. It's not much, but it gives me the second I need to draw out Loki's staff.

In its normal form, it's a simple wooden staff, albeit one set with some golden inlays, along with some diamonds and rubies. Her eyes light up at seeing it, and I point the weapon at her. Once more, a *long* list of options scrolls past my vision, but the weapon is a good one and responds to my mental commands. It knows what I want, and a blast of magic leaps from the end of the weapon.

SNAP!

Spectral ropes explode out the end of the staff and wrap around the hag, dropping her to the ground in the blink of an eye. She struggles to get free, and I slowly walk forward.

"Alright . . . Let's get rid of that." I turn her staff into a bird, which happily flutters away. "And that." Several charms on her belt are transformed into spiders, which crawl away, glad to be free of their master. "Now, what's to be done with you?"

"Kill me," the hag snarls. "If you don't—"

"If I don't what?" I pause. "You'll kill yourself for me?"

"It would be better than Odin doing it," the hag snaps.

I think for a moment. If this were a human woman, I would hesitate over just killing her. In this moment, the only reason I'm really pausing is because I don't like doing what monsters want me to do, but . . . Well, in this case, our goals align.

Blam!

A blast of magic leaps from Loki's staff, and her body falls limp. After a moment, it crumbles into dust and vanishes, and I turn back around to face the top of the tree.

"Alright, Odin," I call out, "enough with the games." I draw in a deep breath and slowly brace myself. "It's your turn now."

CHAPTER THIRTEEN

There's a long pause with no answer. Suddenly, the buildings around the tree trunk dissolve into nothingness. In their place, I suddenly find myself looking at an old man sitting upon one of the top branches, looking out across the ocean. He sighs and jumps down, landing on the ground with a *thud*. Now, don't get me wrong. He's holding a spear twice as long as I am, he must stand a good seven feet tall, and he's entirely decked out in golden body armor. He certainly looks like he could jump right into a battle without batting an eye, despite the white beard and the white hair. He strides up to me, and I give him a nod.

"Enjoying the view?"

Odin sighs and shrugs. "You know something? I've never really liked all the battle and bloodshed. Sure, it was fun for the first little bit, but all it does is destroy things. Countless civilizations, countless worlds, all of it wiped out."

"Which is why you take samples of cultures." I gesture down below us. "Like The Master, and I assume you have other people as well."

"Yes, indeed. I try to salvage at least a bit from the embers that my daughter, Hella, leaves behind." Odin shifts his weight slightly, making his armor clank. "For what it's worth, when this is over with your world, I plan on dedicating a full three branches to your people. It's one of the most diverse worlds I've ever seen. To be driven back from it once, and to nearly be driven back a second time . . ." He chuckles. "Not many worlds can claim such a thing."

"If it really means that much to you, give up the fight," I snap. "Tell Hella to leave with the dungeons. We won't pursue you."

"You can't possibly convince me that Earth is a peaceful place!" Odin laughs. "Your people have enough nuclear weapons to wipe out a dozen worlds. All they would need is an excuse to pull the trigger."

"You've been driven back from our world twice," I remind him. "We're not a peaceful people, and I don't intend to give that impression. All I intend to tell you is that *if* you retreat now, when we do come after you, we might show a bit more clemency." Odin sighs, and I continue. "You say yourself that you don't want this war. Then *end it*. You're Odin. You're the most powerful of the gods, right?"

"That depends on how you count it." Odin sighs again and shakes his head. "In any case, I am not human. You have the option of changing your mind, of altering your decisions. You have the ability to ask forgiveness."

"So do you," I press. "I don't want this war. I don't want

people to die. If Hella comes through that portal into New York, I don't have a clue how many people will perish, but it'll be a lot."

"I'm afraid you simply don't understand." Odin slowly lowers his spear until the tip of it is pointed at me. "I cannot change. I do not want this war, but long ago I made a choice. I made a decision to go to battle, and that is not a state that will ever change. I can't expect you to comprehend it, but it's the truth. It's in my nature, and a person cannot change their nature."

"So, you're saying that you're going to kill me," I snap.

"I'm saying that you're in my realm, and I am the boss of this world, as you put it." Odin's eyes harden. "If I do not kill you, then I will . . . It does not matter, I suppose. I will give you three seconds to prepare yourself."

I nod, then step back and raise Loki's staff. With a flicker, armor appears on me. It's old-time armor, the stuff that a Crusader might wear but sleeker. The staff itself transforms into a shield, and with that, Odin attacks.

His spear whistles through the air as he strikes, and I brace myself as best I can.

WHAM!

The blow is crushing and flings me backward like a toy. I slam into the outer wall of the arena, and my health falls to 50 percent. Loki's staff kicks in and sends a burst of magic that raises it back up quickly, but it's still a bigger hit than I might have liked to take. I snarl and start forward, and Odin chuckles.

Pzzzzzzzzzzzzzzzew!

A great blast of solar energy flares off the spear and punches through the air like a laser. I narrowly dive out of the way, but even being close to the attack drops my health by a rather dangerous degree. I gulp and clamber back to my feet, then charge at Odin with all my strength and speed.

The mighty god laughs and adjusts his aim, then fires another solar blast. I raise my shield, and the staff adjusts several aspects of its existence. With a mighty *pong*, the energy is reflected back and hits Odin in the chest. It doesn't do much damage, but it makes him surprised, which is enough for me.

"Alright, Odin!" I cry out. "Enough!"

I throw the shield as hard as I can but remain connected to it with my magic. The shield hits Odin in the face and bounces straight back to me like a yo-yo. I've seen the trick in movies before and always wanted to do it. As I catch hold of it, Odin snarls and twirls his spear about him. The weapon cleaves loudly through the air, making a powerful whooshing noise that hurts my head. He lashes out at me, and I call upon the power of the staff again.

Flash!

With that, I shrink down to about half my size. The spear passes cleanly over my head without touching me at all, and Odin snarls in surprise. With that, I grow back to full size and transform the shield back into a staff. Before Odin can react, I point it up at his face and fire.

KA-BOOM!

A blast of magic hits him in the chin and explodes, knocking him backward. He lands with a loud *thud*, only to fire another blast of solar energy at me. It goes wide, but it's enough to cover himself as he rises back up. I grit my teeth, then fire several more blasts of magic at him.

Clang!

Clang!

Clang!

Chains burst out of thin air and wrap around his body, chaining his arms and legs together. Odin snarls and smashes free, but it takes him a moment to do so, and that's enough for me.

BLAM!

I fire another blast of magic into his face, a blast that turns into a massive boulder the moment it hits. It splits in two upon hitting him, and Odin is thrown backward once more. I snarl and stride forward, ready for the kill.

Suddenly, a noise splits the air.

Odin is laughing.

"Ah, boy, you have no idea how this makes me feel." He slowly climbs back to his feet. I fire another blast of magic at him, but he simply shrugs it off as it glances off his shoulder. "I haven't had a battle like this in . . . Oh, it's been a while. Thank you, Jason. Thank you, and . . . goodbye."

Odin charges forward and seems to grow in strength and power as he does so. I jump to the side, but I'm not fast enough, and he throws a punch that hits me in the chest and knocks me up into the air. Before I can do anything, he spins the staff and whacks me like he's hitting a baseball, and I'm launched through the air to slam into the tree trunk. A great many things seem to crack under the impact, and my armor dissolves into nothingness.

"Alright, boy! Come and face me now!" Odin snarls and charges forward. Quickly, I grab a tight hold on the staff and send it a few more commands.

Whoosh.

A figure who looks exactly like me stands up from where I'm sitting and charges off to the side. He's fast, and Odin changes direction to chase him down. I, of course, am quite invisible, and I groan as I stagger to my feet.

"Alright, body. Heal up."

With a flash of light, I heal several of my broken bones and stagger away from the trunk of the tree. Off to one side, Odin attacks the image, only for it to dissolve into sparks. In that instant, I become visible again but cloak myself before Odin can find me. He spins around, then laughs and slowly starts to walk forward.

"You have Loki's staff! I knew that, of course, but it's interesting to see you using it so well." He shakes his head. "Very few people can use it effectively, you know. Everyone can perform a few magic tricks, but the thing is a *powerful* weapon, one that most people will only struggle against. You . . . I see now why you have such a reputation."

I scroll through the list of options that the staff presents me. It can create illusions galore, but those aren't going to be useful against someone like Odin. Maybe for a few moments, but he's not a one-hit sort of combatant. That said, there are quite a few *non*-illusion options. One of them catches my eye, and a smile spreads across my face.

"You'll see it even better before I'm through with you." I dissolve the cloak, and Odin spins toward me. With a flicker,

I transform the staff into a machine gun and slowly raise it to point at him.

"A toy from Earth?" Odin laughs.

"A toy from Earth that's been scaled to match your celestial standards," I answer. With a flicker, the staff activates the next part of my plan, and duplicate versions of myself step off to my right and left.

"More trickery?"

"Nope." I shake my head. "These guys are real enough. Fire at will."

All three of us squeeze down on the triggers and send an immense firestorm of bullets at the raging god. The bullets ping all across him, and Odin lets out a roar. I was able to kill Loki with bullets, after all. They're not going to kill him immediately, but they punch through his armor well enough. Golden blood trickles out from his armor, and he charges forward into the storm of bullets.

Now, the trick with creating duplicates instead of illusions—at least based on the description that I read for about two seconds—is that if they wind up dying, *you* die, whereas illusions will simply dissolve and leave you entirely unharmed. I watch as Odin bears down on me, taking more and more and more damage, then give a nod.

"End!"

Both duplicates vanish, and I activate a different effect of the staff. With a flash, I teleport away to the other side of the arena and leave a bleeding Odin to bring his spear crashing down on an empty corner. He snarls and turns around, blood dripping down to the ground.

In that instant, I see something in his eyes.

Respect. Respect and, more importantly, fear.

He knows he's in a situation where he's likely to die. He takes a deep breath and magic begins to flare around him.

[Skill: Bearing of a Knight.]

[Peril Detected.]

Ascalon begins to glow on my back, and my stats increase. I don't know what that means, but I have a good enough imagination to assume that there could be a wide number of different horrible things about to happen to me. Not wanting to waste Ascalon's power, I charge forward, racing across the ground just as fast as I can possibly go. As I do, I transform the machine gun back into a staff, then nod.

"Alright. One more trick."

With a flash, the staff transforms into a dagger, and I grow to the size of Odin himself. My feet shake the ground, and he snarls and comes forward to meet me. With a flick of his wrist, he throws the spear. I dodge to the side, letting it pass harmlessly by, and throw myself at him.

Wham!

He throws a powerful punch into my gut and knocks me up into the air slightly. Had I still been my ordinary size, it would have sent me rag-dolling up into the stratosphere. As it is, my health drops to about 30 percent and I'm brought up short. Odin snarls and hits me a second time, punching me across the cheek.

My health plummets to 3 percent, and Ascalon starts to burn. Odin snarls and lifts his hands, and I stab forward.

Loki's staff, as a dagger, stabs straight through Odin's

armor and plunges deep into his gut. Odin's eyes go wide, and he slowly staggers backward. I rip the dagger out and watch as a great deal of golden blood trickles down onto the ground.

"You're . . ."

"I'm the one who's going to save the Earth. That's right." I nod. "And I'm saving it from people like *you*. Care to give up now?"

Odin doesn't speak, but his eyes harden. I nod, then slash forward. The dagger cleaves through his neck, and with a *thud*, his head falls to the ground. His body hits a moment later, and I allow myself to shrink back down to my normal size.

[You have leveled up!]

[Congratulations! You are now Level 84!]

[You have leveled up!]

[Congratulations! You are now Level 85!]

[You have leveled up!]

[Congratulations! You are now Level 86!]

For a long moment, I just stand there looking at the fallen god. Loki is dead. Odin is dead. That doesn't leave many more between myself and Hella—I hope. I slowly turn away and grab a Pumped! out of my inventory to heal.

One more dungeon cleared. Now . . . Well, I just have to keep going until I make it all the way to the top.

CHAPTER FOURTEEN

I take my time healing up. I haven't slept in quite some time, if you'll recall, and I've been in the dungeon for a long while. In the meantime, I look for a way out, and . . . Well, suffice it to say that I don't see anything. No portal appears, and I certainly don't see a path that might lead to one. I don't know what that means, but it's annoying, to say the least. Am I trapped here? With communication down, I can't just call up Mr. Wang to see how he's doing, nor can I count on him being able to open up a portal to help me escape. To top it off, there's not really any loot strewn around the area, which means I'm mostly just left to wait. Don't get me wrong: I don't mind the slowdown. But as I sit and scratch my head, I don't exactly come up with a plethora of ideas.

[ShadowDancer: So . . . Jason? It looks like things are starting to get bad back in the city again.]

[ViperQueen: Yeah! Thunder, lightning, the whole she-bang! You'd better get back there as quickly as you can!]

[DarkCynic: Yeah, you really should. I don't want to die because you're stuck in Odin's tree.]

I roll my eyes as the chats continue to come through. "Don't you know that I'd open up a portal if I could?" I twirl the staff around my hand a few times. Just for fun, I start transforming it into different things. A spear. A sword. A dagger. I also pick up Odin's spear, which I tuck into my inventory. "Straight from here to the clubhouse, if only—"

ZAP!

A bolt of lightning shoots out of the staff, which at that moment looks like an umbrella, and opens up a portal just a few feet in front of me. I blink in surprise at it, then look down at the staff.

"Right." I slowly stick the umbrella back into my inventory. "I . . . uh . . . forgot that it could do that."

My chat begins to chide me over the fact that I was zapped straight from the tower right into Loki's dungeon, and I sigh. I'm going to take no end of flak for this one, I'm sure, but for the time being, I just need to get going. I slowly walk forward and step through the portal, and with that, I'm sucked away.

The portal journey is a longer one, but with a flash, I come out the other end and find myself standing in the middle of a ring of warriors. There are dozens of soldiers all pointing their weapons at me, and I realize that *they* simply saw a portal suddenly open in the middle of the clubhouse.

"Jason! Is that you or a doppelgänger?" Mr. Wang calls out.

"Uh . . . Ask me a question only I would know the answer to."

There's a long pause. "That's going to be difficult," Mr. Wang finally replies, "since everything you do is livestreamed. Anything that you know, everyone else would know too."

"Fair point." I frown in thought. "Well . . . You know me: if you attack me, I'll only beat you to a pulp. Correct me if I'm wrong, but doppelgängers are like level eighty or something. If I'm actually one of those, I'll be weaker than the original Jason, so . . ."

"So attacking you, either way, won't end well." Mr. Wang shrugs. "When you put it that way . . . Stand down, everyone! Someone check on Jason's livestream to see if this one is telling the truth."

The group of warriors slowly starts to disband. Suddenly, a flash of light explodes through the room and a clap of thunder shakes the club. I shudder and walk up to the windows looking out across the city. Mr. Wang joins me, though I notice that John and a few other warriors aren't all that far behind him. Together, we stare out over a vast gray landscape.

Thick gray clouds cover the entirety of the city. It's not nighttime anymore, but the clouds are so thick that most of the streetlights have turned on, and in general, it just looks dismal. Lightning flashes down from the clouds, hitting buildings and lampposts and cell towers, but it generally doesn't seem to be doing a lot of damage.

"Thor," I murmur. "He's here."

"It would seem that when Odin fell, something was triggered." Mr. Wang nods to me. "Yeah, we were watching your livestream at least that much. Real bang-up job you did with him. Congrats."

"Why, thank you." I bow my head slightly, then return my attention to the storm. "How long has this been going on?"

"Uh . . . I'd say the better part of four hours?" Mr. Wang shrugs. "We've contacted the different news stations and meteorological outposts. Some of them are saying that they can detect things moving about above the clouds, some of them say that they're not finding a thing. We tried to get in contact with the airports—we figured their radar might be better suited for that sort of thing—but they haven't been able to pin anything down yet."

I nod slowly as I work through it all in my head. "So, we don't have any actual sightings of Thor yet."

"No." Mr. Wang shakes his head. "A few anecdotal reports have popped up on the internet, but nothing that I'd consider solid enough to risk sending resources after."

"Great." I continue thinking for a few moments. "When Odin's dungeon appeared, he didn't appear immediately either. His dungeon moved around for a while, dumping out monsters here and there, until I managed to back it into a corner. Thor might be doing the same thing."

"What do you mean?" Mr. Wang looks confused.

"I think it's called psychological warfare." I shrug. "If you can spook the enemy well enough, you can actually cause quite a bit of damage before you ever start firing shots."

"Well, he's certainly got us spooked." Mr. Wang shakes his head. "At least in theory, he could appear at anytime. We're just watching and waiting."

"Then we need to turn that against him. How is everyone else doing?"

"Well enough. I'm having them work in shifts, clearing dungeons and then resting. We've closed down almost half of the remaining dungeons in the city, and with my XP wristbands, they're leveling up quite rapidly."

"Good." I nod. "In that case, keep up the good work." I turn away, and Mr. Wang holds up a hand.

"And what are you doing?"

"I'm going to go get some sleep," I answer. "And, beyond that, I have a Phoenix to attend to."

I soon stagger up to the hotel room where Burnie is resting. I'm more tired than I realize and start to swoon at the sight of the bed. Before I collapse, though, I find Burnie resting on the bed, snuggled up to several pillows. He seems to perk up at seeing me, and I give him a smile and sit down on the edge of the bed.

"Hey." I reach out to stroke the back of his head. "How are you holding up?"

Well enough, Master, Burnie answers. *I . . . I'm ready for the procedure if you are.*

I draw in a deep breath. "And after this, you won't remember me?"

Burnie shakes his head. *I'm so sorry, Master. If that will be too painful, I can just—*

"No." I hold up a hand. "That's alright. I'll be sad, but . . . we can just get to know each other all over again."

Burnie seems to smile, and he gives a nod of his avian head. *In that case, can you please set me over on those bricks?*

I glance around until I find a small assortment of bricks not too far from the bed. They've been laid out in a perfect square. I carefully pick up Burnie and set him down on them, and he sits himself up.

Now, Master, step back. He pauses as I take a few steps back. Without my bidding, my pocket dimension opens and all my pets come walking out. One by one, they walk up and seem to say something to Burnie before retreating to a safe distance. As Bjorn finishes up, Burnie turns and looks me in the eye. *Goodbye, Master. Goodbye, and . . . hello.*

With that, flames blaze up all around him. The fire crackles higher and higher and soon entirely engulfs him. The flames burn hotter, cycling from orange to blue to white, and then . . . with a brilliant flash of light, the fire fades away leaving nothing but a small pile of ash on the bricks. I stare down at the ash, knowing well the legend of the phoenix, and wait with desperate, bated breath.

"Come on, Burnie," I whisper. "Don't fail me now."

There's a long painful pause. Then, slowly, magic begins to flicker around the edges of the ash. A few sparks rise up from it and take on the form of a Phoenix—a small one, mind you, but a Phoenix nonetheless. I can hardly speak, and then . . .

Flash!

With a loud pop, Burnie reappears. He's a fraction of his old size, no more than a chick. He slowly staggers to his feet, then looks over at me.

You're my master?

"Yes, I am." I kneel down and hold out my hand. The little chick flaps his wings, though he can't fully rise up into the air.

I walk forward and let him climb into my palm, and he chirps happily.

Did I just regenerate?

"You did." I smile. "I know you don't remember me, but I know we'll get to know each other well enough."

I look forward to it. You seem like a nice master.

"I sure hope I am." I turn to look at my other pets. "Everyone, meet Burnie."

My other pets walk forward and take turns saying hello to the young Phoenix. Bjorn allows me to place Burnie on his back, and together, they all go back into my pocket dimension to get better acquainted. I watch them go, then sigh and flop down on the bed.

Exhausted by all the fighting, as well as the mental exertion of saying goodbye to an old friend and hello to a new one, my eyes fall shut long before I even have a chance to pull the blankets up over my body.

When I wake up, I feel like I've hardly slept at all, though I know from the clock on the wall that about four hours have passed. There's no one in the room, but the whole building shakes with powerful claps of thunder.

Boom!

BOOM!

BOOOM!

I lurch to my feet as the floor shudders beneath me and stagger up to the closest window. Throwing back the blinds, I find that the clouds over the city have grown even thicker, casting the entire city into a deep pseudo-night. Lightning flashes over and over and over again, and I grit my teeth as I look out upon it all.

"Sir." The voice of Mr. Wang's sister echoes behind me, and I turn to find her standing in the doorway, eyes wide. "I'm sorry, I didn't realize you were awake."

I shrug, then turn and walk across the room toward her. "You were coming to wake me up?"

"Yes," she says apologetically. "I'm afraid things are getting a lot worse, and whether or not you're tired, we—we need you."

"No need to be sorry." I shake my head and follow her out into the hall. "Let's go get this guy."

CHAPTER FIFTEEN

As I run down into the main club, I find things in complete and utter chaos. Warriors rush this way and that, some of them charging out into battle, others limping back in. As I run down the stairs to the main level, a powerful blast of lightning strikes the helipad and causes a resounding explosion that shatters several glass panes. A cold, wet wind blows into the club, and I shudder against the chill.

"Jason!" Mr. Wang looks up and waves at me. "Good to see you up! Sorry to disturb your rest!"

"Not to worry," I say as I jog up to him. He approaches one of the broken panes and, carefully, bends down and touches the shards. With a flash, the window is repaired, and I shake my head. "I imagine that none of us is going to get much rest until we're either dead or the portals have been closed."

"Indeed. I'll get you as much as I can, but it'll likely only be enough to fuel you through the next battle." Mr. Wang fixes up the next glass plane, and I'm momentarily reminded that he is technically one of the warriors as well. The difference is that his powers are limited to fixing things in the real world as opposed to breaking things in the dungeon. Those very powers were how he made most of his fortune back when the dungeons first opened.

I frown as a thought crosses my mind. "Question: if you can fix things, why didn't you just fix the computers and portal generators when Loki smashed them?"

"That's quite simple, really." Mr. Wang shrugs. "He used a skill, some sort of magic, that blocked *my* skill from working. I don't know what it is or was or anything." He chuckles. "Your staff might actually be able to reverse it, now that I think about it." He shakes his head. "Hindsight, and all that. It's amazing the things you think about *after* the chaos has died down."

"Here, here," I murmur, then nod out across the city. Lightning hits another building just a few streets down, and I cross my arms. "What's the situation? When did all this start up?"

"It escalated to this level not more than five minutes ago," Mr. Wang answers. "Came out of nowhere. The airports are reporting that they're detecting something in the atmosphere now too. Some sort of small personal craft is what they're saying, though it's traveling far faster than any registered airplane."

"That would be Thor," I mutter. "How do I catch him and kill him?"

"Excellent question, and one we're working on right now."

Mr. Wang points out across the city to my right. "We're detecting a buildup of energy right over there. We think that's where his portal is going to open, though we can't be certain. Our forces are moving into position just in case. I'd like to keep you here until we know for sure, but—"

Bzzzzzzzzzzzzmmmmmm!

A blast of lightning suddenly shoots down from the sky. I can't see exactly what it hits, but I see at least one building burst into flames, and another one slowly topples to the side in a fiery crash. My jaw drops, and the lightning begins to pulse stronger and faster. Hidden beneath the crackling energies, it seems to flicker with all the colors of the rainbow.

"The Bifrost," I whisper.

"Weaponized." Mr. Wang nods. "If *that's* Thor's portal, I can only imagine what Hella's will look like."

"Here, here," I mutter. I check my level: still eighty-six, which isn't bad, but it is a lot lower than I'd like it to be going into battle against Thor himself. "How quickly can you get me there?"

"Unfortunately, all our Batmobiles have broken down," Mr. Wang apologizes with a small smile.

"Then I'll just have to go on horseback." I quickly walk to the glass door that leads out onto the helipad. "Keep an eye on me! I don't know what I'm going to be walking into, but I somehow doubt that it's going to be anything good. If he's being this bold, darting about in the real world, you may need to be able to respond elsewhere."

Mr. Wang nods, and with that, I draw in a deep breath and walk out onto the helipad and up to the edge of the platform, a light rain spraying against me. Slowly, I look down at the depths below . . . and then I jump.

Once, a jump from such a height would have been fatal. As time has progressed, it's gone from fatal to deadly to painful to mildly inconvenient to epic. When I slam into the sidewalk below, I nod in confirmation that I've officially reached the final stage. Sure, superhero landings are a *little* cliche, but there's a reason they're done so much.

I climb to my feet and bolt down the sidewalk. There's no one out and about, which makes things easier for me. With a flash, Lightfax bolts from my pocket dimension. As she runs past me, I catch hold of her neck and swing up onto her back, and we shoot down the street just as fast as we can go.

Lightfax's hooves pound against the pavement, and we flash down street after street at a simply extraordinary speed. The steed is powerful, and she's only become more so as I've gotten stronger myself. Ahead, I can see the glow in the sky showing where the Bifrost has opened. I grit my teeth and brace myself for battle, wondering what I'll be walking into.

We come racing around one final corner, and I find myself staring into a maelstrom of utter destruction. The Bifrost is pulsing down from the sky and hitting an intersection squarely. It seems to be between an industrial and residential district. Around half a block on either side of the point of impact has been destroyed by fire and lightning strikes, and the destruction is slowly spreading. Civilians scream and tear down the streets away from the blast, while a deep, laughing voice emanates from within. Meanwhile, lines of warriors are rapidly forming up around it, watching and waiting. I swing down from Lightfax as I come up to the rear of the lines, and my steed flashes back into my pocket dimension as I slip through the crowd.

"John!" I call out. Ahead of me, John turns and nods in my direction, and I step up next to him. "What's the deal?"

As if in answer, a bolt of lightning shoots out of the swirling column of deadly energy and hits the street right in front of me. Molten asphalt is blasted up across me, and I grimace and wipe it away. It hurts, but compared to some of the pain I've been through recently, it's really quite bearable.

"The *deal* is that we're waiting." John shrugs. "I can only assume that something's going to be coming out of that thing soon enough, but nothing's appeared so far. Just lots of lightning and fire."

I nod slowly. I almost wonder if I can see dark forms moving about beyond the barrier, but I can't quite tell for sure. High above, I think I can see a portal in the sky itself, the source of the energy attack. If that's the case, it gives me a destination. Yes, Thor is out here for the time being, but if I manage to get inside his dungeon, he'll surely stop his attack on the city. Even if he doesn't, if I can gain access to the Bifrost . . . It's a powerful weapon, to be certain.

"I'm detecting movement!" a police officer calls out from the side. He's holding a radar dish and has it pointed at the epicenter of the blast. "It looks big! There are things coming down from above, and—"

Snip!

An arrow shoots out of the Bifrost and hits the officer in the chest. He staggers backward and falls, and with that, a great roar echoes through the air. Monsters begin to rush out of the Bifrost, and all around me, the warriors let out cries and charge forward to meet them.

[LunarEclipse: Alright, now this is what I'm talking about! Giant epic battle!]

[ViperQueen: Stay safe, Jason!]

[RazorEdge: Punch some monsters for me, alright?]

[GrendleH8tr: Keep your head about you, kid. This isn't going to be nearly as easy as it looks.]

The creatures are odd things. I'd call them satyrs if I had to give a name to them. They look like half-humans, half-goats, with the goat part dominating. They're holding a wide variety of weapons, from bows to swords to clubs and, all things considered, look rather like the low-level things I've been tearing through ever since I came into the dungeons.

"Piece of cake!" I call out to John as we leap toward the battle.

"Right back atcha!" he calls back. "Whoever kills the most of these things wins!"

"Loser buys the other a year's supply of Pumped?"

"Deal!"

I smile, then push onward even faster. I draw out Beowulf's Dagger and hold it tightly in my right hand. As the first of the satyrs comes racing up to me, I throw a powerful slash at its throat.

Wham!

It throws a strong uppercut into my chest and lifts me off the ground. I grit my teeth and stab it in the chest, and it punches me again, actually knocking me sideways. That makes me mad, and I snarl and stab it once more, then pull the blade downward as hard as I can. It's hard work, way harder than it ought to be, and the dagger slashes through the thing's guts. The monster staggers and falls forward, and I move onto the next one.

Next to me, John throws a powerful uppercut into a satyr's chin. Now, I know John. He's got some muscle—and they're eating his punches like breakfast. The satyr slashes John across the chest with a dagger, drawing a great deal of blood, and John growls.

"No you don't!"

He spins and punches it in the chest as hard as he can. This time it's more effective and the monster is blasted backward into the ranks. That said, it doesn't kill it, and more of the things surge forward as I watch.

I dive into the fray, hacking and slashing with my dagger just as fast as I can move. The satyrs are solidly built, that's for sure. I slash one across the neck, and I have to admit a bit of frustration as I only cut through its throat and don't actually remove the whole head. John grabs one of them by the arms, slings it down to the ground, and smashes it into the pavement.

"Anything else and I'd have ripped the arm clean off!" John complains.

"No guts, no glory, right?" I spin and stab one of the things in the chest. It punches me in the face, knocking me backward, and I grit my teeth as blood fills my mouth. I rip the dagger free, then stab it three more times before it falls.

"Yeah, but I'd rather that the guts belong to my opponent!" John calls out.

"Fair point." I take a few steps backward, and several arrows flash over my head. They explode brilliantly as they stick in half a dozen of the monsters, and while I see holes blown in several of them, none of the monsters falls. That's frustrating. I glance over my shoulder to see Ali keeping up the attack, but the arrows aren't doing nearly as much good as I might like.

The story is the same all around me. I watch as one of the satyrs brings a club crashing down on the helmet of a Viking-styled warrior not far from me. The blow caves in the side of the helmet and knocks him to the ground. Any hope of his survival is ended a moment later as the satyrs stab him several times through the chest. Another warrior takes a spear through the gut, and yet another one is struck down by a war hammer.

Things aren't looking good across the board. I slash my dagger through the chest of another of the satyrs, twice, and then step back.

"Alright, then. We're going to have to bring out the big guns, I suppose."

"And why didn't you do that . . . the first . . . time?" John grunts as he struggles to take down a slightly larger satyr. He headbutts the thing, knocking it backward, and then punches it in the jaw. It starts to fall backward, and he snatches the sword out of its grasp, flips it around, and stabs it through the gut. The monster lands on the ground with a sickening *slap*, and he steps back before punching the next monster in line.

"Because I didn't want to cause any collateral damage," I answer simply. "Here, catch! This will probably help you more than me at this point."

I toss Beowulf's Dagger to him. John catches it, then spins and slashes the weapon through the gut of another of the monsters. I lose a few buffs off the trade, but it's a fair enough statement: as my level climbs, the dagger is simply becoming a lower-tier weapon for me. I have more powerful tools at my disposal, and I'm just going to have to make use of them.

Against so large a force . . . I think for a moment, then step back and open up my inventory. Odin's spear falls into my palm, shrinking slightly to fit my stature. A few warriors around me whistle, and the satyrs scream. I smile at them, then point the weapon into their midst.

"Alright, goats. Time to get roasted."

A great blast of solar energy explodes off the end of the spear and cuts through the satyrs like butter. Dozens of them are sliced cleanly in half by the blast, and I swing the spear carefully as I continue to mow down over three-quarters of the pack.

[You have leveled up!]

[Congratulations! You are now Level 87!]

[You have leveled up!]

[Congratulations! You are now Level 88!]

I give the spear a twirl as the solar flare dies down, though I do wince as a building on the other side of the intersection slowly collapses, brought down by my attack. I get a few more kills when the collapse buries several satyrs under several dozen tons of rubble, and I hope that I didn't take out any people along with them. In any case, that's taken care of, which makes the fight a great deal more manageable.

I charge into battle once more, this time filled with more confidence. All around me, the warriors rally and do the same, throwing themselves into the fray with gusto. The remaining satyrs are forced steadily backward toward the portal, and I make sure to make it as harrowing as possible.

Several near the rear break rank and charge for the safety of the Bifrost. I point the spear at them and fire a blast of energy. It cuts through them, and the rest snarl and face us with renewed fury. One of them attacks me with a sword, and I only *just* block the blow with the shaft of the spear. For several long seconds we duke it out, with the satyr attacking and slashing just as hard as it possibly can. I hold my own and then see an opening. Quickly, I spin the spear around and stab it through the gut. The spearhead pokes out its back, and the thing slowly goes limp. With that, I fire another blast of solar energy and hit another escapee while *also* cutting the corpse from the spear.

"You know, you're really not bad," John says with a smile as he stabs the very last satyr through the neck. It gurgles and staggers, and he rips the blade out. The monster collapses in a heap, and I slowly look around, surveying the damage. There are hundreds of bodies, civilians and satyrs and warriors alike. Some have been burned by the fire of the Bifrost. Some have been cut up, some beaten, some don't show any noticeable injuries but are quite dead nonetheless.

"Really not bad." I smile and hold out my hand, which John shakes. "I'll take that as a compliment."

[LunarEclipse: Jason, you're way more than *that!* He should be thanking you for saving his life!]

[ShadowDancer: LunarEclipse? That's exactly what he's doing.]

[ChaosRider: I don't get it.]

[DarkCynic: It's a guy thing. A buddy-cop sort of thing.]

[ChaosRider: Uh . . . I still don't get it, but whatever.]

I laugh as I look the messages over, then slowly turn to face the Bifrost.

"You going through it?" John asks me. He can see the glint in my eyes and crosses his arms tightly.

"I think so." I nod. "I know Thor is on this side of the portal, but if I can get in there, I might be able to lure him back through. After all, if I'm threatening to blow up his entire flagship . . ."

"It's a risk." John shrugs. "If he stays here, he'll be able to run amok without anyone who can challenge him."

"I know," I mutter. "I just—"

With a flicker, the Bifrost begins to shrink. Ordinarily, that would be welcome news, but I have to admit that it makes me nervous. It reduces my time to make a decision.

"Go!" John shouts out. "Go! We'll handle Thor if he does show himself. Go burn his home to the ground!"

I nod, then charge toward the lightning. It starts to shrink faster, and I put on a burst of speed. A moment later, I dive into the torrent of energy and find myself sucked upward, like I'm being abducted by aliens. With that, I'm carried away . . . onward and upward, toward whatever might be waiting for me on the far side.

CHAPTER SIXTEEN

Light blazes all around me, dazzling my eyes and making my head spin. It's really something else, and I find myself drawn ever upward by an unseen hand, pulling me along. It feels similar to being sucked through a portal, but without being dematerialized.

[DarkCynic: Whoa! That's sort of pretty.]

[RazorEdge: Yeah!!! I love it!]

[GoldenShield: I've got to admit, sometimes I wish I could be a warrior. This is totally one of those times!]

Suddenly, though, I reach the top of the Bifrost and hit the portal itself. Which is when I'm reminded that the beam of energy was being projected out of the portal down to the street below and it wasn't a portal in and of itself. Lightning explodes across my body as I'm sucked into the portal, and *that's* much the same as before.

I know I've said it in the past, but these portals are *weird*.

Your whole body turns to soup, and while you do come out the other side looking more or less like you did when you entered, you never quite know if the flesh making up your eyes was once part of your knees or if the part now composing your gut used to be part of your brain. It always leaves me a bit discombobulated, and this is no exception.

Thankfully, the portal itself is short, and I'm quickly spat out the other side. As I land on the ground, I hear a startled gasp along with a clank of armor, and I quickly look about.

The portal opens into a small courtyard. Just in front of the portal is a glittering diamond set upon a pedestal, which has a number of glowing rainbow beams of light shooting out of it. That's the Bifrost projector, I'm certain of it. Behind that, I can see a rather grand castle rising up from the midst of what seems to be an elegant city, though as I'm down in a courtyard, all I can really see are the peaks of golden buildings poking up here and there. In any case, what I can see is rather beautiful, and I have to say that I'm impressed by it.

Of course, surrounding me, standing in front of the broad gates that lead *out* of the courtyard, are quite a few guards. They're all wearing shiny golden armor and have their hands on their swords.

"Well, well, well," a woman's voice echoes through the air, and I glance around as a female warrior slowly walks into the area. She's tall, almost a head higher than the other guards, and wears a helmet that almost entirely conceals her features. Frankly, the only way I know she's female is simply by her voice.

"Let's see . . ." I hold up a finger. "You'll be Freya?"

"Sif," the woman counters. She slowly approaches me. She seems coiled like a snake, ready to strike at a moment's notice. She's no one to mess around with, I'm certain of that. "Welcome to my trap."

"Trap?" I raise an eyebrow. "You know it's usually not a good idea to trap prey stronger than the trap itself, right?"

[ShadowDancer: OOH! Burn!]

[ViperQueen: I don't know if that's *really* that good of a burn. Possibly accurate, but kind of cliche.]

[RazorEdge: Yeah . . . You can do better, Jason.]

I snort as I watch the chat, then turn my attention back to Sif. "If that's the case, why don't you just sit back and explain your little trap?"

Sif shrugs. "It's really pretty simple. We knew you wouldn't be able to resist charging through the portal, even though you knew Thor was already on the other side. Too much promise of loot, of glory. So . . . we brought you here." She reaches out and picks up the diamond, and the lights flicker and die away. In turn, the portal closes as well, which is a problem. "And now you're trapped and Thor can cause as much chaos as he desires."

"Then I'll just have to kill you and get back to him quickly." My mind whirls. I knew ahead of time that this was a possibility, but I was really hoping that I was wrong. "Hand over that diamond and we'll get down to business."

"How about I *don't?*" Sif starts to back away. One of the gate doors opens for her, and she starts to stride off. "Guards, deal with him."

With that, I bolt forward. The guards respond and slam

the gate door shut long before I can get to Sif. Quickly, I draw out Odin's spear and plant my feet.

"Anyone feeling lucky can certainly try me," I snarl. "Anyone who's smart can open those gates and let me get after Sif."

There's no response other than for the guards to lock ranks. They stare down at me, a dozen in all. This is going to be a tough fight.

Well, so be it. I can handle it.

I activate the spear's solar flare and blast the guards with a great torrent of energy. They all raise their shields, blocking the attack. It knocks them backward and staggers them, but it doesn't kill any of them. Well, that's fine by me. I didn't need them to die by it, anyway.

All I needed was a bit of cover.

Quickly, I switch out the spear for Loki's staff, and before any of them can recover, I cloak myself and slip off to one side. As they glance around and find themselves alone, they begin to quake, but none of them breaks formation. They're trained well. I scroll through the options available to me, try-ing out one quick idea before I engage them. If I can use the staff to open up a portal straight back to Earth . . . Well, I can always come back here *after* I've taken care of Thor.

[Error: Loki's Staff cannot open portals in and out of Asgardian Dungeons. This may only be accomplished by Bifrost Crystals.]

I was afraid of that. I quickly transform the staff into a machine gun, then uncloak myself and open fire.

Tat-tat-tat-tat-tat-tat-tat-tat-tat-tat-tat-tat-tat-tat-tat-tat-tat-tat-tat-tat-tat-tat!

Bullets spray across the courtyard, blasting holes in the walls and pinging straight through the shields of the guards. They all dive for cover, and several of them fall in pools of golden blood. As the gun winds down, several of them charge at me, and I spin to face them.

Flash!

I transform the staff into a dagger, then rush forward to meet them. It's a much stronger dagger than my others, and as the first guard slashes at me, I duck under the blow, then come up close. I stab him clean through his armor, deep into the gut, and shove him backward. He stumbles and falls, and with that, I spin onward to the next challenger.

"Flank!"

Two more guards approach slowly, taking up a position on either side of me. Fire glints in their eyes, and they slowly start to move around, ready to attack from either side. I keep a close eye on both of them and begin to allow more magic to flow through the staff. One of them senses it and charges, and I fire a blast of spectral ropes at him. They wrap around his body like a spider's web, and the second soldier screams and charges as well.

I allow the tied-up soldier to fall to the cobbles, then spin and slash at the second one. My dagger meets his sword, and a great explosion of sparks erupts throughout the courtyard. The guard staggers slightly, and I lunge at him.

Flick!

A dagger appears in *his* hand, and he stabs me in the gut. That hurts—a *lot*—and I groan as I stab him in the same place. He grits his teeth and pushes, and I do the same. It's a battle of endurance.

The only difference is that I have Loki's staff, and all he has is an Asgardian dagger.

With a flicker, I transform my dagger into a sword. There's a sharp clang from inside his armor, and the guard slowly falls to the side, dead. I stagger back away from him, then spin to face the other guards coming my way.

They're a bit more cautious, and rightly so. That said, if they knew much about Loki's staff, they would have charged into battle instead of playing it safe. I spin to face them as I transform the sword back into a staff and fire several blasts of explosive magic at them. The concussive explosions knock the guards down, scattering their ranks, and I charge forward as hard and fast as I can.

The magic is fun, but at the end of the day, I'm a dagger guy, so I transform the staff back into a dagger as I come upon the first guard, the one I had tied up. He's just staggering to his feet, and I slash open his throat before he has a chance to fully stand up. Another guard, recovering from the blast, stands up and lashes outward with his sword.

He's fast, this one, and I take a step back as the blade cleaves through the air. He seizes the chance and presses hard, forcing me to take step after step after step backward. He snarls as he pressures me, passing over the bodies of his comrades as he does so.

"You're nothing but a dog," he snaps.

"Some of my best friends are dogs," I retort. "You're the one who's not going to walk away from this alive. Throw down your weapons, take me to Sif, and—"

I sense movement off to the right, and I glance in that

direction to see a guard charging at me full tilt. He has his sword drawn back to run me through and stabs right as he comes up to me. Thankfully, I have just enough warning to step forward and use my dagger to parry the sword quite easily. The guard passes behind me, and I spin to attack him as he does so. My dagger punches into his chest, straight through the armor, and I slam him to the ground. Now, part of why I do this is because it looks cool, but mostly it's because of the *other* guard performing a powerful slash against me. Dropping to the ground lets the sword pass over my head, and I pull the dagger out and spin.

I hit that guard across the knees. I don't cut them clean through, but I draw blood, and the guard screams and falls. I quickly stand up, transform the dagger into a pistol, and fire two quick shots through him. He collapses, and with that, I move on.

There are only three more guards left standing, and they quake in their boots as I approach. I raise the pistol, then nod at them.

"Alright, time to make a deal. Take me to Sif and I'll leave you alive. Fight me and you'll regret it. It's up to you."

The guards don't hesitate for even a moment and charge me in one motion. I sigh, then transform the pistol back into a dagger and go to work. The first guard strikes, and I parry the attack and slash him across his gut. The other two try to flank me. One slashes high, one goes low. I jump backward, narrowly avoiding both, and attack the one on my right.

Slamming up against his torso, I get far inside his range of attack and manage to put him down within only a few seconds. The last guard shakes visibly, but he stands his ground as I turn to face him.

He doesn't remain standing for very long.

[You have leveled up!]

[Congratulations! You are now Level 89!]

As the last of them clatters to the ground, I let out a long breath, and my chat explodes.

[ShadowDancer: Yeah, Jason! That was just about the coolest thing I've seen today.]

[LunarEclipse: I'd like to see him do it again!]

[ViperQueen: Frankly, I'd like to see him take down Sif and then get back to New York. I don't live all *that* far away, and things are getting hairy out here. That storm is *bad*, and Thor is going on a destructive rampage as we speak.]

Horror shoots through me as I read that last message. "Can anyone send me some pictures? Videos?"

Almost instantly, I start getting messages. As I open them up, scenes of utter destruction fill my vision. Burning buildings, cars flying about like they're being thrown by a tornado. Here and there, I can see a dark blur shooting across the sky, but it's moving so fast that I can't really see it properly. That said, given the fact that the dark blur is shooting lightning, it's not too hard to figure out who it is.

"Alright, then." I draw in a deep breath. "I'll just have to get back a little faster than I'd planned."

With that, I stride over to the closed gates. They're locked, and I punch them as hard as I can.

[Error: Gate requires a key to open.]

"Then I won't open it." I grit my teeth together and throw

another punch. The stone around the hinges cracks, and I draw in a deep breath. Two more punches later, the pillars crack and the whole thing comes crashing down.

I'm left with a clear path up to the palace and no time to lose. I charge off without another moment's hesitation. I have a world to save and a god to kill.

Anything more than that I can deal with at a later date.

CHAPTER SEVENTEEN

The road ahead of me is a long one, stretching out for several hundred feet before turning sharply off to the right. It's lined with houses made from bricks of gold, which I have to admit are rather pleasing to look at. Here and there, I can see monsters lurking in the shadows, but I ignore them all. I have business to take care of.

As I charge down the road, a few more guards step out into view. A few of them shoot arrows at me, while several others rush out to try and block my path. I ignore them all and simply charge straight through.

"It's been a while since I tried to speedrun a game," I comment as I come around another corner and find myself facing the immense doors of the palace. "I think the last one I tried was Space Marines seven point five."

[DarkCynic: Oh yeah! I tried to speedrun that one too!]

[ViperQueen: What? I didn't even know that was a game.]

[ChaosRider: It was a fun one! Only a few people know about it. It was kind of a terrible game, but if you did a speedrun, it was entertaining.]

A sense of nostalgia fills me as I read the messages in the chat. Unfortunately, I don't have the time to really trek down memory lane. I focus on the doors ahead of me and draw upon my remaining strength.

I let out a shout as I race up the steps, then throw a powerful punch at the door. Splinters blast outward upon impact, and the doors are both thrown open, crashing against the stone walls beyond. I breathe heavily as I slowly step inside and find Sif standing in the middle of an immense throne room. She looks just like before and is holding the stone in her left hand.

"You know, I left those unlocked just for you," Sif says as she raises an eyebrow.

"You didn't leave the last one unlocked," I answer. "Now, hand over the Bifrost Crystal so I can get out of here."

"Tsk." Sif shakes her head. "I can't do that, and you know it."

"But you know something's about to happen." I twirl Loki's staff around my palms. "You wouldn't have left the door unlocked otherwise."

"You have your priorities, and I have mine." Sif slowly draws out her sword and drops into her stance. She places the crystal back into her inventory and raises an eyebrow again. "I need to protect Hella and Thor. I'll give my life to do it. You're trying to protect your Earth, and you'll give *your* life to do it. There's only one solution, but I'm not going to make it easy for you."

"Fair enough." I transform the staff into a dagger. "Come at me."

Under other circumstances, I might try to question her about the nature of the palace, the attack upon Earth, or other such things. Right now, though, I just want to get the fight over with so I can get back home. Quickly, my eyes sweep around the room. She has the crystal, and she knows I need it, which means that she'll likely do more than *just* fight me. Running away is a good way to prolong a fight since I'll have to chase after her if I want to have any hope of getting back home.

Sif reaches up and adjusts her helmet slightly, then nods. After a moment, she charges forward, pounding across the ground. Her boots clang against the stone, sparks flying from her heels, but as she comes at me, I can see several openings and weaknesses. I'm quite certain that they're only there to bait me, but if I can take advantage of that fact . . .

I don't do anything at first. As Sif reaches me, she executes a flurry of attacks that are almost certainly designed to feel me out. They come high, low, and from both sides. I parry a few but mostly just evade. I don't want her to figure out my true capabilities. As she comes to the end of her attack, I feint to the left, which is one of the places she was leaving open. She reacts almost instantly and spins to take advantage of me falling for her trap, but in a classic double cross, I'm ready for it and manage to land a slice across her shoulder. The blade doesn't do any real damage through her armor, and I frown as I disengage.

"Loki's scepter, eh?" Sif recognizes the weapon as she spins away from me and takes up her stance again. "Not too shabby, but it's weaker than my gear. Loki was the lowest of all the royals. The only reason he wasn't downgraded to a simple rift boss was because he managed to beat Hella in a game of cards. But"—she shrugs—"rely on that thing too much, and all it'll do is make sure you wind up dead."

I shake my head. "We'll see about that."

Sif attacks once more, this time not leaving anything open. I parry a few more of her attacks and lead her off to one side as I try to plan my next move. Then, as I manage to put myself between Sif and the rear entrances to the room, I suddenly erupt forward just as hard and fast as I can.

Sif's eyes go wide beneath her visor as I hit her with extreme force. My attacks come hard and fast, and she's driven back toward the rear wall. Her face becomes a mask of anger and concentration, and her own attacks and blocks start to come faster. Suddenly, I feint backward, then lunge at her. She manages to whack my shoulder with the flat of her sword, but I make it up to her right away: my dagger flashes in the light, and I stab her in the gut and slam her back against the wall. More golden blood trickles down to the ground, and I sneer at her.

"How's this for a—"

Blam!

I don't really know where the explosion comes from, but I find myself flung backward with the force of a cannon. I bounce several times off the red carpet of the throne room and slam into a pillar, which drops my health far out of the comfortable green and yellow portions of the bar. Sif pushes herself away from the wall, and I raise the dagger-shaped staff.

"Alright, Sif. Time for some tricks, then."

I fire several blasts of rope magic from it. They wrap around Sif, but she only blasts them away with a similar explosion effect. I switch over and launch another concussive attack, but she shrugs it off as though it were a light mist. I'm starting to get annoyed now. This is an entity who actually seems as difficult to defeat as a god, which doesn't make things look good for me.

"You know, I actually had hopes that this would be a good fight." Sif flings several small balls at me. They separate and stick to me, several on each arm and a handful on my legs. Tiny binders bite into my skin to pull them flush against me, and electricity explodes across me.

"Ahh!" I fall to my knees, struggling to stay upright. "You'll . . . regret—"

"No." Sif smiles as she reaches me. "No, I don't think I will. You, though, might very well rue the day that you decided to take on the heir to the—"

I raise the dagger and teleport myself to the other side of the room just as she strikes. The impact of her attack shatters the pillar that I had been standing in front of. She spins to find me and chuckles as I heal myself.

"You're weak, you know that."

"I'm strong enough to beat you."

I charge forward as I transform the dagger into a gun. I know it's not going to do anything, but it makes me feel good to shoot her several times. The bullets ping off her armor and bounce around the room, and she simply laughs. She braces herself as I transform the staff into a dagger once more, and with that, we come crashing together.

I strike with fury and stab her in the side even as she slashes me across one arm. Blood from both our bodies drips down onto the ground, and she snarls.

"You are nothing."

"A lot of people have said that to me." I grab her arm as she starts to spin away. It makes her stumble, and I yank her backward as hard as I can, then stab her in the chest. She gasps in pain, and I see her eyes light up.

Blam!

Another blast of magic knocks us apart, and Sif breaks for a small doorway at the back of the throne room. I follow along behind and switch out Loki's staff for Odin's spear as I do so. Racing through the doorway, I find myself in a massive banquet hall, with a table set with dozens of places and a *great* deal of food. Sif is near the other end, running toward a set of double doors, and I point the spear at her.

Foooooom!

A great piercing blast of solar energy tears through the table, cutting it clean in half, then slashes across the doors, making them shift slightly on their hinges, and locks them together. Sif spins around, anger in her eyes, and she snarls.

"I was wondering when that might come out."

Howling with fury, she charges back at me, sword flashing in the air. As she attacks, I strike back with the spear. It's an incredibly light weapon, thankfully, and I block her attacks with ease. Suddenly, though, she ducks past the spear and stabs me in the stomach. The blade sinks in a lot deeper than I'd like, and she shoves me backward.

I find the world spinning and fall to the ground. Smiling

with triumph, she steps over me and raises the sword to finish me off. Desperate, I lift the spear up and fire another blast of energy. I miss Sif, but I *do* cut through a large chain that's hanging an enormous chandelier from the ceiling. It comes crashing down where the table used to stand, and while it doesn't hit either of us, it *does* make Sif jump.

Which is just what I need.

I roll out of the way before she can strike and force myself back to my feet. Sif snarls and leaps forward, then drives her knee into my face and smashes me back into the wall. I respond by letting off another blast of energy from the spear. This time I lose my grip on the weapon as I do so, and it comes clattering down. But, as it does, the blast hits Sif in the head.

To her credit, it doesn't actually kill her, though it *does* melt a good portion of her helmet. The molten metal runs down her face and into the main body of her armor, and she screams.

I let out a shout as well, then lunge forward and punch her in the gut as hard as I can. I'm sure it doesn't do much on its own, but with the other wounds I've inflicted, she stumbles backward and turns. She takes off running once more, and this time I let her. Quickly, I open up my inventory and chug several Pumped! bottles, then take off after her.

Injured or not, she's still fast, and I find myself behind her. The chase winds through the long halls of the castle, through elaborate pleasure gardens, through chamber rooms, more banquet halls, and kitchens. Finally, we burst out into a wide courtyard surrounding the castle. We seem to be on the back side of it, with a low wall looking out over the rest of the city. A high guard tower rises above the area, with a flag flying from its peak. Sif charges toward the doors of the tower, smashes through, and starts running upward. I see her pass by several windows on the way up, and I slowly draw to a stop.

[DarkCynic: Better be careful, Jason! That's probably a trap!]

[IceQueen: Yeah! She'll wait at the top to stab you or something!]

[ChaosRider: Better not go in there!]

[GoldenShield: Maybe try to climb the outer wall?]

An idea comes into my mind, and I let out a long breath. "No, I'm not going to climb the outer wall." I shake my head. "I'm going to bring the outer wall down to me. Blub?"

With a flicker, my pocket dimension opens, and Blub bounces out and into my hand. He starts to inflate, and I look up at the tower. Suddenly, I see Sif appear on the top level, looking down at me. I should probably explain that the top floor of the tower is open at the sides with a roof overhead, which is likely designed to prevent enemy arrows from killing the guards from above.

"You should have followed me inside!" she calls down. I frown, and Sif takes a step back. A moment later, a *massive* crossbow pokes its nose over the edge of the wall and tilts down to point at me. I jump out of the way, and—

PEW!

A brilliant flash of energy explodes in the courtyard. The blast sends red-hot fragments of gravel sparking across the area, and I charge toward the tower. Sif fires twice more, both of which go over my head. I suddenly see her plan. She wants me to come up to the tower, at which point she'll have me at point-blank range. Alternatively, I could back up and be a sitting duck.

Thankfully, I have an alternative that she can't anticipate.

As I rush up to the doors, I throw Blub inside, then turn and use Speed to dash away. From high above, I hear Sif's laugh, and a blast hits the courtyard just next to me. The explosion rings out . . . and then an even more powerful one shakes the whole area.

I fall to my knees as Blub explodes, and I spin around to see the whole tower crumbling. High above, Sif screams and tumbles down as stone cracks and breaks around her. Countless tons of stone pour down on top of her as it crashes into the courtyard, and I let out a whistle.

[IceQueen: Now that's how you take care of business!]

[RazorEdge: Yeah! Go Jason!!!]

[FireStorm: If I hadn't seen it myself, I wouldn't have believed it.]

I walk slowly and purposefully toward the rubble. Stone begins to shift, and, slowly, several chunks of the old wall are shoved aside. Sif rises up from the destruction, worse for wear. Her armor is dented, and she's covered in the golden blood of her people. Still, her eyes are filled with fire, and I know she's not going to yield.

It almost pains me to raise Odin's spear and hit her squarely in the chest with the blast of solar energy. Light radiates all about the courtyard as the torrent of heat fights against her armor. She grits her teeth, but she can't move to evade, and the heat ray melts through her armor within just a few seconds. With a piercing scream, Odin's spear brings an end to her life, and she falls flat upon the ground.

[You have leveled up!]

[Congratulations! You are now Level 90!]

I lower the spear as she dies and crouch down next to her. Slowly, I pick up her sword and slide it into my inventory.

"Loki's staff, Odin's spear, Sif's sword. I'm getting quite a collection," I joke as I open up her inventory and start to scroll. "Wonder what'll be next?"

Given who I'm fighting, I have a *very* good idea what'll be next, but that's a bridge to cross when I get there. It takes me longer than I'd like before I'm able to find the Bifrost Crystal in Sif's inventory. There's a *lot* of junk in there: trinkets and trophies from her previous battles. I'm sure they all meant something to her, but I'm clueless about them, so I don't bother. Plus, it's not really all that cool to take a trophy from something that you didn't kill yourself.

When I have the Bifrost Crystal in hand, I square my shoulders and slowly stand up.

"Alright, everyone." I smile as lights start to flicker out of the crystal. "Time to get back to Earth."

CHAPTER EIGHTEEN

The Bifrost Crystal gives a sharp explosion of light, and a portal forms in front of me. I waste no time racing forward and jumping into the flickering portal, and I go shooting off toward my beloved home. Belatedly, I hope that using the crystal is as simple as activating it. If not, well . . . I've seen how destructive the Bifrost can be. *Hopefully,* I didn't just open up a Bifrost beam into a residential area or something.

I come shooting out the other side of the portal and find myself caught in the brilliant Bifrost column, then come crashing down into the exact same spot I left earlier. The beam fades away, and I tuck the crystal back into my inventory. Slowly, I look around, trying to take stock of the situation. All the dead bodies are still there, minus some of the human ones, which seem to have been cleaned up. Otherwise, all appears exactly the same. The clouds are still thick and low and are roaring with thunder. The city is dark: only a few lights appear on some of the tallest skyscrapers. It looks to me like every-thing has lost electricity, which, all things considered, prob-ably makes sense.

"Alright, everyone." I start walking forward. Lightfax appears next to me, and I climb onto her back. "I need to know where to go. Where's Thor? Where's—"

Rrrrrrrrrrrrrrrrrrrrrargh!

A powerful cry rings out, and I look up to see a massive form pass over my head. It's black as night, but with the flashes of lightning backlighting it, I can make out a distinctive form that I would know anywhere.

A dragon.

I know, I know, it's getting less shocking with each one that shows up, but I can't control that fact, and besides, drag-ons come in a whole host of shapes and sizes. This one in particular must be two hundred feet long, though it's hard to say for sure. I can't really tell how high it's flying, other than to say that it's below the clouds.

"Follow that thing," I order Lightfax. "Everyone! How many monsters has Thor unleashed on the city?"

[DarkCynic: I'm not really sure. A lot of them!]

[IceQueen: Uh . . . I think there are two. There's the giant, and then there's this titan thing.]

[GoldenShield: Yeah. Thor himself vanished about the time you killed Sif. I think he might have sensed it. That's also utter speculation. I'm just repeating what I saw on John's feed.]

"So, John was fighting Thor?" I ask. "Someone send him a message and get him to this dragon, pronto. Ali too. I could make use of her for a few things."

My chat responds in the affirmative, and Lightfax shoots off even faster after the dragon. I try to heal up as best I can on the way, but it's hard. I don't know where this dragon is heading, I don't know what the plan is, and I just want to minimize as many casualties as possible.

KA-BOOM!

The dragon suddenly lets out a brilliant blast of lightning. Below, a great swath of buildings explode into flame. I grit my teeth as I see what looks to be a factory collapsing in on itself. The dragon spreads its wings wide and comes down for a landing, and I find that I can see it better in the flames.

It's huge, a blue-black color, and it wants to kill people. That's all I need to know.

Lightfax puts on another burst of speed, and we come racing across a bridge and up to the area where the dragon is sitting. To my dismay, it's landed next to a power plant, down in the industrial part of town. I've dealt with monsters and power plants before, and it's not usually a good combination. The monster flares its spines out, taking no notice of me, and spreads its wings to cover two of the immense reactors.

"Hey!" I call out. "Get away from there!"

The dragon glances in my direction, then snorts and closes its eyes. Suddenly, electricity explodes upward from the power plant and flows into its body. As it finishes drinking from the plant, the dragon steps back. Now electricity arcs from spine to spine, scale to scale, and as it opens its mouth, lightning blossoms inside.

[ShadowDancer: Squeeeeeee! It's a Thunder Dragon!]

[ViperQueen: REALLY??? I'd been hoping to see one of those, but they're SUPER rare!!!]

[RazorEdge: This is going to be great!]

I'm not entirely sure that I agree with the assessment, but there's not much I can do about it. Quickly, I draw out Odin's spear and charge the dragon while remaining on Lightfax's back. After all, charging a dragon on horseback while wielding a spear is a *classic* way to slay the things.

Ka-boom!

Another blast of lightning erupts from its maw and explodes across the ground. Lightfax desperately tries to jump out of the way, but the electricity catches her legs and sends her sprawling. I leap free and bounce several times, avoiding most of the attack, and come up holding the spear firmly in my hand. The dragon chuckles, then spreads its wings to take off.

"Oh no, you don't." I raise the spear and fire a blast of energy up at the thing. It hits the dragon in the face, knocking the great head slightly to the side. With that, it chuckles slightly and turns back to face me.

"Now you have my attention, little one," it says. I glance over my shoulder to see Lightfax struggling to her feet and staggering through the portal into my pocket dimension. "That's Odin's spear. Not many people could have taken it from him, and he lends it to no one."

"I suppose you might call me a special case, then," I answer back. "Surrender now, get out of here, and I won't kill you."

The dragon begins to laugh. "A joker! A joker. Thor will love you, if you survive long enough for him to meet you."

The great beast slowly stalks toward me. As it does, I notice that its tail is trailing closer to the power plant, and a great deal of lightning begins to arc into its body once more. "The question now is what *I* should do to you."

"You can fight me, but I'll win. I killed Odin. I killed Loki."

"Odin was washed-up. Loki was a joke," the dragon spits at me.

"How about Sif?" I draw out her sword, holding it in my other hand. "Gaze upon it, if you will!"

With that, the dragon's eyes narrow. "Sif was no one to mess with. I sense her blood upon the weapon—hers and yours both. It was a mighty struggle, and one that you won fairly and squarely." The dragon pulls itself upright. "If that is the case, we shall speak no more. You must be destroyed."

Great. I've oversold my case. I tuck both of the weapons back into my inventory as I activate Speed and dash out of the way. A torrent of lightning blasts the spot where I was just standing, and I run toward the beast as hard as I can.

The dragon sees me coming and flaps its wings, then launches itself up into the air. It laughs and turns away, and I draw out Loki's staff. I point the weapon up at the great beast and send it a few commands.

"Get me up there."

A single spark flashes out of the end of the staff and shoots across the sky. A moment later, I find myself teleported up to the dragon's back, right between its wings. The monster doesn't seem to have noticed me, which is fortunate. Instead, it simply chuckles to itself as it angles for the densely populated downtown portion of the city.

"And now they will know destruction," the dragon murmurs to itself. "Now they will know death."

I bend down and feel around the dragon's scales. They're thick and have grown so close together that there isn't a half-inch gap between them. An idea hits me, and I open up my pocket dimension and allow Blub to come out. He starts to inflate, and I wedge him between several spines protruding from the dragon's back. When he's inflated enough to stay in place, I take a firm hold on Loki's staff and transform myself.

With a flash, I'm turned into a falcon. I spread my wings and shoot up into the air like a bullet, and I watch the immense dragon fly off into the distance, toward the city.

I send a mental command to Blub. *Not now . . . Not yet . . . Now!*

Blub explodes with all the force that he can muster, and an immense nuclear eruption suddenly joins the lightning in the sky. The dragon's wings crumple, and it tumbles from the sky, knocked down by the sudden, unexpected blast. My aim is perfect, and it comes crashing down into one of the long channels of water that separate the island from the rest of the city. Several bridges shatter under the impact, and a massive wave washes up onto the streets on both sides.

Slowly, the dragon starts to stand up, and I come flashing down. I land on a rooftop nearby and transform back into a human, then stand and watch for a moment. Several nearby warriors draw their weapons and begin to fire arrows and bolts of magic at the thing, and the dragon shakes itself as it slowly rises up.

"You will not take me down!" the beast roars loudly. "I am

not a mortal, not one that can be struck from the Earth like a common dog!"

A great blast of lightning erupts from its body and flares down the channel in both directions, sparking off boats and guardrails and supports. It *also* arcs up onto the street itself since, you know, the dragon *did* splash a whole bunch of water up onto it. The beast snarls and starts to pull itself up out of the water, and the warriors all fall, writhing in pain, as the electricity does its work.

"Now you will die! Once you are gone, I will find the impudent wretch who—"

I back up and pull Odin's Spear out of my inventory as I do so, then race forward and jump out into space. I sail through the air perfectly and come crashing down onto the head of the monster. As I land, I stab the spear down into its head, piercing the scales just above its left eye.

With that single bit of momentum, I shove the spear downward as hard as I can, trying to crack through the skull and put an end to the beast. It snarls and rears up and lets out a blast of lightning that explodes against a nearby office building. I fire another blast of solar energy into the monster, and it stumbles, and with that, I rip the spear back out and jump to the ground.

"You filthy—" the dragon snarls and spins to look down at me. I can see the left eye turning red. I've wounded the creature, at least to some degree. It opens its mouth wide, and I point the spear upward.

PEEEEEEEEEEW!

Energy streaks off the spear and hits it in the mouth,

driving deep into the gullet of the beast. The dragon snaps its mouth shut and pulls back slightly, then simply draws in a deep breath and thunders forward.

I hardly have a moment to blink before it scoops me up in its claws and blasts off into the air. The acceleration is fantastically painful, and I feel several bones pop loudly. I don't think anything breaks, though, which is nice. The dragon snarls as it rises up into the sky, then pauses as we break through the clouds and shoot up into the light of the day.

I have to admit that I'm stunned. Below the clouds, it's so dark that it feels like night. Above the clouds, the sun is just a smidge past noon—one o'clock, maybe? Stretching out below me like something solid is a great rolling plain of clouds. There are hills, some valleys, and all of them pitch black. Lightning flashes upward here and there, looking like brilliant, momentary trees.

And then the dragon folds its wings and we go plummeting down.

The air whistles around us, and my heart rises into my mouth. I squirm about as I try to break free, but the beast has too tight a grip on me.

[DarkCynic: Jason! Use the thing!]

[ChaosRider: Oh! If only Burnie were here!]

[ViperQueen: What exactly do you think BURNIE could do here?]

I lose track of the chat as we shoot back down through the layer of clouds and come crashing down into the city. I see a building below me—I don't have a clue which one—and then . . . we hit.

I can't really describe the hit itself. I'm smashed downward through layer after layer after layer of building. Pipes wrap around me, concrete crumbles. I'm caught between the impossibly powerful grip of a dragon and the rather impervious nature of modern architecture. Finally, we come to a halt, and Ascalon blazes with warmth.

[Skill: Bearing of a Knight.]

[Peril Detected.]

"You think?" I groan as the dragon lets go of me and withdraws its claws. Rubble comes pouring back down around me—I have no idea how much. There's an office chair pressed into my back and a computer screen wedged against my chest. Somehow I'm still alive, though I admittedly don't really know how that's happened.

[Peril Increased.]

My health is sitting at a fraction of a percent. I'm fairly certain that I was only saved by my Bearing of a Knight skill. Likely, it just increased my damage resistance as I took more and more damage. In any case, I now need a great deal more strength. I flex my muscles as I try to move the immense load on top of me. A few things shift about, but not nearly as much as I'd like.

"Come on," I groan as I slowly start to push myself up once more. "You can do it."

[Peril Increased.]

"Come . . . on!" I shout. "The world is depending on you!" Something snaps under my feet, and the pile of rubble shifts. "NOW!"

CHAPTER NINETEEN

Ooooooooooooooooooow!

Balder's howl cuts through the pile of rubble like a knife through butter, and suddenly, I'm being blasted back upward just as fast as I came down the first time. A large column of stone crashes into my head, but I shove it aside with my increased strength. Up I go as the debris all around me is pulverized by Balder's cry, and finally, I'm launched upward through the top of the pile.

Given that I find myself surrounded by skyscrapers, I can only assume that the pile of rubble intended to be my prison was once a skyscraper as well. At this moment, I see the tail of the dragon whipping around a corner as the beast leaves, satisfied that I'm not going to make any more trouble for it. I stagger down from the pile and suddenly hear screeching tires.

"Jason!" John pokes his head out of a Jeep that comes roaring up to me. "You alright?"

"I'm alive," I mutter as John tosses me a few Pumped! bottles. "That Thunder Dragon is a piece of work. Any ideas what can take it down?"

"Mr. Wang says that it's weak to cold damage," John answers. "Think old Bjorn could give it a whirl?"

"I'll see what he can do." I nod. "Go around and head the thing off. Stay safe, don't engage it directly, but see if you can get it to stop moving."

"On it."

The Jeep's tires screech once more as it goes shooting off down the road. I watch John go, then open up my pocket dimension and call for Bjorn to step out. As he does, I start running down the sidewalk after the dragon, and Bjorn moves to keep pace.

"Did you hear that?" I ask him. "Any chance you could freeze something that large? Or, at the least, slow him down?"

Bjorn doesn't answer for a moment. *Maybe, Master. That thing is awfully large. I might be able to knock it down a few pegs, but it's going to be difficult.*

"Is there any way I could make it a smidge easier for you?" I ask as we go racing around the corner. We're just in time to see John's Jeep come flying out in front of the dragon, about three blocks down. The dragon says something in its low rumbling voice, but we're too far away to make it out properly. "We've got to stop this thing. If we were in a dungeon, I'd just keep attacking it until it gave in, but we're destroying a *lot* of public property here."

Bjorn thinks, then answers, *If you could get it into the ocean, I could use the natural cold temperatures of the water to my advantage. If I targeted the water instead of the dragon, it would create—*

"I don't need the science. I just need to know that it can be done." I nod down to him. "Get to the waterfront and get ready."

Bjorn nods, then turns and bounds away. I race down the street as fast as I can, getting ready for whatever's next.

[IceQueen: Hey, Jason! How exactly are you going to lure the dragon into the water?]

[LunarEclipse: Don't pester him! I'm sure he has a great plan!]

[ChaosRider: Yeah! Jason always has a plan!]

I don't have the heart to tell the chat that I *never* have a plan. I don't have the faintest idea how I'm going to get the dragon into the water, but I know I have to try anyway. Down the street, John rips a fire hydrant off the sidewalk and throws it into the dragon's face, spilling water all across the street. The dragon roars and fires a blast of lightning at my friend, and I'm given an idea.

No, it has nothing to do with water or fire hydrants at all. It does, however, have to do with throwing things.

I flex my muscles, then rush over to a taxicab sitting on the edge of the street. It's already taken a lot of damage. All the windows are smashed out, the seats have been charred—I mean . . . it's not going to run again, even if I don't do anything to it. Quickly, I rush over and grab the bumper and yank upward as hard as I can.

PING!

The bumper rips right off. I frown, then shrug and throw it at the dragon as hard as I can. It sails true and bounces off the dragon's rump. Unfortunately, the beast takes no notice of it. I scowl, then walk around to the side of the car, bend down, and grab the chassis.

This time I'm able to lift the taxi off the ground. Have I mentioned that my strength has increased by a *lot* since I first got my powers? The taxi sways a bit in my grip, and I grunt as I throw it into the air. With that, I rush forward, pounding along the street just as fast as I can.

The dragon snarls and bends forward, searching for John, and the taxi hits it in the back of the head. It smashes down onto the monster's long spikes, sticking to the dragon, and the beast roars and spins around to face me. Hatred rages in its eyes, and I smile.

"It's me again!"

I grab a fire hydrant as I pass, rip the thing right out of the sidewalk, and fling it at the dragon as hard as I can. The hydrant hits the dragon in the nose with a loud bong, making it stagger backward. It shakes its head slowly, then closes its eyes. A great blast of lightning shoots out the back of its head and blasts the taxi into molten slag.

By that time, though, I've reached the monster.

I jump upward and punch it in the nose as hard as I can. It doesn't do nearly as much to the dragon as I might like, but I do manage to snatch hold of one of the spikes, then swing myself up onto the head of the dragon. It snorts and begins to charge up its attack, and I scramble over the back of the head and slide down the neck. The dragon turns its head around, trying to catch sight of me, but I run all the faster as I dash down the length of its back toward its tail. As I do so, I pull out Sif's sword and drag it down the spine. It sends up sparks as it cuts a long gash through the scales.

Huh. That weapon's stronger than I thought. The dragon howls in pain and lets off a blast of lightning, but I jump into the air and avoid it. As I come down, I call out for Lightfax and land on her back as she shoots out of my pocket dimension. With that, we tear down the streets.

"Fiend!" the dragon snarls, then takes to the air, chasing after me as we race through the abandoned streets of New York. It flies low, its wings and claws smashing the tops of buildings as we go past. Ahead, I see the harbor looming and start to try and calculate my options.

"Alright, Lightfax, I need that dragon to *not* see me for about three seconds."

Lightfax snorts and tosses her mane, and she suddenly spins and shoots down an alley. At that moment, I pull out Loki's staff and cloak us. The moment we're invisible, I create an illusory me that rides off on an illusory Lightfax. With that, we come to a stop and stand as still as possible as the dragon shoots overhead.

Carefully, we walk back to the end of the alley and ride down to the waterfront. There, I can see my illusion shooting down the road, nearing the ocean. It leaps over several barriers, clatters down the pier, and reaches the water. I give it a nudge, and the illusion flashes off across the water itself.

It's a bit of a stretch, but let's be real: we're dealing with monsters here. I have to imagine that the dragon has seen crazier things than a horse running on water, you know? The dragon does seem to pause, but it simply flaps its wings and races on faster after the fleeing Jason. I ride all the way up to the water to watch, and together, Lightfax and I behold the dragon suddenly folding its wings and dropping down onto my illusion with immense force.

I reappear with a flicker as the illusion is broken. Out on the water, a plume of water shoots a hundred feet into the air as the dragon plunges below the surface. With that, Bjorn howls loud and long, his cry coming from about a hundred feet down the docks. I watch as a layer of ice grows across the surface of the bay, and I hold my breath.

"Do you think it worked?" I ask Lightfax. She doesn't answer, and I slowly climb down. Lightning flashes from deep within the harbor. The flickers of light show me the bottom of the sea floor, and I can see the shadow of a shipwreck, which is interesting but hardly something that merits any undo curiosity at this exact moment. The lightning continues, and I see the form of the dragon thrashing around, twisting and turning this way and that.

Bjorn's howl continues. Bits of ice float to the surface from where they've formed down below. More spouts of water shoot upward here and there. And then . . . suddenly . . . everything goes quiet.

John's Jeep pulls up next to me, and he leans out the window. "Nicely done. Looks like you really took care of business."

"I haven't gotten any XP from it yet," I murmur. "That

tells me that it's still at least a little bit alive, and that's concerning to me."

"Huh." John pops the door open and climbs out. He's holding Beowulf's Dagger tightly, and his eyes sweep across the water. "Well, while we're waiting, would you care to challenge me to an arm wresting contest? That was some serious muscle when you threw the taxi, and I'd love to see how we really stack—"

Foom!

A spout of water explodes upward from the pier only a few hundred feet away from us, and a dark form emerges from the water. It's humanoid but probably stands eight feet tall. As it turns and looks at me with one yellow eye and one bloodied eye, I realize that I'm looking at a dragonspawn. Somehow, the Thunder Dragon has escaped by transforming. It's still covered in scales, has claws instead of fingers, and so on, but it's a whole lot smaller.

"You," it hisses and slowly starts forward, thumping across the deck. "You're going to pay for this, you know!"

"I think it was less terrifying as a dragon," John mutters.

"You're telling me." I draw out Sif's sword and take my stance. The weapon feels heavy in my hands, but the dragonspawn pauses as it catches sight of the blade. It's terrified of the thing, and that makes it valuable even if I personally don't love it. The dragonspawn takes a stance as well, flexing its claws and barring its teeth. There's a long moment where we simply stare at each other . . . and then the dragonspawn charges forward.

The monster is simply terrifying as it leaps at me. It can

move *fast*, and as it reaches us, it slashes at me with unfathomable force. I jump backward, but it catches me on the arm anyway, knocking me to the side and slamming me to the asphalt.

The pain is enormous, and my left arm almost goes entirely limp. John shouts something, though I don't make it out, and the dragonspawn's claws latch down around my injured arm. I'm flung upward into the air a moment later, only to be struck by *something* with extraordinary force.

I'm knocked clean into the street, where I bounce several times as I come to a stop. Slowly, I rise back to my feet, and the dragonspawn snarls and advances. John picks himself up from the ground from down the block, but he's still a short distance away.

"Wretched boy!" the dragonspawn hisses. "Do you have any idea how long it'll take me to grow into a full dragon again? You've ruined me!"

"Be grateful that you're not dead," I snap.

The dragonspawn hisses, and I get the feeling that it would have appreciated if Bjorn had killed it outright. Well . . . I can work with that.

I charge forward as fast as I can, with a bit of help from Ascalon. Sif's sword gleams in the light, and I draw back to attack with all due force. The dragonspawn rushes forward to meet me, and we crash together in the middle of the street.

The sword flashes through the air, and the dragonspawn leaps back to avoid the blow. I stagger a bit as the blow sends me off-balance, and the creature takes advantage by flashing forward to slash me across the chest. I cry out in pain and fall backward, and it follows, pressing the attack. As I recover, I brace myself and lash out, and I strike it across the left arm. The sword bites deep, and thick black blood trickles down to the ground.

Wham!

John leaps into the fight from the side and punches the dragonspawn in the side of the head. It's knocked slightly to the side, where it hisses and spins back with an extraordinary amount of force. By then, though, John and I are both in mid-strike, and the dragonspawn's eyes go wide with fear.

John stabs it in the right side while I slash it across the left. More wounds open, and it's forced backward. We press the attack as quickly as we can, forcing it down the street and backward toward the docks once more. The dragonspawn looks nervous, but there's not much it can do.

And then I hear Bjorn howl once more.

A spear of ice erupts from the dragonspawn's chest, punching through it like a lance. That makes the monster come to a stop, and it slowly looks down. John pauses slightly, but I don't hesitate for a moment.

"AHHHHH!"

Sif's sword flashes once more, and the dragonspawn's head falls to the ground with a dull thunk. It rolls a few times, then comes to a stop, and the dragonspawn's body follows after a few seconds.

[You have leveled up!]

[Congratulations! You are now Level 91!]

I whistle softly, and John gives a nod.

"The bigger they are, right?"

"Something like that," I snort, then turn away. "Alright, then. That's one of the monsters down. I think I heard that there was a titan mucking around somewhere?"

"Off to the west, yeah." John nods. "Are you up to heading out to it already?"

"If I pause, people will die," I mutter. "Let's get going. I don't plan on stopping until Thor lies dead."

CHAPTER TWENTY

John nods to me, then runs off to find his Jeep. I check my HUD to make sure that I didn't get any reward for leveling up and confirm that nope, there's nothing new. I suppose the system just expects people at this level to make do with all the new unique loot they're pulling from the bosses. I pet Bjorn a few times, then let him go back into the pocket dimension. A few seconds later, John comes screeching up, I climb inside, and we shoot off across the city.

I've always been told that driving anywhere in New York City takes forever. Well, for once, I actually find the roads to be pleasantly clear. John's Jeep rumbles through potholes and over small piles of debris as we fly desperately toward the west. There, I see flames rising in the sky, and we're a lot further away than I'd like to be.

"Where'd you get this ride?" I ask as we fly over a bridge that's somehow still standing.

"I found it. It still had the keys in it, so Mr. Wang told me to take it and he'd repay the owner once we manage to get the portals closed." John shrugs. "I don't know who it belongs to, but I imagine they'll be happier being alive than having the Jeep in one piece."

"And hey, maybe you'll actually get it back to them without too much damage!" I point out. At that exact moment, a bit of rubble falls from a building high above, bounces off the ground, and smashes out one of the headlights. "Well . . . I suppose 'too much' is somewhat relative."

John only laughs and leans back in the driver's seat. "How have you been, anyway? Everyone keeps talking about seeing you do this thing or that thing on your feed, but I haven't actually gotten a chance to talk to you in like . . . Pfft, I don't know. Must have been back when you were still working with Mr. Wang on that stock-market warrior-for-hire thing."

I laugh a bit at the memory. "You know, that was only like three days ago, but it feels like an eternity. Everything's just been going so fast, you know?"

"Yeah." John chuckles and nods. "Frankly, if we can make it through the next day or two, I'm going to go find a bar, walk inside, and not leave for at least a week. I'm not even going to get drunk. I'm just going to kick my feet up, order all my meals there, and enjoy the lack of utter chaos around me."

"I might join you." I shake my head in amusement. "When that happens, I'll tell you all about everything. Deal?"

"Deal." John slows the Jeep as we rumble through another rough patch. "Sorry about that. And . . . looks like we're almost there."

I nod and lean forward. We're entering the "suburbs" of New York: the places outside the main body of the city that don't appear on television nearly as much. We're mostly flying through residential neighborhoods and leaving the skyscrapers far behind.

Ahead, though, the skies are orange. Flames raging wildly down below light up the underside of the thick, overcast skies. Against that backdrop, I can see something slowly walking along. It looks almost like the void behemoth that I fought right before the gods showed up, but I can't tell for certain.

"And there we have it," John mutters. "Alright, so here's what I know about this thing. It's a good two hundred feet tall and seems to be some sort of lava elemental or something. It hasn't taken any notice of anyone. It hasn't been affected by tanks and missiles, but it also hasn't engaged and destroyed the people who have attacked it. It's moving pretty slow, about twenty miles per hour, and is stomping in a line north by northwest. The police have already evacuated all the affected areas, which means that we're good to destroy things."

"Within reason." I hold up a finger. "Just because we won't kill anyone by blowing up a house doesn't mean we should do it."

"Obviously." John stares at me like I'm stupid. "You think I don't know that?"

"I know you do, but I also know that we both have livestream chats watching our every move, and I'd rather make sure that *they* know we're not going to be raining wanton destruction on the city before the internet goes and blows things all out of proportion."

[ShadowDancer: Don't worry, Jason! We'll defend your honor!]

[IceQueen: Yeah! Nothing to worry about! Just go do what you need to do!]

[ChaosRider: *checks to make sure that my house isn't affected* Yeah! Go for it!]

I laugh at ChaosRider's message, then turn my attention forward.

We soon close in on the titan. The thing is simply enormous and is slowly lumbering forward as though it's out for a leisurely stroll. I can hardly even see its head, nor can I really tell if it has facial features or if it's just a blob of putty. In any case, the skin of the creature is blackened stone, and a warm lava-like glow exudes from dozens of cracks all over its body. It emits a low rumble as John starts driving parallel to the thing, about a block away from its path.

"Alright, I'm going to swing around in front of it," John calls out. "If you have even the slightest idea how we're going to take it down, I'll happily accept suggestions."

"It looks to me like attacking a mountain." I whistle. "But there's nothing to it. We've just got to take it down."

"If only we could get Thor's hammer *before* we knock it down to size!" John chuckles.

"Oh, trust me, I'm right there with you."

I grit my teeth as John roars around a corner, and we drive right up in front of the thing. I hop out, and John drives down the block a bit further to keep the Jeep away. I look up at the thing as it continues to slowly march along.

"Pets?" I ask. "Any good ideas?" Nothing comes back, and

I sigh. John walks up next to me, and for a moment, we just wait. Slowly, I pull out Loki's staff and nod up at the thing. "Get ready."

"For what?" John asks.

"Anything," I answer simply. With that, I activate the staff, and in the blink of an eye, we're teleported up to the head of the mighty beast.

I land on one shoulder, and John lands on the other. The head is enormous, a good twenty feet tall in and of itself, and the monster snarls softly. I can't tell if it's detected us or not, but I suspect so. John nods to me, then rushes forward and punches the side of its head as hard as he can. Stone explodes under his fist, and the whole monster shakes slightly. I respond by drawing out Sif's sword and slashing it through *my* side of the head.

That gets its attention, and the titan rumbles to a stop. It snarls, then twists its head to the side. As it does so, black stone cracks and falls away, and I find myself staring into two eyes that blaze and crackle with an energy almost unfathomably powerful. It's like looking into the sun. More stone cracks across the mouth, and the creature speaks.

"Who are you, you who challenge the mighty—"

I don't wait to hear any more but lunge forward and slash my sword across the face of the creature from bottom to top. The titan doesn't yell, but it does snort, and the fire burns hotter.

Before it can do anything, I attack with fury, and my sword flashes brilliantly left and right as I land long cuts across its face. The monster opens its mouth and roars . . . and in that moment, I realize that I should have planned better.

A blast of fiery air hits me like a sledgehammer, and I'm lifted off my feet and cast out into the air. It doesn't actually do that much damage, but all of a sudden I'm falling, and that's a problem. Quickly, I spread my arms and legs as I try to control my flight. About halfway to the ground, I manage to slam into the creature again, and I slash outward with Sif's sword.

The blade bites deep into the monster's body, and I carve a long deadly path down the side of it as I plummet to the ground below. As I hit the earth, I roll away, then look up to see the gash glowing from the internal fires. The titan huffs, then lifts up a massive foot to squash me. I smile and turn to run . . . only to realize that I have nowhere to go.

I've landed inside someone's backyard. The fences are tall and made of wood, and the only gate is barred by more than one drawbar. I take the only option I see and bolt straight through the back door.

The wood explodes into splinters as I crash through. I feel sort of bad as I smash through a kitchen table, knock a doorframe slightly asunder, slam into a wall and knock down several picture frames, and finally come crashing out again through the front of the house. That said, when the titan's foot comes crashing down on the house a second later, the entire thing is obliterated.

"That's enough," I mutter as I charge back toward the foot. Sif's sword gleams in the firelight as several nearby houses spontaneously catch fire, which I can only assume is some sort of latent power possessed by the titan. "Time to end this!"

High above, the titan yells once more in anger, and I have

to guess that it's struggling with John. I attack the monster's ankle—which, I should point out, is *substantially* thicker than my sword. That said, I do a good enough job and slash deep into the thick flesh. Lava pours out, and I jump back out of the way, then attack again with force. This time I hit just above the original cut and inflict a second wound on the mighty beast.

I don't know how detrimental it is, but the thing certainly lets out a scream that shakes the very foundations of the Earth. I teleport back up to its shoulder, where I find John clinging on for dear life. His claws are dug deep into the flesh as the monster blasts him with the same stream of air that it used to try and dislodge me.

"Hey!" I rush forward from the other shoulder and drive Sif's sword deeply into the creature. The torrent of hot air on John intensifies as it screams once more, and he's blasted clean off the shoulder and into the air. It swings its head around to try and get to me, but I keep hold of the hilt, so I just get swung around to the other shoulder.

The moment I feel something solid under my feet, I draw the sword back out and drop down, then wait and back up. The monster turns its head once more to stare at me with an extraordinary intensity and fury, and I charge forward.

It doesn't have a chance to hit me again as I jump upward, then climb up the features of its face. A moment later, I'm on top of its head, where I drive the sword deep into its skull. The sword sinks in all the way to the hilt, and I drop down and hang on as the titan begins to buck around, trying to knock me off.

Suddenly, I see the thing raising a hand to swat at me. Now, I should note that although this isn't exactly the most nail-biting fight I've ever had, it's certainly one of the most terrifying. I mean, if you were a grasshopper trying to attack a full-sized human, that would be no easy task, to be certain. I whip out Odin's spear and brace it against the top of the skull as I point the spearhead out at the approaching hand.

Wham!

The palm of the titan's hand impacts the spear, and lava bursts free and comes cascading down. I swing out of the way, still holding onto the hilt of Sif's sword, so that I'm halfway dangling off the side of the thing's head. The titan roars again and pulls its hand back—and the spear along with it. The second hand raises up from the other side, and I desperately try to think of a way to knock *it* away. I had been planning on using the spear to punch straight down into the skull, but now that *that's* not an option . . .

I'm certainly running low on ideas, so I yank the sword back out and slide down the side of the head as the titan slaps itself loudly with its hand. It snarls under the impact, and I suddenly realize what mosquitos must think when we humans slap ourselves in the ears. It's kind of funny . . . And that gives me my idea.

"Hey!" I run up to the ear of the monster, on the side of the head with the injured hand. "Hey, I'm right here!"

The wounded hand flashes through the air, faster this time, and I follow its trajectory. When it hits the side of the head, I grab hold of Odin's spear and rip it back out with as much force as I can manage. The titan howls in pain once more, but I don't really care. I have the spear back, and that's the important thing.

Now . . . for the tricky part.

Quickly, I dart forward around the front of the head. The chest falls away straight down, of course, but I slam Sif's sword into the thick flesh and hang on as hard as I can. As I swing into the right position, I drive Odin's spear into the monster just beneath its neck and sit back to wait.

Thankfully, I don't have to wait long.

A powerful hand flashes through the air, and I pull Sif's sword out and drop. As I whistle downward, the titan punches itself in the chest and drives the spear into the core of its body.

This time it doesn't cry out in pain.

Instead, it simply freezes and stands there as though it's been shocked. When I land, it slowly starts to sway. John runs up to me, but I wave him back.

"Get to the Jeep, now!"

We both fly to the vehicle and dive inside. John fires it up, and we go racing off down the street. Behind us, the titan slowly starts to fall. Fire bursts through its skin as it melts into lava, and John shouts out and punches the air in excitement. Of course, that action accidentally punches a hole straight through the roof of the Jeep, but . . . minor details, I suppose.

The titan hits the ground with a thunderous crash, and lava pours through the streets like rivers of fire. Houses explode and burst into flame, trees are transformed into candles, and our Jeep nearly gets consumed as well. John puts on a burst of speed, though, and we narrowly race away from the edge of the fire as the lava slows to a crawl.

"Want to go back and look for your spear?" John asks as we race off into the growing darkness.

"No time," I murmur as a brilliant flash of lightning pierces down into the inner city. "I've got a god of thunder to catch. After he's done, we'll see, but"—I shrug—"for now, we've got to stay focused. Thor, if you're listening to this . . ." I pause for dramatic effect. "I'm coming for you."

CHAPTER TWENTY-ONE

The Jeep roars back toward downtown New York, tires squealing as we shoot around corner after corner. The vehicle is solid. It bounces up and over piles of rubble with hardly a delay, and several times we have to crawl over fallen trees and such things. Ahead, if it were possible, the sky grows even darker and the blasts of lightning become even more intense. My stomach flutters, but I force it down.

[ShadowDancer: Alright, Jason, you're going to want to head for Central Park.]

[ChaosRider: Yup! That's where Thor just landed!]

[ViperQueen: He looks like he's there for business, that's for sure.]

I nod slowly at the chat, then turn to John. His lips are tight, and he pushes the vehicle on even faster.

"Central Park?" he asks me. "My chat is saying the same thing."

"Then let's go knock him down a few pegs." I stare out into the inky darkness, lit only by the flickering lightning and the pale beams of the Jeep's headlights. "Are you going to join me?"

"If you want me at your side, I'll be there, but I sort of figured I'd be best on the sidelines." John shrugs. "I've gained quite a few levels over the last few hours, but you're still way above me."

"I just hope I'm leveled enough." I draw out Loki's staff, still in its dagger form. It's such a small thing, but it's so powerful. In the hands of the right person, I imagine that it could be the single most powerful weapon in the multiverse. In my hands . . . Well, it's powerful, but I'm not a natural trickster. Suddenly, an idea pops into my head, and I quickly cast an effect with the staff.

We're invisible as we come racing up to Central Park, and an illusory Jeep is driving about fifty feet ahead of us—until a bolt of lightning strikes it from above. The blast opens up a rather large crater in the street, but the real Jeep just rumbles through it without stopping. As we flicker and appear, I hear a crack of laughter, and something dark shoots through the air. Suddenly, a man lands right in front of us and holds up his hand.

John slams on the brakes, but it's not enough, and we slam into Thor a moment later. He doesn't move an inch. He simply stands there as the front of the Jeep crumples and wraps around his hand like plastic wrap. He slowly lowers his hand, then walks around to my side of the car. John hops out and backs up, but I don't dare.

"Why don't you step out?" Thor reaches out and grabs

hold of the door. With hardly a hint of effort, he rips the door off and tosses it to the side. It lands with a crash, and he motions for me to emerge. I nod and step down, then turn and look up at him.

He's just about as "Viking" as you could imagine. He's wearing an outfit made of hide, with a cloak slung over his back. A helmet with two horns sits upon his head, and a golden mustache and beard hang down his chest. He's draped in chain mail, with vambraces wrapped around his wrists and greaves on his ankles. I don't see his hammer, but I assume that he has an inventory like everyone else. He still has an odd smile on his face, and I cross my arms.

"That was a nice little trick there." Thor nods down to me. "Reminds me of someone."

"I'm afraid he's dead now," I say with a shrug, hoping that playing the strong game will work with him.

"Oh, I know. He'd sure never have given that thing to you." Thor chuckles. "Pesky little brat. Can't say as I'm sad to see him gone."

I keep my countenance. "No brotherly love has been lost between you, I see."

"I respect strength. I don't respect tricks." Thor's expression starts to grow stonier. "Loki was a trickster, but he wasn't strong. That's why you killed him. I threw that lightning bolt at the Jeep to test you, to see if you could survive it or not. Since you *did* kill Loki, and got rid of that little pest for me, I decided to reward you."

"Reward me with this conversation, by not killing me outright?" I raise an eyebrow.

"Indeed." Thor nods. "Your time is drawing short, though. Prepare yourself for battle! It will be the last one you ever—"

Something clicks in the back of my mind. Maybe it's a noise, maybe it's something in Thor's face, but I quickly step to the side. Thor's hammer—I know the name starts with an *M*, but I don't really remember anything beyond that—flashes through the space where I was just standing and smacks into Thor's hand. He raises an eyebrow, and I shrug.

"I used a trick, so you used one. I didn't defeat Loki because I'm easily taken down by tricks."

"Fair enough!" Something changes in Thor's eyes, and he twirls his hammer around his wrist. With a flick, he tosses it up into the air, then catches it again. "Let us do battle!"

He doesn't hesitate but swings the hammer at me with all his might. Let me just be clear: it's a *lot* of might. I jump backward and it misses by a mile, but the force of the wind is still enough to press me back. I start slowly walking backward, and Thor smiles.

"You're fast. Let's see just *how* fast, shall we?"

He's toying with me. I brace myself, but before I can do anything, he throws his hammer right at my chest. It hits me firmly and blasts me backward about forty feet or so. I hit the ground hard and jump back to my feet just in time to see the hammer snapping back into his hand. He throws it once more, and it flashes across the sidewalk, sending out a shock wave as it does so. I race forward, then dodge to the side. It whistles as it flies down and smashes into a building, then comes flashing back with simply extraordinary speed. I dodge once more, though only just, and charge at Thor just as fast as I possibly can.

"You've already survived longer than most!" Thor laughs as he swings the hammer at me again. I transform Loki's staff into a dagger and dodge several wide hammer attacks, then stab him deep in the side.

Well . . . I try to, at least.

The dagger doesn't exactly penetrate all that deep due to the rather impervious nature of his armor. I do draw a little bit of blood, which trickles in a golden rivulet to splash down onto the ground, but it's not much. Thor laughs, then spins and hits me in the shoulder. I'm lifted clean off my feet and slung back into the Jeep, where I hit so hard that the vehicle rocks up onto its side before crashing back down. There's a *huge* dent where I impacted, of course. Slowly, I stagger forward, and Thor lunges to attack again.

This time he performs an overhanded strike and brings the hammer crashing down at my head. I dodge to the side, but the impact against the street sends out a shock wave that makes me stagger. As Thor stands up, he flicks the hammer sideways at me, and it hits me in the chest and knocks me backward. Thor snarls as the hammer snaps back into his hand, and he gives it a twirl. I see something moving behind Thor and brace myself. I need to keep his attention for a moment longer, that's for sure.

"Why won't you go down?" He throws the hammer again, and I let it knock me backward onto the street once more.

"I guess I'm just not a guy who stays down easily." I shrug as I climb back to my feet. "You know, you've already survived against *me* longer than most do."

Thor chuckles, and he gives his hammer a twirl. "Touché."

CRASH!

The Jeep suddenly comes crashing down on Thor's head. It was thrown by John, who had been hiding in the shadows, of course. Thor snarls and casts it aside, where it screeches on the asphalt, sending up a spray of sparks. As he draws in a deep breath, I attack with all due force, slashing at him just as hard as I can.

My dagger slashes across his armor, drawing more sparks. He swings his hammer, and I slash open his arm just below the vambrace. More blood drips down, and Thor lets out a curse before trying to crush me again. I spin out of the way, then stab at his side. I hit the same wound I opened up earlier and manage to draw it open just a bit further. Thor gasps under the blow, and I get the feeling that he's not used to taking such damage.

"Did that little scratch hurt you?" I brace myself as he charges at me. He swings wildly, and I dodge and slash him across the side of his neck, between the bottom of the helmet and his shoulder. It's far from a kill shot, but it makes him scream all the more. "I would have expected more from such a great god as you—"

Wham!

I have to admit, I was asking for that one. The hammer hits me in the gut, making me double over, and Thor grabs the back of my shirt before I can say a thing. His hand balls into a fist, and he punches me in the chest so hard that bones break. I'm thrown up into the air by the force of it, just in time to see John rushing into battle.

At that moment, chaos seems to break loose. John leaps

up into the air and throws a punch, hitting the unsuspecting Thor in the chin. The god is knocked aside slightly, and I land with a *thud*, then attack with all due force. He backs up as we both unleash attacks. I land several strikes on his torso, and John punches him more than a few times. He's far from fading, but he's certainly being driven backward.

"You two aren't bad!" Thor snarls, then jumps backward and throws his hammer. It hits John, bounces and hits me, then snaps back to Thor's hand. We're both knocked off-balance by the hit, and Thor attacks again with a fury. He truly looks like a mad god now. Eyes wild, hair wild, he spins to wind up and throws the hammer at me. I dive to the side, and the weapon plows a *long* furrow through the asphalt of the street.

John snarls and rushes forward, then hits the momentarily defenseless Thor in the chin. As Thor's head is knocked up into the air, I cloak myself. I don't create a double or an illusion or anything, I just make myself turn invisible. As Thor comes back down, he grabs John by the arm, twists, and throws him through a window. With that, he glances around, looking for me.

Wham!

I punch Thor in the back of the head, knocking him *forward* slightly, just as his hammer comes whistling back to his hand. The motion causes Thor to stumble, and the hammer misses his hand and slams into his chest. He groans and doubles over, and I bend down and grab hold of the handle of his hammer.

"Don't you even *think* about it." Thor reaches out and grabs hold of the handle too, his larger hand fitting perfectly over mine. He snarls and climbs to his feet, but I maintain my hold. Slowly, Thor starts to twist, but I fight against him, twisting in the other direction. This . . . I've done some hard things before, but this might just take the cake. Thor's muscles are like *steel*, and it takes every last ounce of my effort to maintain my grip. Sweat beads out across my forehead, and pain lances up and down the length of my arm. We stand there, desperately fighting against one another . . . And that's when I notice lightning starting to flicker in the sky.

It comes down and hits the handle of the hammer an instant later, and in that moment, my whole reality becomes nothing but white pain. Lightning courses over the two of us, but it affects *him* far less than me. I drop to my knees, and he successfully twists the hammer out of my hand—snapping my wrist in the process. He shoves me backward, and I fall to the ground as he raises the hammer high over his head.

KA-BOOM!

A blast of lightning shoots down from the sky and wraps around the head of the hammer, cloaking it in light. I stagger to my feet, and Thor smiles and points the hammer in my direction.

KA-BOOM!

Every last watt of energy is blasted into my chest, and I'm knocked flat on my back. When it fades away, I find that I can't move. Not a single limb will obey my commands. No, it's more than that . . . I can't breathe. My vision swirls and begins to fade, and I fight against the darkness.

I will not go like this!

I will not die like . . .

I will not . . .

I . . .

CHAPTER TWENTY-TWO

Skill: Bearing of a Knight.]
 [Peril Detected.]
[Notice: You have 1 HP remaining.]
[Notice: Your arms are crippled.]
[Notice: Your legs are crippled.]
[Notice: Your head is crippled.]
[. . .]

A *great* many notifications scroll past my vision as I slowly rise back to alertness. I don't know how long I've been knocked out, but I don't think it's been very long. I hear John shouting out in the distance, and I slowly stagger to my feet.

[DarkCynic: HEY, EVERYONE!!! Jason's back online!]

[ViperQueen: Whoa! I honestly thought he had died!]

[ShadowDancer: I knew he hadn't. There was no death notification. I did think he was *going* to die, though.]

I shake my head as I look around. Flashes of light come

from deeper in Central Park, and I draw in a deep breath and take a step forward. My boot crunches on some broken glass, and I pause for a moment. If I only have a single point of health left, I really don't want to die from stubbing my toe, especially since just about every part of me is crippled. I pause and open up my inventory and pull out my last three Pumped! bottles. I chug them just as quickly as I can, then slip forward.

The blasts of lightning grow louder as I slip through the side of the park and race along the paths that lead through the trees. Suddenly, I come over a small hill to find Thor standing tall, while John and a couple other warriors cower in front of him. They're hemmed in by a living fence of lightning as he laughs and shoots bolts down at them every few seconds.

"Alright." I pause and crouch down as Thor laughs and taunts them. "I'm going to need everyone for this one. Are you all ready?"

My pups all nod as they come out. Burnie flutters out and lands on my shoulder, and he pecks at my ear.

Master, can I help at all?

"Just watch and learn. I don't know how this is going to go, but until you get a whole lot stronger, you're mostly going to have to sit out, I'm afraid."

Burnie nods, though I can tell he's disappointed. I watch Thor closely for a few moments more, then slowly rise up, draw out Sif's sword, and charge toward him.

I don't call out any words of warning. Instead, I simply brace myself, then tear straight through his little fence of lightning, jump upward, and slash at him as hard as I can. He turns and sees me, but his eyes only show mirth and a little surprise . . . at least until he registers Sif's sword in my hands.

The blade hits his left arm and slices clean through. Golden blood splashes on the concrete as the arm smacks against the ground, and he howls and steps backward.

"You—I—"

I snarl and lunge forward, stabbing at his chest, but he throws his hammer with his right hand. It hits me, and at such close range, I'm knocked backward several feet by the force of it. This time I manage to keep my footing, and I snarl as the hammer flashes back into his hand.

"Everyone! Now!"

Thor snarls and throws the hammer again, but as it leaves his hand, a powerful shock wave hits him from the side. The hammer whizzes off into the forest, knocking down several trees as it does so, and I stab him as hard as I can. The sword is driven deep into his gut, where ice crystals almost immediately begin to grow across his armor. Astrid adds her own voice to the fray, and a crack opens up in the ground below. I shove Thor inside, and he tumbles downward. Eyes wide, he snarls and lunges for freedom, but Astrid closes the gap over him a moment later.

Now, I'm not stupid enough to think that the ground can hold him for long, but it gives me a few seconds to think. I turn and wave at John, who escorts the other warriors away just as fast as he can move. My pets come charging down to me, and we pause to wait.

[FireStorm: Can I just say that this is the most epic battle ever? Like, of all time?]

[RazorEdge: I dunno. Doesn't seem like all that much is happening.]

[DarkCynic: Yeah, but like . . . It's *Thor*. Against Jason.]

I don't have a chance to comment, as the hammer suddenly comes flashing back to the clearing and hits the ground. Gravel explodes up into the air as it smashes through the crust of the Earth and plunges down to wherever Thor fell, and I brace myself.

"Only a few seconds now. Get ready!"

Everyone nods, and I fall into position. The ground trembles . . . shakes . . .

With a mighty blast, Thor erupts from the ground just behind me. His eyes blaze with lightning and fire, and he throws the hammer at me as hard as he can. It hits me in the back and slams me forward even as my pets all spin around to attack him.

Gabe howls and blasts Thor with powerful rays of light. His flesh blackens and burns under the intensity of the attack, and he holds up his hand as he tries in vain to shield his eyes. Bjorn howls and causes ice to grow across Thor's body—which in no way prevents him from being burned by Gabe's light. Balder blasts the god with shock waves, hitting him from the back, the front, the side.

Thor is getting attacked from all angles, and he doesn't really seem to know what to do. His eyes are wild, and he waves his hammer about. Lightning flickers and pulses, but it doesn't quite know what to strike and what to avoid. Thor snarls and throws the hammer, but it only destroys a park bench before flashing back to his hand. We have him on the ropes.

"Alright." I nod to them. "Let me have him."

The attacks cease, and a dazzled Thor is left standing alone as I attack as hard as I can. Sif's sword cleaves through the air, and I slash him across the chest. Thor snarls, and he raises his hammer and calls down another bolt of lightning. It hits him squarely, charging him back up, and he roars.

"No one defeats the mighty Thor!"

With that, he throws himself into the fray, swinging wildly. For a few long instants, we're locked in battle. Sword against hammer, steel against stone, man against demon. Thor draws in a deep breath and lifts his hammer, then swings down. I rise upward, and, whether by chance or some unconscious choice on my part, I slash straight through his wrist.

Thor gasps as his right arm is cut short as well. The hammer falls to the ground, sizzling and crackling, and he steps back. I lunge at him, intending to run him through, but he turns and flashes off through the trees, escaping as fast as he can go. I watch him, then slowly bend down and pick up the hammer.

[Mjölnir]

[Rank: SSS+]

[Details: Can summon lightning. Will return to the hand after being thrown. Devastating power.]

"Wonderful." I toss the weapon lightly in my hand, then rush forward after Thor. "If only it came as a dagger."

No one answers my cry, although I would honestly be concerned if someone did. In any case, ahead of me I suddenly hear a sharp call, along with the bleating of . . . goats?

I race out into a clearing to find the wounded Thor

climbing into a small chariot. A team of goats is hitched up to the front of it, and he looks over to see me closing in fast. His eyes are wide—this time with fear.

"No, you don't!" I spin and throw the hammer as hard as I can. It breaks the sound barrier as it flashes across the clearing, then hits the chariot with extraordinary force. The vehicle is knocked slightly to the side, but it's magic too, so it looks about the same as hitting an ordinary car with an ordinary hammer. Thor calls out something in a language I don't recognize, and the goats all lunge forward.

With a flourish, they shoot off into the sky, rising upward toward the clouds.

[ShadowDancer: HE'S ESCAPING!!!]

[GoldenShield: Come on, Jason! You aren't going to let him do that on your watch, are you?]

[RazorEdge: GET HIM!!!]

I throw the hammer again, and it sails upward before slamming into the chariot once more. Again, there's very little response, and the hammer smacks back into my hand an instant later. I grit my teeth and look down at the thing.

"Let's see here . . . I think this can be used to fly . . . So . . ."

Engines roar in the sky, and a jeticopter suddenly flashes into view. It comes down to the clearing, and the door pops open to reveal Ali standing there, smiling.

"Does someone need a ride? Twenty cents a minute with a ten dollar down—"

"Put it on Mr. Wang's tab. He pays everything for me anyway." I run forward and jump up into the copter. The pilot pushes the levers forward, and we shoot off through the sky at an extraordinary clip. I don't see Thor, but that doesn't mean much. "Do you have him?"

"We're tracking him on radar, sir," the pilot answers. "It looks like he's . . . Well, he's actually getting close to the club."

"Then get us there!" I call out. "I don't care how, just get us there."

The engines roar, and we flash through the darkened skies. I see the dark shadows of skyscrapers ahead and realize that I can't really *see* any of them. The plane's radar suddenly comes in handy as we zoom through the streets, dashing around buildings with ease. I stare ahead, watching . . . And then something appears.

"There!" I point past the pilot, down below. "There he is! He's staying low!"

"Can you hit him with your lightning?" Ali asks as I slide open the door to the jeticopter and gauge the distance. He's ahead of us by a good hundred feet or more and maybe a hundred feet below us. There's no way I can jump it, but I do want to watch him closely.

"Maybe." I shake my head. "I haven't exactly had time to experiment with this hammer thing. I'd rather not test it out in the middle of a densely populated area."

"Fair enough." Ali frowns. "Then tell us what to do. Do we wait for him to stop?"

"No. If we do that, he'll just wreak havoc. He's injured, but he's still more powerful than probably anyone except me." I think for a moment, then nod to Ali. "Teleport me over there."

"With my arrows?" Ali looks shocked. "But—"

"He can detect the use of Loki's staff. I can't risk using *that* to teleport across." I shrug. "You can do it."

"If I fire a teleporting arrow and I miss—"

"I know the risk. You'll just have to come get me, and we'll track him down again." I point down at him as we tear around a corner and flash down a larger street. Ahead is the club . . . along with countless people. "Ali! Now!"

Ali nods, then draws out her bow and fits a silver arrow to the string. She draws it back, then points the bow down. "Alright . . . Hang on . . ."

I touch my hand to the bow, letting my fingertips just *barely* brush the wood. Ali focuses . . . and then, carefully, lets fly.

Twang!

The arrow flashes off like a bolt of lightning, vanishing into the darkness. I hold my breath as we wait. I can't see it anymore. I don't know when it might—

FLASH!

I suddenly find myself falling, then scrabbling against the side of the chariot. Desperate, I grab hold of one of its wheels—it isn't spinning, since we're in the air—and it swings around to the bottom, where I hang on for dear life. The goats all let out sharp bleats, and the chariot swerves sharply to the right, reacting to the weight change.

"You again?" Thor sticks his head over the edge of the chariot. "You just won't leave it alone, will you?"

His eyes blaze with lightning, and he fires several bolts down out of his eyes into my body. My arms twitch and I nearly let go, but I manage to hang on. Thor begins to charge himself up again, and I pull upward with all my might, then swing into the chariot.

Thor screams, and blasts of lightning shoot down all around, sparking off buildings, starting fires, and smashing windows. Then he discharges a massive blast into my chest. I stumble and collapse into the front of the chariot, near the reins. Thor lets up on the attack, then closes his eyes. He mutters some words once more, and his right hand regrows.

The moment his hand has formed, he slumps backward, exhausted from the effort but now a bit more deadly. I gulp, and Thor reaches out to grab me. Before he can manage it, I reach up and grab one of the reins, then pull sharply as hard as I can. The goats react, turning on a dime, and the chariot yaws through the sky as it changes direction suddenly. Thor falls against the side, nearly tumbling out, and I lunge forward.

As I do so, I pull the hammer from my inventory and swing it upward to smash him in the chin. The blow lifts him from the chariot and flings him out into space. I glance at the goats, then jump out as well. The goats, following straight along, smash into a water tower on top of an apartment building. Water explodes across the area, and the goats frantically climb for the sky. I, though, tumble down to land in the street.

Crash!

I land on a car and smash the roof flat. As I climb down to the street, I see Thor about two blocks away, staggering to his feet. He's just regrown his other missing hand and is staggering toward me, barely able to walk.

With a cry, he holds out his arms, and lightning arcs from the nearby buildings, then courses through his body, making him light up quite brilliantly. "You may have my hammer, but I am the god of thunder! I need no—"

Wham!

I throw the hammer, which hits him in the chest and bounces right back to my hand. Thor staggers, and I spin and throw it once more. This time it hits him in the face and knocks him flat on his back. As he starts to rise, I throw it into his face again, this time smashing him down into the asphalt. He groans and slowly rolls over, and I throw it one last time.

Smack!

The hammer slams into his palm, and he chuckles and slowly starts to rise once more. His hammer, now firmly in *his* grasp again, blazes with lightning.

"You foolish human! I turned my back and you couldn't pass up the opportunity to—"

His voice trails off as I stab Sif's sword through his chest. It's true, I hadn't passed up on the opportunity, but that's because he was telegraphing his intentions to grab the hammer when I threw it. Giving him the momentary victory was enough to distract him, and now . . . Well, he may be a god, but he still has a heart, and now it's been pierced by Asgardian steel.

Blood gushes out from the wound, and I rip the sword out of his chest. He falls to his knees, and I see a word pass over his lips. I don't know what it is—probably "please"—but I ignore it. With one final blow, his head falls from his shoulders, and the mighty Thor collapses in a heap, dead.

[You have leveled up!]

[. . .]

"And there we have it." I let out a sigh and slowly turn

away. There are more notifications, but I ignore them for the time being. Instead, I hold out my hand and the hammer flies to my palm, recognizing its new owner. "Time to get back home. Only one more left . . . And I have a feeling that she's going to be the hardest of the lot."

CHAPTER TWENTY-THREE

It doesn't take me long to get back to the club. As the jeticopter lands on the helipad, the clouds begin to break, letting the sun stream through. The sudden change, seemingly from the dead of night into broad daylight, certainly throws me for a loop. Eyes burning in the sudden light, I make my way inside, where I find utter chaos.

Technicians and warriors run back and forth, frantically fixing things up. Wires are strung from wall to wall, stretched from the upper levels of the club down to the floor, and even run up the side of the building itself. Mr. Wang stands in the middle of it, arms crossed, looking back and forth over the chaos.

"Jason!" Mr. Wang turns and smiles. "You did it!"

"I did something, alright." I stretch, popping my shoulder as I do so. Every bit of me is sore, but I know I'm not going to have time to rest until later. "What's all of this?"

"The short answer is that we're turning this place into the

biggest switchboard that New York has ever seen." Mr. Wang smiles. "We still haven't gotten any sensors online, so for the time being, we're setting *this* up. If anyone catches the faintest hint of Hella, we'll know about it here. We have people scanning social media and open phone lines, and there are people in contact with every newspaper, weather station, and television network in the area. We also just have people out and about looking for whatever they can find."

"Wonderful." I nod, acknowledging the success. "Do you have any good news for me?"

"The good news, I suppose, is that the last dungeon in the city was just closed." Mr. Wang shrugs. "There's not a single dungeon left other than Hella's mysterious still-cloaked dungeon." He pauses, and a smile spreads across his face. "Mind telling me what level you managed to reach?"

I open up my interface and spend a moment scrolling. "Uh . . . It looks like I'm level ninety-four." My heart twists, and I frown. "Ninety-four. Interesting."

"Why is that interesting?" Mr. Wang asks.

"Because I need to be level ninety-five in order for Hella to appear." I shrug. "I'm just trying to think . . . If I stay at level ninety-four, and all the other dungeons are gone, then maybe this is the best course of action. Hella can't come through to attack us, and we can't get through to attack *her*. Seems like a win-win, right?"

"Maybe." Mr. Wang frowns and shakes his head. "I think you're forgetting something, though. Hella has already proven her ability to attack people in other places. Yes, she usually attacks her own people, but I would imagine that if she so desired it, she could probably find a way to start attacking the Earth from her realm."

"Not to mention the fact that the prohibition technically only applies to *her*," Elrith says as he strides up to us. "She has countless minions inside that thing, including a level ninety-nine Dire Wolf. It's the most powerful thing in the multiverse, second only to Hella herself."

"Great." I cross my arms and start to pace. "So, she really could open things up at any time."

"Yup." Elrith nods. "My guess is that she'll probably try to wait for a few hours to see if you can find a way to level up. If you can hit level ninety-five, then she can march through the portal herself, which will be *way* more fun than letting her generals do all the work, but—"

"But if she can't, she might as well get the job done," I murmur. "And she has the ability to open up her dungeon for everyone else?"

"I think it unlocked when you hit level ninety."

"I sure wish I had known that fact earlier. In that case, we need everyone on high alert."

"I'll give the order, of course," Mr. Wang confirms. "Don't worry, Jason. As soon as she appears, we'll be ready."

I take a deep breath as a thought strikes my mind. "Elrith, why don't you tell me about your journey through the portals. Did you ever experience anything that might help us out? Did you ever encounter Hella?"

Elrith frowns but starts to talk about his birth in a lowly dungeon composed mostly of swamp. I don't really listen to his description and do a handful of things instead.

First, I disconnect my livestream camera from my physical body. Second, I create an illusion of myself standing there and talking to Elrith. Third, I step backward, out of the illusion, until I'm standing half a dozen feet back. I can still see my camera floating there in the air, a disembodied little thing transmitting what my illusion sees, and Elrith's eyes suddenly widen slightly in recognition. It takes me an instant longer to use Loki's staff to do the same for Elrith, and, careful to stay out of the range of the camera, he comes over to join me. Now my illusion is hearing the riveting tale of Elrith's journey through the Desert of Dinn while I get to have a conversation with the *real* Elrith.

"What's the point of this?" Elrith hisses softly. "If you don't want to reveal your plans, why not just turn off your chat for a few minutes?"

"Because then Hella will know that I have secret plans," I answer. "I'd rather avoid that possibility for as long as possible. She watches my chat, at least a little bit. I want to be able to hit her entirely unexpectedly."

"How do you plan on doing that?" He seems intrigued by the idea, to be certain, though still quite skeptical.

"Simple." I hold up Loki's staff. "Is there any chance that I could use this to teleport straight into Hella's dungeon?"

"It would be suicide, but yes." Elrith frowns. "Why would you want to do that? Wouldn't it be better to be on the front lines when Hella opens the doors?"

"Maybe." I shake my head. "I don't know, though. She knows I'm here, and she's been watching me for a long time. When she opens up that portal, she's going to send something that's designed to guarantee her success."

"Right. And if our strongest warrior isn't with us, what then?" Elrith asks. "She'll tear through our lines and leave nothing but a smoking crater for you to come home to."

"Hmm." I look down at the staff. "I just have a feeling that it could be a good idea."

"Unless you go inside and hit her *before* she sends anything through the portal, I don't think it's a good idea." Elrith shrugs. "Now, if you *did* do that, you could potentially prevent her from emerging at all. The portal would open, you'd come out dragging the head of that giant wolf, and you'd be the biggest hero that Earth has ever seen. I'll admit, it's a nice fantasy, but I just don't know. That's a *lot* to take on, even for you."

I think for a moment, then shrug. "What are the alternatives? Play her game and probably get smooshed anyway? I really think this could give us the best shot at survival."

Elrith nods slowly, then sighs. "I'll let you do it on one condition."

"Oh? And what's that?"

"You take me along as a guide."

I don't have a good answer for that. I don't really want to take Elrith into the dungeon, but if that's the deal I'm going to get, that's the deal I'm going to get. I nod slowly, and Elrith and I both walk back over to our illusions. We step back into our bodies—which is a rather odd experience, just so you know—and I reset everything.

"And that's how I came to you." Elrith nods with finality.

"Wonderful." I smile. "Can someone in my chat record all that? Maybe in an audiobook?"

[IceQueen: I can, I can! Ooh, this will be fun!]

[ShadowDancer: No, let me!]

[RazorEdge: I'm a professional ghostwriter! I can take the basic format of it and add in some extra dialogue and things, maybe make it a bit more exciting!]

The chat explodes with excitement, and I turn away. Slowly, I walk up to the glass windows and look out across the city . . . watching . . . waiting.

The next several hours are filled with preparations. I don't know if Hella *has* to wait for a certain length of time, if she's trying to spook us, or if she's making preparations as well. What I *do* know is that this is the battle of a lifetime. All the battles up until this point, every boss battle, every skirmish, all of it has been preparation for this. All of it can be counted in numbers, in XP, in damage dealt, in bodies, weapons, and drops of blood.

All of it has been a deposit toward this one single fight. If Hella wins, the Earth burns. If *I* win, the Earth is saved.

It's really that simple.

Mr. Wang is a whirlwind of activity. He's on the phone constantly, making first one call and then another. Ali stays busy sending warriors this way and that way, lining up guards in different quarters of the city and making sure that everyone can respond quickly. John has a small strike team of the ten highest-ranked warriors in the country, second to me. They spend the time training, healing, and doing everything possible to make sure that they can respond the moment the dungeon opens.

Me? I do a lot . . . and I do nothing.

What my *chat* sees is me lying on a couch, eating some food, healing, and generally trying to recover from my last several battles. None of them begrudges me the rest since I've been through the wringer and have taken down a great many god-level monsters, each of which could have razed the city to the ground. Of course, I'm far from idle, and while my illusion stays nice and comfy on the couch, I drill with as many people as I can. I work on some sparring lessons with John and his team, I give some pep talks to Ali and her group, I participate in a few of the phone calls, and I read up on as much Norse mythology as possible. There's actually surprisingly little that we know firsthand; most of the legends actually come from much later or have been invented by modern authors. Who knew, right? In any case, it's a lot to take in, but I do the best I can.

After all, the world might be counting on it.

I should probably mention that pretty much everyone except me keeps their chat turned off for the sake of security. That way none of their viewers sees the real me. I mean, they flick the chats on and off and tell their viewers that they're going into important security meetings and things, which keeps everyone pacified *and* increases the feeling of mystery for our viewers. No one dares log off, that's for sure. For that matter, Mr. Wang informs me that, worldwide, almost six billion of the world's eight billion people are watching us. No pressure, of course.

The sun is just setting when it all starts to come together. I'm working on a drill with John's squad when an alarm starts to blare. I quickly run back to the couch and "pick up" my illusion and camera, before running to the general assembly area, which is an auditorium deeper within the club. As we run inside, Mr. Wang takes the stand and draws in a deep breath.

"Everyone!" he calls out. "We have just received word from the dungeons. I repeat, we have just received word from the dungeons."

I glance over at Elrith, who's right next to me. He turns slightly pale and balls his hands into fists.

"It came in the form of a video message," Mr. Wang continues. "If my techs have managed to get it working, we'll view it. Now!"

The lights dim, and a projector beams an image onto the back of the stage. There, I catch my first glimpse of Hella, goddess of death. My blood runs cold, and I feel my hands inching toward my weapons.

She's sitting on a stone throne, one with iron spikes coming out of the back and sides. On either side stands a wolf, though I don't really think that either of them is the level ninety-nine one. Either way, they're obviously quite powerful, with black hair and red eyes. Hella herself . . . She wears black robes, and her skin is dark and cracked. No, not cracked . . . scarred. One particularly large scar runs across her left eye. A crown made of bones sits upon her head. She's absolutely hideous. You know how sometimes evil queens will still look beautiful and terrible all at the same time? Not Hella. She just *oozes* evilness and darkness, and I know that she's no one to mess with.

"Greetings, inhabitants of Earth." Her voice is cold and harsh. "I have sent this recording to many, *many* other worlds, and I will do so again in the future. I know many of you are confused about why we attacked your world, why we burned it, and why we intend to raze it to the ground. The answer, of course, is simple: I am perfecting my army." Her words are precise and rehearsed. There's not a thing about her that isn't intentional and planned. "I have gone from world to world for many years now. When I arrive, I bestow power randomly upon the population. This power is then used to fight against us. Yes, I lose dungeons, sometimes half of my forces, but when I'm done, I have a more powerful force than before. How does this happen? Simple: right now, you are being offered a chance to come and join me." Her voice grows more powerful. "Across your world right now, portals will be opening up. Anyone and everyone is welcome to enter, to join my glorious army. Civilians will be used as . . . I suppose you would call it cannon fodder: the filler monsters for my dungeons in the next world.

"Don't worry, you'll be given powers too, so there's always a hope for your survival. Warriors, meanwhile, will be allotted command posts that will be awarded based on their respective power and on merits that they've gained over the last several weeks. I do hope you *all* will consider my message. The portals will remain open for two hours. As soon as they close, my personal dungeon will open, and your world will be reduced to ash. I suggest that you not tarry long in your decisions."

With that, the message ends. A murmur breaks out around the room, and Mr. Wang holds up his hands.

"Everyone! Everyone! Quiet!" The room grows quiet, and Mr. Wang continues, "That message was broadcast to the entire world. We haven't yet received any reports of portals opening, but—"

An aide bursts into the room. "They just did! They just opened up! They're here!"

At that, the room falls deadly silent. Everyone looks to Mr. Wang, who doesn't say a word. My chat is silent as well, and I know that the world is watching him. Sure, some people are going to run to the portals and there are other people who will fight no matter what, but . . .

"Well, Hella, if you're watching, know that you came to the wrong planet." Mr. Wang clears his throat. A small smattering of applause breaks out, but he holds up a hand, and silence descends once again. "Humans don't give in so easily. Open your portals. Open them wide! That will only make it that much easier for us to charge into your domain and tear you down from that throne. This is Earth, and I can tell you, Hella, that every human with blood that runs red will fight to defend it. We will fight, and we will defeat anything that comes our way." The room starts to cheer, and Mr. Wang pauses it once more. He stares directly at me, and I know that he's speaking straight through my chat to the ears of Hella herself. "We'll win, or we will die trying."

CHAPTER TWENTY-FOUR

The room explodes with cheers, and Mr. Wang shouts out instructions.

"Everyone, to your posts! Watch out for those portals! Do your best to stop anyone from going through. Try to talk down any civilians, and use force on any warriors. We're not going to add anyone to her army, not if we can help it." Mr. Wang's voice grows louder. "This is the final battle, everyone! This is what you'll remember! This is the day that your grandchildren's grandchildren will be talking about. This is the day that will define the rest of your life! Did you hide, or did you fight? Did you flail about, or did you make every strike count? Did you cower in fear, or did you swallow your fear, crush it just like one of the monsters in the dungeons, and charge into battle?"

He continues shouting, but by this point, everyone's growing far too loud. Warriors and civilians alike surge back out of the room, pouring through the complex, and rush down to the streets. I make my way out onto the helipad, where I'm able to watch the whole of the city. There, I carefully form my illusion, place my livestream camera inside it, and then step back. Once I'm confident that it's good, I walk backward until I'm out of earshot. The chat continues to roll, but, thankfully, it doesn't have a clue what I'm doing.

[GoldenShield: SQUEEEE! This is going to be the most epic, bestest fight of all time ever!]

[DarkCynic: Yeah! This is going to be GREAT!!!]

[IceQueen: Only problem is that after this, we won't have anything nearly as cool to watch. I mean, no monsters, no dungeons, no livestream, you know?]

[LunarEclipse: Sorry not sorry, but that's totally okay by me.]

I have to agree with LunarEclipse. I sort of like being a celebrity, but I'll gladly go back to my ordinary life if it means that the world is safe.

I step back into the club and slip around to the side, avoiding the prying eyes of other warriors who might notice that I'm in two places, and find Elrith. He's in a small command room, where security cameras are keeping an eye on everything in a two-block radius.

"You ready?" I ask Elrith as I pull out Loki's staff.

"I believe so." Elrith whistles softly. "How much of my backstory did you actually listen to?"

"Not much," I admit with a smile. "Why?"

"Because while I've never actually seen Hella, I *have* been inside her dungeon. Once." Elrith grimaces. "I was being a stupid teenager, following a dare. Jason, the things I saw in there . . . you can't unsee them."

"Then why are you coming?" I ask him.

"Simple. I know my way around that place." He holds out his hand, and I hand him Loki's staff. A complex diagram appears in the air above it, which shows the position of dungeons in the interdimensional space relative to New York. "There's not a bit of me that wants to go back, but if I can save even a single life, I'll do it."

"Well, the world thanks you." I nod. "How—"

"Right here." Elrith raises his right hand while holding the staff with his left, and a *massive* dungeon suddenly appears in the diagram. "There we go. The Queen's Dungeon."

"It's enormous." I whistle. "How did we not see it with our sensors before?"

"It uses a specific frequency of . . . Well, it uses magic to keep itself hidden. This staff and a few other magical artifacts are the only things powerful enough to see through it." Elrith smiles at me. "Don't ask what the others are. Suffice it to say that I had a friend who belonged to a rich family, and their dad kept one on his desk."

I chuckle. "Sounds like our version of stealing the car keys to go out joyriding."

"Something like that. The only difference is that we *quickly* lost all joy." Elrith begins zooming in on the dungeon. "She's added to it, it looks like. Wait a moment . . . I know . . . Here we are." He nods at the screen. "Right here."

"Just get me inside."

"Will do, boss." Elrith takes a deep breath. "And . . . hold on to your hat."

With a flash, lightning bursts from the staff and wraps

over the two of us. We're carried away, sucked down a long portal and on to the battle of our lives.

The portal isn't a long one, thankfully. When we come crashing out, the smell of mold fills my nose, and I gag. I find myself in a small jail cell, with a floor covered in moss and mud and the walls slick with a thick slime. The door looks like it rusted shut long ago, and the bones lying on a moldy cot in the back of the cell show me clearly how much attention was paid to the prisoner here. Slowly, I stand up and walk to the cell door. I'm rather missing the startled cries of my chat—I can still see their messages, of course, but they're commenting on things happening back in New York.

"What is this place?" I murmur as I glance out through the cell door. The room here is large, with a handful of cells set up around the perimeter. There are more bones or desiccated corpses in the cells I can see into from my own. Nothing alive has been imprisoned here for years.

"I know it as the Starving Chamber," Elrith answers. "The only things to eat here are slime and the bodies of the people who have died before you."

"It's awful." I shudder.

"It's actually one of the more pleasant ways to be killed around here." Elrith turns to the back of the cell and frowns. "Now . . . let me see if I can remember this." He taps a few bricks, then a few more. There's a rumble, and a hidden door cracks inward. "There we are!"

I blink in surprise. "A hidden door in a prison designed to starve people to death?"

"Another of the horrible tricks that Hella plays." Elrith shrugs. "When she tosses the people in here, she tells them that there's a secret way out. People spend all their time tapping bricks and pushing bolts, trying to find the secret. It prevents them from using their time to actually break out."

"And how do *you* know about it?" I ask as we slip into the passage.

"My friend's father worked for Hella. Pretty high ranking," Elrith answers. "Why do you think we were able to get our hands on something like that? Now pipe down. You'll have lots of questions, and I'd rather spend our time getting to Hella instead of getting you answers."

I nod and swallow my curiosity as we move along through the passage. It's long and dark, and if it wasn't for Elrith's breathing, I would wonder if he was even there. Finally, we come to the end, where another false wall waits for us. Elrith presses a few more bricks, then carefully inches the door open *just* a crack.

He looks through for a long moment, then nods and slips out. I follow, and my jaw falls open in horror. We're standing in another torture room, and I suddenly realize what Elrith meant when he said that the Starving Chamber was among the more humane ways to die.

A handful of torture racks are spread around the outside of the room. Half a dozen monsters are stretched across them, and . . . It's hard to even describe. Their flesh has been mostly peeled away and tacked to the wood next to them, their muscles flayed, razor blades and knives poked into their bodies at key points. And yet, they're still alive. Weary eyes follow the two of us as we slip through the room, heading for the door on the far side. Minotaurs, satyrs, one human—they're hardly recognizable. I feel a great stab of pity for them, but Elrith urges me onward. At the door, we slip out into a hall, and I start trying to get a feel for the place.

The hall has been carved through the solid rock, which means that we're below ground, at least in some sense, and it's narrow, so there's no chance to hide if we're seen. I can hear muffled voices and shouts off in the distance, but I don't see anyone and move forward all the faster. Elrith holds up a hand to slow me, then points to a doorway ahead. I frown but nod, and we step up, pull the door aside, and walk in.

The moment we set foot inside, my blood freezes, but Elrith doesn't flinch. We're in an armory with a great many weapons, sets of armor, and other battle equipment. A blood elf and a small troll are sitting on a bench nearby, pulling on Norse-style armor and chatting quietly. As Elrith and I enter, they glance over, but Elrith simply walks to one of the lockers and starts taking down armor.

"Hey!" the blood elf says with a cackle. His skin, as his name suggests, is red, and black blood vessels are visible beneath the surface. His fingers are long and spidery, and his fingernails narrow to talons. "Who let the wood elf in here?"

The troll snorts and nods. "Yeah, and the meatbag. Seems a little early." He stomps over toward me. "I thought it was still going to be a few months before your kind got sorted through the training dungeons and assigned roles."

"Maybe they're sneaking around." The blood elf snickers.

"A wood elf? Sneaking?" The troll laughs and punches the

blood elf in the arm. "I ain't never met a wood elf that could do anything other than sneeze on their enemies. And then they'd apologize for it!" He turns away. "Wood elf. Sneaking. Pfft."

"I agree." Elrith nods as he takes out a helmet and tosses it to me. "Wood elves would never lower ourselves to sneaking. We follow the proper laws of combat and engagement."

"Never *lower* yourself?" the blood elf sneers. I suddenly have the feeling that I'm going to need to remove his head, but I restrain myself. "You're saying that we're lower than you?"

"Course he is!" The troll suddenly becomes more interested in the conversation again. "I ain't never met a wood elf that thought other folks were as good as they were."

"Yeah? Then maybe we ought to knock him down a few pegs," the blood elf snarls softly. "Maybe we ought to show him just how *low* he can go."

"Good sirs." Elrith pulls out a pair of boots and pulls them onto his feet. "Forgive me for any offense I've given you. Not that I think I truly gave any real offense, since if I actually deigned to craft a proper insult, I would do so in a way that would go over your lowly heads. After all, everyone knows that blood elves and trolls have as much brainpower as the majority of sapient creatures. Which is to say that you'd struggle to know which end of a sword was used to dissect your opponents were it not for the number of times that you, yourselves, had been injured by them."

He bows low, and the troll snorts. "That sounds 'bout right. Thanks for groveling."

The blood elf stares at Elrith for a bit longer.

"That's it." Elrith nods. "You can work it through, I'm sure."

"I think he's saying that we're stupid." The blood elf glances over at the troll.

"Is he?" The troll frowns. "I never know with these things. Is it good or bad to be stupid?"

"You . . ." The blood elf puts his hands on the side of his head, then sneers as he turns back to Elrith. "You're going to pay for what you've—"

Elrith gives me a small nod, and I draw Loki's staff in the form of a dagger. It flashes through the air and removes the blood elf's head in the blink of an eye. The body sways and falls to the ground, and the troll snorts in surprise. He pulls a club from his inventory, but before he can do anything with it, I draw out Thor's hammer and throw it at him as hard as I can. The blast smashes him into rubble—trolls are made of stone, after all—and the hammer snaps back into my hand.

"You know, for a pacifist, you're awfully fine with *me* killing people." I collect Loki's staff from where it landed, then start pulling on the armor that Elrith hands me. In a moment, we've disguised ourselves as members of Hella's army.

"Desperate times, desperate measures." Elrith shrugs. "In any case, I do believe that we need to—"

Blam!

The door flies open as two minotaurs come walking inside. Elrith doesn't waste a moment and rushes up to them.

"Please! They've been attacked!"

"Must be an infiltrator in the dungeon," one of the minotaurs says. "Get into rank. I'll alert the proper authorities."

They turn to walk away when, suddenly, my chat lights up.

[DarkCynic: Uh . . . Jason? How did you just teleport from the helipad to a dungeon?]

[ChaosRider: Wait, are those minotaurs???]

[FireStorm: I'm confused . . . Wait . . . We were watching from the perspective of an illusion, weren't we?]

[ShadowDancer: WHAT??? THAT'S THE MOST EPIC THING EVER!!!!]

[Originalgoth: I'll admit . . . I'm impressed. That doesn't happen often. Guards?]

The minotaurs suddenly freeze, and I see them turn back around.

"Alright, Elrith," I murmur. "The jig is up . . . And we've got an army that's about to come looking for us."

When Elrith answers, his voice is tight. "Then maybe I'll just have to remember how to hold a sword after all."

CHAPTER TWENTY-FIVE

The two minotaurs grunt and draw massive battle axes out of their inventories. Without hesitation, they charge at me, grunting and swinging their weapons. I don't know if they don't consider Elrith a threat at all, or if they just consider him to be *less* of a threat than me. Whatever the case, they both attack with all the force they can muster.

That proves to be their mistake.

I've long since grown strong enough to slay minotaurs in my sleep. The first one growls and brings his axe down in an overhanded stroke intended to cleave me from top to bottom. I once more draw out Loki's staff in the form of a dagger and slash upward to meet his strike.

Crack!

The axe smashes into bits against the far stronger dagger. The minotaur snorts and stumbles back, and the second one attacks. I think he had already started his swing, otherwise the fear in his eyes tells me that he might have backed up. In any case, the blade is aimed for my chest, and I slash outward to block. Another *crack* sends that axe shattering into metal slivers, and both minotaurs are left defenseless. They glance at each other, then, bare fisted, charge at me with all their might.

Two strikes later, they're dying at my feet. I slowly put the staff back into my inventory, then step up to the doorway, where I hear a great many snorts, roars, and other terrifying noises that signal Hella's entire army is bearing down on our position.

Shing!

Elrith draws a small sword out of one of the lockers and gives it a practice swish. "It's been years since I last held one of these."

"Mind telling me why you're so set on being a pacifist?" I ask as we run out into the hall and start jogging toward the noise. After all, if they're going to get to us eventually, we might as well make it on our terms.

"If you order it, I, as your loyal servant, will tell you," Elrith answers curtly. "That said, if you don't mind, I'd rather wait until the dungeons are defeated and that livestream camera is out of your head."

"Fair enough." I smile at him. "You'd better live that long."

"It would be my great pleasure!"

Ahead of us, the hallway curves and I see shadows dancing across the wall. I grit my teeth and plunge forward, taking the lead. And then . . . the tide of battle comes crashing upon us.

Two more minotaurs lead the charge, huge and burly, with thick clouds of steam puffing out of their nostrils. The first swings his axe, the second draws an enormous sword. It doesn't help either of them. My dagger slashes straight through the axe, then cuts through the minotaur's throat. The sword is parried with ease, and I stab him through the chest. Both of the monsters fall, and I press forward.

Next in line are the elves. Lots and lots of elves. Most of them are blood elves or dark elves. All of them are armed with swords, though I *do* see quite a few bows. None of them can get off a shot, though, in such close quarters. In any case, my dagger flashes faster than they can attack, and I steadily cut my way through them.

The monsters are coming fast, pouring around the corner at a run, and I brace myself in the middle of the floor and slash as fast as I can. Bodies begin to pile up around my feet, and a barrier of sorts slowly forms. I huff with the exertion of such constant battle, but I don't dare take a rest. Finally, the pile of bodies grows as tall as I am. A few of the elves still try to scramble over the top, but that makes them easy prey, which only makes the pile grow taller. Finally, the tide of battle slows, and I step back. I can still hear the monsters shrieking and crying out in other places, but I can't really tell where they're coming from.

"They're going to come around the back," Elrith calls. "This way!"

He runs in the other direction, and I follow. I think I see a couple elves scrambling through the gap behind us, but I don't have time to deal with them right now. We run past the armory, past the secret entrance to the prison, and around a corner to a *long* narrow hallway that runs for a good two hundred feet. There's a small door at the end, a door that seems to me to be vibrating with energy.

"They'll come through there in just a moment." Elrith nods in the direction of the door. "They'll be all lined up for you."

"I appreciate it." I draw out my staff in dagger form and hold it in my left hand, then take out Thor's hammer and hold it in my right, hiding it behind my back. As I do so, I see several blood elves coming up from the other direction.

"Don't worry." Elrith twirls his sword. "I'll keep them off you."

I nod in his direction, then turn my attention back to the door at the far end. Elrith's sword crashes against steel, and I hear the blood elves screaming. Suddenly, the door bursts open and a great many monsters come surging in.

They're a mixture of elves, satyrs, dragonspawn, and an assortment of other such vile creatures. I hold out the dagger, readying myself, and watch as the monsters draw closer and closer and closer. And then . . . with all my might, I spin and throw the hammer.

BONG!

The weapon flashes down the hallway, flickering with lightning, as it knocks monsters flat onto the floor and plasters them across the walls. At the very end of the hall, a particularly large werewolf has just stepped through when the hammer first obliterates the head of a stone golem and then smashes through the werewolf's chest. The werewolf staggers, then groans and falls forward to land on the ground with a loud crash.

[DarkCynic: That. Was. EPIC!!!]

[IceQueen: Please, Jason, can we see lots more stuff just like that? It would totally make my day!]

[FireStorm: YEAH!!! Lots of monster kills! I'm going to record all of this and put together a montage, if that's alright.]

I hold out my hand, and the hammer flashes back through the hall, returning to its sender. I give it a twirl, then smile and wait for more of the monsters to come.

Surprise, surprise, they decide to hold off.

"We need to get moving, Master." Elrith spins and cuts down another blood elf, then points down the hall. "They're probably bringing in some sort of ranged weapon. It's not something we're going to want to get caught by."

"Fair enough." I charge forward. "You alright?"

"Well enough!"

"Good!"

I flash down the hall, leaping over bodies and slipping in pools of blood. As I reach the door, I catch a glimpse of a particularly large *something* being lugged into place, and I charge through, ready for anything.

Sitting there on the ground is what looks to be a cannon of some sort. It almost looks like an energy cannon, really, though I can't tell that for sure. Several satyrs are busily hooking it up to several power cells, while a wide assortment of other creatures stand at the ready, filling the hall. They all snort in surprise, and I leap forward, then kick the barrel of the cannon aside. It spins to point at the army just as the satyrs pull a lever.

PEW!

A great blast of green energy spears through the crowd and

vaporizes a great many warriors with a single strike. The satyrs are left looking horrified, so I relieve their anxiety by removing their heads. As the last one falls, I slash my dagger across the power cells and get rewarded by a burst of sparks flickering from the metal canisters.

"Quick! Dive!"

Elrith spins back into the hall while I simply charge into the fray of monsters as they mill about in confusion.

KA-BOOM!

The power cells explode violently and blast a dozen monsters into nothing but pulp. I smile and stand up, then quickly get to work.

I should probably explain what the hallway itself looks like. It's wide and broad and looks quite useful, if you know what I mean: very few frills, just a long and broad corridor that looks to be quite heavily traveled. As such, it's packed to the gills with monsters eager to flay Elrith and I alive.

We decide to return the favor.

I hack through werewolves, through vampires, through wraiths and goblins and kobolds. Orcs and dwarves join the fray, mindlessly pressing forward. Honestly, it becomes hard to keep track of everything. There are always more monsters surging forward, always more combatants ready to carve us up, so I just hold my dagger even tighter and slash all the harder.

"Jason!" Elrith calls out. He's fighting against a skeleton and parries an attack with what looks like casual ease. With a flick of his wrist, he cuts off the head of the monster, then brings the sword crashing down to smash the rest of it into powder. "We need to get out of here. She'll have more than enough troops to keep us busy for the next ten years. It'll give us plenty of levels, but it won't do anything to get rid of Hella."

"Fair enough." I slash through the neck of a humanoid chimera. "Which way do we go?"

"Uh . . . That way." Elrith points off to my right. "That's where her throne room is located and where they'll be assembling to go attack Earth."

"Works for me." I nod. "In that case, I need everyone to move!"

There's no response, obviously, and I pull out Thor's hammer and throw it as hard as I can. The weapon blazes through the hall, crackling with lightning, and blasts aside dozens, if not hundreds, of monsters.

[ShadowDancer: HE DID IT AGAIN!!!]

[RazorEdge: This is the Jason I love to see!!!]

[GoldenShield: I'm going to be rewatching this battle for the rest of my life. This is seriously the coolest thing I've ever seen.]

A rift forms through the middle of the group, and I charge in that direction as fast as I can go, slipping and sliding through the thick of battle. Elrith follows along behind, and, as the hammer snaps back into my palm, I find that we're actually being given a fairly wide berth. The monsters were sent here by Hella to kill us, but . . . if we're escaping, they're not *technically* obligated to stop us, so they're not going to do so. I imagine that they're just as scared of Hella as they are of me, maybe more so, and see in me an opportunity to be rid of her.

Whatever the case, we come up to a corner in the hall—I notice a large crater in the stone where my hammer hit—and spin around it, then cover another short distance that leads into an antechamber of sorts. Two enormous double doors there open up into what seems to be a simply *massive* room, though I don't see many more details than that. Guards slam the doors shut as we come around the corner, and with a grunt, a large stone troll drops down from the ceiling and lands on the ground with a crash.

"And who might you be?" I ask as we run up into the antechamber. The ceiling is tall, the floor broad. The troll carries a massive club and looks down on us with disdain.

"I'm sorry, but I cannot let you in to see the magnificent and glorious Hella." The troll bows low. "You must be conducted back to your own realm, where you can await your grand destruction."

I open my mouth to respond, but Elrith holds up a hand, walks past me, and bows his head.

"Good sir, you are obviously a man of culture."

"But of course." The troll snorts, even as a large blob of snot slips down out of his nose. I try to avoid gagging, and my chat explodes with snickers and other comments.

"Then you must know how important it is for us to see your great and lovely queen." Elrith bows. "We would love to go back home—we really would—but you see, we've come a long way and been through quite a lot. Please, if you would, it would be a great favor to us if you would stand aside. As one doorman to another?"

The troll shrugs. "I understand that you've been through

a lot, but without an appointment, I'm afraid that I can do nothing."

Elrith nods, then sighs. "Then I'm afraid that all our efforts will be for naught. If we cannot get an appointment, it will all be doomed."

The troll nods, then frowns. "What will be doomed?"

"Oh"—Elrith shrugs—"you know."

The troll blinks several times. I can see that he's intrigued, and I suddenly realize that Elrith really *is* quite talented in a great many ways.

"No, I don't know."

"You don't know?" Elrith gasps. "But certainly, you *know?* Everyone knows! Someone of your position *must* know!"

"Ah! I know everyone knows." The troll straightens up. "And . . . that something . . . it's . . . Well, you might as well tell me, because I *know.*"

"But of course, except that I can't, because . . . Well, you know." Elrith holds up his hand.

"Ah! I do!"

"And that's why we must see the queen."

"I wish you had just said so in the first place!" The troll turns and grabs hold of the door handles and pulls the doors wide open. "There you go! Hope you can—"

The guards, looking up at the troll like he's grown a second head, slam the doors back shut.

"They're going to try to kill the queen!" one of them shouts.

The troll shakes his head, and he looks down at us. Elrith glances at me and shrugs.

"It was worth a try. Trolls are *very* easy to outwit. The other people that are placed in the room to make sure the trolls don't get tricked . . . They're quite a bit harder to outwit."

"I see." I brace myself as monsters crowd around the back-side of the room, watching the fight about to go down. "Then we'll just have to do this the hard way."

CHAPTER TWENTY-SIX

B*LAM!*

The troll is flung backward straight through the doorway from the impact of Thor's hammer. The blow smashes a great deal of his stony flesh, and he blasts the doors clean off their hinges. The doors flatten several dozen monsters standing on the far side, and with that, Elrith and I have a clear passage into the throne room.

[You have leveled up!]

[Congratulations! You are now Level 95!]

"Welcome, Jason. Welcome, Elrith."

Hella's voice cuts through the room, and I have to force my body not to tremble. Slowly, we walk into the room, and I do my best to stay focused. It's hard to do since the room is so impressive, but . . . well . . .

The cavern must be a good quarter-mile long and nearly as wide. At one end is nothing but flat rock and some crystals, which makes me convinced that it's where the portal will open up. At the far end is a massive throne. The throne itself, which we saw in the video, sits upon a pedestal that rests a good forty feet above the main floor, accessible via a long flight of obsidian steps. Standing in ranks between the throne room and the portal area are thousands upon thousands of monsters. I mean, it's seriously hard to express just how many monsters there are. Smaller monsters stand in lines, and rows of trolls and dragons and other large monsters are placed in between the blocks of smaller ones. Massive hallways, a dozen at least, branch off in every direction, allowing for monsters to flow in and out of the room in quite a large volume. It's a place designed for war, for intimidation, and in this moment, it's doing both of them quite well.

A relatively small area, maybe fifty feet wide, has been cleared in front of the throne itself. That's clearly where we're supposed to go, and I slowly walk in that direction, a feeling of inevitability filling my soul.

[ShadowDancer: Whoa . . .]

[IceQueen: That's what's coming for the Earth???]

[ChaosRider: Mr. Wang? You'd better make sure you have plenty of warriors ready, 'cause this is going to be CRAZY!!!]

[Moneybags: Jason? We'll get as many of them as we can, but we'd sure appreciate it if you could knock that army down a few pegs. Bright side: it's nice to know ahead of time!]

I nod at the messages as Elrith and I slowly walk to the base of the throne. We find ourselves looking up at Hella, who's honestly rather hard to see since she's so high up, and her voice comes booming down.

"Jason Lee. Elrith. Long have I desired to meet both of you."

I bow my head. "Well, for what it's worth, you've been on my radar for about as long as I've been on yours. Since I couldn't kick you out of the chat using the system, I suppose I'll just have to manually remove you from . . . well . . . life."

Hella laughs, though it doesn't sound like a particularly *mirthful* sort of laugh. "Few are this brazen in your position, Jason. I hope you know that."

I can only shrug. "I figure that it doesn't matter what I say. You're going to try to kill me. I can either have a little bit of fun with it, or I can just stand here and spend the rest of the time dreading it. One of those options puts me in a better position to survive."

"A wise perspective on life." Hella slowly rises from her throne. Her two wolves both rise as well, growling down at me. They don't attack, though. I don't know if that's a good thing or a bad one. "Well, you've come here. What's better is that you've killed so many of my army that you're now level ninety-five, which means that I can enter your wretched world. I have only a few more minutes to wait until my ultimatum runs out."

"Wait all you want," I snap. "You're not getting anyone from Earth to enter your little army."

Hella only smirks at me. She doesn't brag about how many people have already come through, but she doesn't have to. If she had simply given me the number of warriors that had defected, I would have called her out for lying. As it is, I have to assume that she's telling the truth.

"Not to turn the conversation away from you, Jason,

but I do need to turn my attention to Elrith for a moment." Hella glances down at my friend. "The leader of all inter-dimensional resistance to me. He's like the dungeon version of Mr. Wang. Did you know that, Jason? He's been a thorn in my side for the better part of two millennia now. For that matter, he's a big part of the reason we withdrew from Earth all that time ago. I've wanted him in my throne room for that whole time, but he's evaded capture."

Elrith doesn't say anything, but his lips stretch in a smile. "You've racked up quite a debt, Hella. The time has come to pay up."

"You think you have something that can fight against me. You all believe that you can stop me." Hella slowly starts to walk down the stairs. Thunder crashes loudly as she does so, and lightning flickers around the corners of the cave. "You know, though, that you can do no such thing. You cannot defeat me. You cannot stop me. I am inevitable. I am death—death to a thousand worlds."

"And you won't stop until you've burned every last one of them down." Elrith shrugs. "We know, we know. You got mad that Heimdall kicked you out of Asgard, so you decided to burn down everything else in a violent rage, and—"

Hella stops on the stairs and starts to laugh. "You think that Heimdall kicked me out of Asgard? You really believe that? Oh, you're a laugh! Heimdall? Come down and show these . . . ruffians . . . just how upset you are at me."

As she turns to walk up the stairs once more, Elrith leans over and whispers in my ear, "Take him down quickly. He learns from watching his opponents and can adapt his style of combat to compensate. That said, he'll have more than enough XP to level you up to a more comparable level to Hella."

"You tricked her?" I blink in surprise.

"Nah. I just know what buttons to push." Elrith shrugs. "Two thousand years of studying an enemy will give you a *lot* of data about them. Anyhow, have fun."

I nod and draw out Sif's sword just as a golden individual crashes down in front of me. I give a start and jump back and find myself looking at Heimdall, guardian of the Bifrost.

He appears with a burst of rainbow lightning, which certainly coincides with what I know of his role in Asgard. He's entirely clad in golden Asgardian armor, similar to what Sif wore, and wields a massive sword. His skin is pale, so pale that it almost looks translucent, and his eyes are a milky white.

"You misunderstand what happened between Hella and I." Heimdall slowly walks forward, letting the tip of his sword drag against the stone. Alright, so the fight is starting with barely a hint of buildup. "You are a fool to come here!"

He lunges forward and slashes at me with extraordinary force. I raise Sif's sword and block—at least, I try to. The blow hits hard enough to knock me backward several steps, and I sway as I try to keep my balance. Heimdall attacks once more, hard and fast, then spins and attacks *again*. He's fast, fast and powerful, and I find myself struggling to keep up.

"Then why don't you explain to me what really"— I gasp as he attacks with an overhanded blow aimed at my neck—"happened."

"Gladly," Heimdall snorts. "Hella and I hatched the plan to take over the dungeons and rule the universe. I sent her forth from Asgard not as an exile but as a glorious general making ready our plans to conquer all the known worlds."

"Right." I raise an eyebrow as he attacks once more. "And the fact that she's your general totally explains why you're fighting at *her* behest. Shouldn't it be *you* on that throne?"

"You understand nothing." Heimdall strikes yet again. Doesn't this guy run out of stamina and need a break? All monsters have some sort of a pattern, but he's not letting up. Suddenly, he steps backward, gives the sword a twirl, and then attacks again, hard and fast.

Right. The previous attacks were just feeling me out. I'm not great with a sword, so I just accidentally showed him all my weaknesses. I have to use the Speed skill to block his attacks as he presses relentlessly, hacking and striking and doing everything in his power to cut me down to size. Sweat runs down my brow, and I grit my teeth as he forces me steadily backward.

"Hey, Heimdall!" Elrith shouts as he lunges up and stabs at the warrior's side. Heimdall spins and slashes out with his sword and cuts Elrith's own sword clean in two. The blade clatters to the ground, and Heimdall seems suddenly triumphant. I take the moment to attack with fury, and suddenly, Heimdall is the one on the defensive. If Elrith *was* intending to say something, it's been obscured by the change in battle.

I press the attack as hard as I can, feeling him out. The only problem is that I don't really see any weaknesses in his guard. His eyes, for being blind, can see everything in the universe, or something like that, and he employs it well in his defense. If I go high, his sword is there to block. Low, it's there. Middle, back, front, there's not a place he can't guard—and with an effortless ease that makes me look like a novice. If I'm going to take him down, it's going to take a whole lot more effort than I've ever put into something before.

Only problem is . . . I just can't think of a plan.

"You're weak, Jason." Heimdall suddenly lunges forward and executes a blinding series of attacks faster than I can follow. I'm knocked backward, and he snorts as we lock blades. "Do you know what your biggest issue is?"

"Not knowing when to stop?" I shrug. "I'm told that it's a strength as well as a weakness, but you know how—"

"Your weakness is not being willing to rely on others," Heimdall snarls. "Not that I'm complaining, mind you, but look at Hella. Look at me. We have an army, and we have a plan to destroy your whole world. And look at you. Alone. One man in a dungeon. One man with the weight of the entire world on his shoulders."

A smile spreads across my face. Heimdall frowns, and he squints. "What is it?"

"You." I shrug. "You can see everything . . . and yet, you can see nothing."

"How so?" Heimdall snarls.

"Simple. I'm not alone," I answer. "I have all the help I could ever want."

Something flaps down to land on my shoulder, and Burnie joins the fight. Heimdall glances over at him with his blind eyes, and the level-one Phoenix spreads his wings and puffs a bit of flame into the monster's face.

It's not much, but it makes him blink, and we break

swords. I glance over at Elrith and toss him Sif's sword. He catches it with ease, and I pull out Thor's hammer and smash it upward into Heimdall's chest. He's knocked backward by the blow, and as quickly as I can, I spin and throw it into his gut. It doesn't really injure him, but it knocks him backward a few feet. He snarls and charges at me as the hammer returns to my hand, but by then, Elrith has joined the fray.

For being a pacifist, he's exceptional with a sword. Sif's blade gleams in his hand as he steps in to duel with Heimdall. Metal rings against metal, and the shouts of battle ring out across the area. Heimdall gasps and staggers backward, and Elrith presses the attack, muscles rippling in the light.

"You're . . . incredible!" Heimdall gasps.

"I ought to be." Elrith spins, and their blades clash together just in front of his face. "I have the most powerful master in the multiverse and the best group of fellow warriors that an elf could want."

A powerful howl splits the air, and Balder steps out of my pocket dimension as he blasts Heimdall with a shock wave from behind. Heimdall gasps and staggers, caught between Elrith's sword and Balder's attack. Astrid appears as well with her own howl, and Heimdall's armor starts to glow red.

"I'll give you one chance." I draw Loki's staff and transform it into a dagger as I walk up toward Heimdall. "Turn against Hella and we'll let you live."

Heimdall snarls, and he looks at me with fury in his eyes. "I would rather die than join the likes of you."

"Fair enough."

As I charge forward, Heimdall lets out a shout, and a blast

of energy ripples outward from his body. Elrith is knocked backward, Balder and Astrid are both knocked flat, and I'm slammed rather hard in the chest. With that, Heimdall attacks me with fury, his sword blazing harder and faster than ever.

Only now, I'm wielding a dagger. Plus, I just got a good morale boost from my friends showing up, which is always a plus.

Heimdall attacks with force, his sword cleaving through the air, but I dodge him half a dozen times. I'm faster now, and he sees it. He's going to have to change his tactics, and that's really all there is to it. I see him adapting, preparing for a faster strike . . . And there it is: his sword swings low and flashes across my stomach to gut me. If I had dodged like before, he would have gotten me.

As it is, I jump straight forward, right past his sword, and stab him in the throat.

Golden blood trickles down the blade and over his armor, and he gasps. Before he can do anything, I draw out Thor's hammer with my free hand and whack him in the chest, and he's blasted back into the stairs with enough force to send up a spray of obsidian gravel. He falls silent and motionless, at least for a moment. Then he slowly starts to rise, and I give the hammer a twirl.

"I'd stay down if I were you."

Heimdall groans and sits up. I spin and throw the hammer as hard as I can straight into his face.

This time he doesn't get up.

[You have leveled up!]

[Congratulations! You are now Level 96!]

[You have leveled up!]

[Congratulations! You are now Level 97!]

[You have leveled up!]

[Congratulations! You are now Level 98!]

"You're most welcome," Elrith says from off to the side, giving a small bow. I slowly look up to where Hella sits upon her throne once more. Her wolves have risen up again, and her eyes look . . . unsettled. I imagine it's been a while since she lost *this* many warriors all in one go. She slowly raises a finger, and a blast of lightning flashes across the far wall and opens up the portal.

"Behold, my armies!" she cries out, her voice thundering across the room. "Go forth! Go forth and leave nothing left alive."

CHAPTER TWENTY-SEVEN

The portal forms. It's a proper rift portal; huge and ugly, it stands a good fifty or more feet tall. All across the room, the monsters cry out, snuffling and snorting. Elrith runs up next to me, and I grimace.

"You're not thinking of . . ." He frowns. "She's just trying to distract you."

"I know, but she's desperate." I shrug. "I have to stop these things from going through and razing the planet."

"They can't destroy the planet without Hella," Elrith argues.

"They can probably still destroy most of New York," I counter. "I don't know how many people are left, but there are still millions upon millions of survivors. I owe it to them to make sure that this army doesn't go anywhere."

[ChaosRider: Jason against a whole army? This is going to be incredible!]

[ViperQueen: YEAH!!! You can do it!!!]

[ShadowDancer: Just go charging into battle! Your kill count is going to be *incredible* after this!]

[Moneybags: Jason, you do what you need to do. You're not going to be fighting alone anymore.]

I read the last message, then slowly turn toward the portal. Monsters are marching in ranks toward the flickering energy, preparing to cross over and attack the city. Suddenly, though, the energy starts to flicker a bit brighter and figures start to emerge.

"For Earth!"

"For Jason!"

"Wipe this scum from our planet!"

"*AHHHHHHH!*"

Dozens—no, hundreds of warriors pour through the portal at once. They come like a flood, swords and bows and shields and clubs and axes all at the ready. The front lines crash together, and a great cry rings out. The noise of battle explodes through the chamber, and I smile.

"Now that's what I'm talking about!" I shout.

[Moneybags: What are you talking about? That was just the opening salvo. Behold!]

My jaw drops as the portal opens up again and two jeticopters come roaring through. They fly about halfway over the army of monsters, then turn their engines downward and blast the ranks of evil with a torrent of jet-wash. I see the doors pop open and gun barrels poke out, and I frown.

"But . . . ordinary guns don't really work against monsters."

Elrith holds up a finger. "Technically, that's true. That said, if you take weapons out of the dungeons, melt them down, and then make bullets out of that metal, they actually become quite effective." My jaw drops, and Elrith shrugs. "You're not the only one who can make secret plans. Mr. Wang is *quite* the one-man think tank, and Paul knows his way around pyrometallurgy."

The guns let loose with devastating force and hundreds of bullets cut through the lines of assembled enemies. Undead fall in heaps right alongside slimes, wolves, giant crows, golems, gargoyles, trolls, harpies, and more. The sheer destructive force is unprecedented, and my jaw drops at it all.

"Impudent humans!" Hella screams down from her throne.

"I'd say that we're at least bothering her," Elrith quips. He pauses, then shrugs. "I suppose you could go join in the fray if you'd really like to."

"Honestly, I wouldn't mind seeing if I can gain another level or two before I have to fight Hella herself," I answer. "Every little bit helps, you know."

"Fair enough."

With that, I draw out my dagger-shaped staff, give it a twirl, and charge into the ranks of monsters. Most of them don't even see me coming, and I don't give them an opportunity to repent—they've had their chance. This is the final battle. This is the defining moment for humanity. This is where it matters, where it counts.

A line of trolls looms ahead of me, and one of them turns around and frowns.

"Hey, that's the—"

I slash out across his belly as I approach. The blast rippling off the blade carves straight through him *and* takes the heads off half a dozen monsters in the next row. As they all fall, the trolls lumber forward and bring their clubs crashing down. I dodge out of the way, then rush forward and jump onto one of their clubs, then spring up into the air. My blade carves him open, and I spin to deliver the next hit. Another blow cuts him in half, and I rush down the line.

None of them even touches me, and as I reach the end, the trolls slowly topple over, crashing down one after another in an immense heap. With that, I rush forward once more and carve a long path through the monsters as I head toward the front lines, where our lower-level warriors are still struggling against the beasts.

Two small dragons have formed up to challenge them. I see John fighting against the creatures with dozens of other warriors behind him. Ali fires an explosive arrow into one of them, while the second roars and lunges down at John. John punches the monster in the jaw, then slashes it across its throat. The monster groans and falls flat, then starts to pick itself up again.

Shing!

I flash forward and cut off its head. The second dragon looks down at me, then lifts a claw and slashes across my chest.

Crack!

The claws shatter into bits, and the dragon looks down in horror. I grab hold of the paw and slam it down, then slash through the dragon's neck. The beast flails for a moment, then collapses, dead, and I sheath my blade and slowly turn to John.

"Showboat," he snorts as a chimera jumps out of the

crowd. He punches it in the nose and insta-kills it. I turn as a stone golem lumbers up, then throw a punch into its belly. The whole thing is blasted into rubble, and bits and pieces of shrapnel shoot out through the army to kill half a dozen more monsters. I turn back to John, and he laughs.

"What's the situation outside?" I ask as the monsters surge around us. A warrior screams as a large scorpion stings him in the arm. I jump over, grab the scorpion and rip the tail off, then crush its head. The warrior's friends quickly hand him some antivenom, and he nods to me before pushing himself back into battle.

"Mr. Wang has two more jeticopters ready to gun down any monsters that happen to make it through. There are a few warriors, too, but they're lower level," John answers. "All told, I think we're in pretty good shape."

"I agree, except that I think we need to move." I nod at Hella, who's now pacing back and forth next to her throne. "We're all in a cluster right now, and that makes us vulnerable."

"What do you think?"

I pause in thought, then nod as I see magic beginning to flicker around Hella's hands.

"On me! Everyone, follow behind! We're forming a wedge!"

The jeticopters seem to respond to my call and pull off to the side, then turn their guns back toward the entrance. Meanwhile, I charge forward, straight up the middle, as warriors flash behind me and form an immense wedge. Monsters press on every side, but the humans stay strong. Our blades are sharp and fast, and we cut down hundreds of the beasts as we press forward.

I cry out as I cut through a troll, a dragon, and countless minions. I'm performing the same actions over and over and over—so many of them that I can hardly keep track of it—but still, onward I go. Hella lets out a powerful blast of magic from her throne, and lightning bolts rain down across the area where we were just standing. Several monsters making a break for the portal are cut down as a result, actually, but Hella seems not to care. Instead, she begins charging up once more, and I fight on.

We're certainly outnumbered, but we're not outpowered. With a roar, several larger dragons thunder out of one of the many corridors leading into the room. They spread their wings and seem to be preparing an attack. Suddenly, more lightning blasts down from above, and this time Hella doesn't miss. Lightning explodes through our ranks, arcing from warrior to warrior to warrior. It hits John and I, certainly, but neither of us are really affected. Others, though, crumple under the blast. The warrior who was healed from the scorpion stumbles, and a minotaur slashes through his chest with a sword. Another warrior is obliterated altogether. Sure, some of the monsters around us are killed as well, but we take the larger hit.

As the lightning passes, I turn and shout at John, "We need to separate! If she does that again, we're all toast!"

"We've already separated too much!" John calls back. "Look! More monsters are coming in through those tunnels, and they're running for the portal!" I look, confirming that it's true. The jeticopters are stemming the tide for the moment, but . . . since we moved, the monsters have been taking advantage of our absence and are doing everything in their power to break past. Now, I *had* to move everyone or Hella would have just deep-fried us with her lightning. But now that we're gone, there's no one to protect the entrance . . .

The situation gets worse when a single bolt of lightning arcs from Hella's throne and hits one of the jeticopters. It whines as flames break out over one of the engines, and slowly, it starts to tilt. I see the pilot and gunners jump free, and it comes crashing down, where it explodes violently across the ground. Flames pour across the stone, shrapnel fills the air, and the concussive wave from the explosion hurts my chest. I see a hundred or more of the monsters fall dead, but still, it's not enough. And now we're down a jeticopter.

"Jason!" Elrith cries out as he suddenly appears at my side again. Sif's sword gleams in his hand, and he nods an acknowledgment to John. "Take out those two dragons, and I'll get these warriors to safety."

"You have a plan?" I ask.

Elrith smiles softly. "*We* have a plan. Just do it—trust me."

I nod to him, then break away through the monsters. Behind, I hear the warriors shouting as Elrith leads them toward one of the side tunnels. A few more of the warriors fall, but they seem to be doing better. As I charge the dragons, though, I have to wonder about Elrith's plan: the monsters all scream in delight and charge at the portal, since the last several barricades have now been removed, but there's nothing but a single jeticopter in the way now—and its steady stream of fire can only do so much. They crash toward the portal, scrambling, screaming, raging.

FOOOOOM!

A new blast of lightning erupts through the air and another portal opens right in front of the first one. I blink in surprise, but a smile breaks across my face as a stone giant steps out and lifts a huge club. It screams something in a language I don't understand, then charges forward as it swings the club with astonishing force. Monsters are sent flying like bowling pins, and with that, a torrent of creatures comes pouring out of the new portal.

Elves, a great many of them, come racing through armed with bows and guns and all sorts of other things. A torrent of projectiles pours forth and tears into Hella's army like a child through tissue paper. More giants thunder through. I see a small group of robed individuals, led by the one who fought me in the World Tree, The Master. Blasts of magic and lightning flash from his staff, and I smile again.

"Now *this* is what I'm talking about!" I turn back toward the dragons and put on a burst of speed. "Hella, we're coming for you!"

The two dragons snarl as I approach, and one of them bends down and opens its mouth wide.

Foooooom!

A blast of flame comes roaring out. I charge straight up the middle of it, hardly feeling anything more than a warm breeze, and jump up onto the top of its head as I come through the blaze. It doesn't even realize what's happened before I slash through its neck and sever its head from its body.

As the beast falls, its body flails about, and I use the momentum to launch myself at the second dragon. The beast snarls and turns to me, spreading its wings. I hit it in the chest and carve my dagger through its body, and it falls, dead, as I land on the ground.

[You have leveled up!]

[Congratulations! You are now Level 99!]

I let out a long breath, then slowly turn toward Hella's throne.

She's standing there, at the top of the stairs, staring down at me.

Her eyes are filled with hatred, filled with fury.

I smile, then charge forward through the ranks of beasts and monsters. Not a one can stand before me, not a one will dare step into my path. There are plenty who can't get out of it, sure, and those I cut through with ease. In any case, within a few moments, I arrive at the base of the long black stairs.

At the top stands the queen of the dungeons.

At the bottom stands Earth's champion.

Who will come out alive? There's only one way to find out. I slowly start up the stairs, and she slowly starts down.

[IceQueen: This is it!!! This is really IT!]

[RazorEdge: Whoever wins this battle will decide the fate of all humanity!]

[GoldenShield: I can't watch! I have to watch! I can't watch! I have to watch!]

[GrendleH8tr: Just . . . watch yourself, kid. You've got this.]

I draw in a deep breath. I know I've got this.

I *have* to have this.

Millions—no, billions are counting on it.

CHAPTER TWENTY-EIGHT

Hella and I meet in the middle of the long flight of stairs. No love is lost between us as we stare at each other, watching each other's every move. For a moment, neither of us speaks. Finally, Hella lets out a long breath, and she nods down at the chaos unfolding in front of the portal.

"I suppose you think you've already won, don't you?"

"Not at all." I shake my head. I don't dare look away from her, that's for sure. "Let's say that you beat me right now. You'll probably have to leave Earth without destroying it. Sad for you, but hardly a loss in its entirety. You'll have to spend a few millennia rebuilding your forces, but you'll be back. New generals. New troops. I hardly believe that Loki, Odin, and Thor weren't replaceable."

"You're a smart one."

"I haven't gotten to this point just by being strong," I snarl softly. "I don't take any risks I don't have to, but I don't waste the chances that I'm given. All you want to do is burn and destroy. You think you're a cold, calculating queen, but you're nothing more than a wannabe warlord, a titan gloating over the ruins of a cold and dark galaxy."

"And what makes you think that?" Hella snaps.

"It's simple," I answer. "You want to be more than a queen. You want to be a goddess. You want to be *worshipped*, but no one is going to worship the goddess of death. No one is going to worship someone who can be, and has been, defeated. Thus, your only course of action is to go through the multiverse and cut down anything and everything that stands in your way. You won't be able to rest easy until your goal is accomplished, and that won't happen until there's only one entity left in the entire multiverse—*you*. Then, and only then, will you be able to worship yourself in peace."

Hella's face twitches, and I know I've hit the mark. Maybe I'm not right on *every* subpoint, but I'm close enough that it's making her angry.

As I've learned, both from experience and from watching other people, anger only makes you more ineffective in battle. Temporarily more powerful, sure, but at the end of the day, you're far more prone to make mistakes. Somehow, I have a feeling that I'm going to need her to make as many mistakes as possible.

"You know nothing," Hella finally hisses.

"Denial." I hold up a finger. "That's the first sign of a guilty conscience."

Hella snarls, then draws out her sword. It's long and black, made of obsidian. It seems to have a reddish tinge, from the blood of the countless people who have died upon it. I brace myself, and she snarls again and steps back.

"Get him."

Her two wolves bound down from her throne, claws sparking on the stairs as they close in on me. I shrug and brace myself, then lash out as they leap at me.

My dagger-shaped staff cuts through the two of them like a hot knife through butter. Their body parts clatter down the stairs, and I spin back to Hella, only to realize that it was a trick. Her sword is already in motion, and it hits me in the chest with unfathomable force.

Whether by design or by accident, the flat of the blade hits me instead of the edge, and I'm lifted off my feet. I flash through the air, flying over countless stairs, and slam into the ground far below. To my delight, I *do* flatten several monsters. As I stagger to my feet, though, a hush seems to fall over the room.

Yeah, she hit me with the flat of the blade intentionally. She wanted to send a message to everyone watching, to her troops as well as mine. Slowly, she walks down the stairs, eyes blazing with fire, and begins to speak.

"If anyone here would like a lesson on what it means to stand up against me, hear this," Hella says forcefully and powerfully. "You cannot. I am the goddess of death. I am inevitable. Everyone is only alive for a short time, no matter how they try to extend their miserable existence. Death? Death comes for everyone." She laughs softly. "Death cannot be stopped. I am here, and you will all come to me."

"Uh, point of order!" I hold up a hand. "If death cannot be stopped, then it'll come for you too."

Hella snorts, though I see her face twitch. "I am the master of death."

"Then bring back your friends." I shrug. "I've killed a whole lot of people, including your top generals. If you're the master of death . . . prove it."

Hella's face becomes stony. With a scream, she jumps off the throne and sails to the ground, then lands with a powerful crash. Cracks spread out through the stone. She marches toward me, lightning blazing in her left hand, and I brace myself.

"Jason!" Elrith calls out. He throws Sif's sword back to me, and I catch it nimbly. I hold it tightly in my right hand, then draw out Thor's hammer in my left. It's not how I ordinarily dual-wield, but it'll have to work for the time being.

Hella attacks with fury and force. She swings high, and I flash up to meet her, where I catch her sword perfectly upon Sif's blade. A loud crack rings out, and a shock wave explodes through the room. The blades lock for an instant, and I throw Thor's hammer into her chest. She's battered back slightly by it, just enough to break the contact, and I spin and throw it again the moment it returns to my hand. This time Hella is ready: she parries the hammer and sends it clattering across the room to crash into the corner. Before I have a chance to recall it, she attacks again, and I parry once more.

This time she attacks coldly and slowly, slashing high, then low, then across. I parry or dodge each blow and find myself gasping with the effort. The blows are *so* powerful that each one nearly knocks the sword from my hand. I'm also pretty sure that I can see Sif's sword getting dented by the stone sword, but I'm not certain. In any case, I don't have the time to stop and check it. I have to fight, and to fight hard, and that's all there is to it.

I grit my teeth as Hella pauses her assault, and I launch myself forward. Both of my hands close down over the hilt of my weapon, and the clatter of steel upon stone rings out through the room as I swing at her again and again. I'm slowly becoming familiar with a sword, and my strikes are becoming more and more precise. I still don't manage to land a hit on her torso, but I do force her to defend herself more closely, which is nice. She snarls softly, then suddenly breaks back and holds out her hand.

ZZZZZZZZZZZAP!

A powerful blast of lightning flashes out and hits my sword, arcing down it like a lightning rod. My right arm falls limp, and the sword clatters to the ground. Hella smirks and rushes forward, and I'm left standing there.

Bong!

The hammer, which I finally call back to myself, catches her in the back. She's spun around by the force of the impact, and the hammer snaps into my still-functional left hand. Before she can recover, I throw the hammer again and hit her in the face. Her head is snapped back, and the hammer returns to my fist again. As she raises her head once more, staring at me with unbridled fury, I see blood trickling down her lip, down her chin, and dripping to the floor.

Unlike the other gods, it isn't golden. No, it's black, and it hisses as it hits the stone and starts to burn a hole through.

"Blood." I raise an eyebrow. "And here I thought you'd just be a desiccated corpse, being Death and all."

Hella responds with a scream. She lunges forward, and I parry her sword with Thor's hammer. It's far from perfect, but it does the job well enough. Slowly, she forces me backward, and I wish that I could just call the sword back to my hand as well. Suddenly, she snarls and lunges forward, then locks her blade underneath the head of the hammer. I grit my teeth as I fight back against the blade, against her strength, and she begins working to twist the hammer out of my grasp, pressing downward in an angle that my hands can't hold as well.

"Getting desperate if your only way to kill me is to disarm m—"

CRACK!

The hammer explodes under the force of her sword, and I'm suddenly left holding nothing but the weapon's wooden handle. I move to block, but she reacts too fast and spins around to perform a perfect slash across my chest. I'm knocked backward once again, but not nearly as far this time. Blood, an immense amount of it, drips down the front of my armor and onto the floor. I gasp in pain, and Hella presses the attack, striking again and again. She aims at my neck, and I only just manage to spin out of the way. At that moment, though, she fires a blast of lightning into my side. I stumble and start to fall, only for her to aim a kick into my chest. The wound flares up with unfathomable pain, and she kicks me up into the air to come crashing down on my back several feet away. Monsters and humans alike gasp in horror, and she slowly advances, letting the blade drag on the ground, sending up a spray of sparks.

"Is this how you thought you would go, Jason?" Her voice

is soft. "Is this how you thought you would end things? Lying on the ground, whimpering, crying out for the sweet release of death?"

"Yeah, I'm not doing any of those things," I groan as I start to rise. She whacks me across the side of the head with the flat of her sword and slams me to the ground once more. I taste blood in my mouth, and my health drops dangerously low.

"You will be," Hella snarls. "Kneel before me."

"Not a chance."

She slaps the sword across the side of my head once more. "I said *kneel!*"

"And I said you're deluded." I grit my teeth and stagger back to my feet. "Well, I didn't exactly *say* it, but—"

Hella's face grows stormy, and lightning begins to flicker from her fingertips. Ascalon grows warm across my back, and I draw in a deep breath.

[Skill: Bearing of a Knight.]

[Peril Detected.]

[Increasing Strength by 200%.]

[Increasing Dexterity by 300%.]

[Increasing Health Regeneration by 1,000%.]

[Increasing Damage Resistance by 500%.]

[. . .]

Hella lets out a scream and lightning blasts down around me. It tears up the stone around my feet. It arcs from fingertip to fingertip, from arm to arm. It *hurts* more than I can describe, but . . . I stay standing.

I stay upright.

And the moment it dies down, I move.

Hella seems shocked as I bolt out of the attack, dive past her, scoop up Sif's sword, and lash out at her. She's unable to block as I slash her across the stomach, drawing more thick black blood. She gasps and stumbles backward, and I press the attack. This time she blocks, but just barely, and I snarl and advance.

"You will *not* possess the Earth!"

"And I say that I *will*."

It's like arguing with a toddler. She screams as I slash across her shoulder, then she lunges forward rapidly. I block the attack, only to see the blade of Sif's sword shatter. Long, thin razors slash across my cheeks and forehead, and the broken pieces of the blade clatter to the ground. Hella smirks, then spins as she aims another blow crossways at my chest. I raise what's left of my own sword to block, and once more, her blow smashes straight through. Now I'm bleeding profusely and have exactly a quarter of a sword remaining. I smile, though, as Hella twirls her sword and takes a step back.

"You've fought well, Jason," she snarls. "But it ends here."

With that, she flashes forward and stabs at my stomach. This time, instead of blocking, I let her come.

And as her sword slams straight through my gut, I stab what remains of Sif's sword deep into her neck, just above the clavicle. She gasps, and a great deal of blood begins to leak down her front. Meanwhile, my world grows dizzy, and darkness begins to creep into my vision. Both of us let go and stagger backward, trying to stay upright.

Elrith is at my side immediately, grabbing my shoulders, holding me tight. Hella staggers back and collapses on the stairs. Another warrior, sensing an opportunity, charges forward, but she raises a finger and shoots a bolt of lightning through his chest. He collapses, dead long before he hits the floor, and I groan.

"Get it out of me," I murmur.

Elrith nods and steps around to my front, then pulls the sword out of my gut. Immediately, he begins applying a salve to my wound, and I gasp in pain. My health is sitting, once more, at a single point. The strike through the gut, by all reckoning, should have killed me. I don't know why it didn't . . . but I'm glad enough for that fact.

"Alright, Master. You've done well." Elrith starts to pull me away. "We'll take her from—"

Rrrrrrrrrrrrrrgh.

A massive form begins to emerge from behind the throne, and I look up to see Fenrir, thirty feet tall at the shoulder, slowly emerging from cover. Brilliant green eyes stare down at me, and he snarls softly, showing fangs that are as long as my torso.

"Master! You have to get out of here," Elrith orders.

"Do you have a Pumped!?" I ask him. Slowly, I reach out and take hold of the hilt of Hella's sword and wrap my fingers firmly and painfully around it. In front of me, Hella reaches up and rips the hilt of Sif's sword out of her throat, then slowly sits up. Her wound heals, slowly and surely, leaving a long scar across her already disfigured countenance.

"Right here." Elrith hands me a bottle. I bite the lid off, then guzzle it as I feel my health begin to rise. Across from me, Hella holds out her hands, and lightning begins to flash to her body as she recharges herself. Fenrir growls and steps forward, and I slowly turn to look up at him.

I'm fairly certain that I could kill one of the two of them, but if they attack me together, I'm toast. About that, I don't have a speck of doubt in my mind.

[ChaosRider: How's Jason getting out of this???]

[ShadowDancer: I thought for sure that he won when he stabbed her through the throat! I mean . . . come on, lady, just die already!]

[ViperQueen: I'm so scared. I feel like all of our lives are hanging in the balance right now.]

I close my eyes for a moment, and a single plan springs into my mind. It's not much of one, but . . . There's a skill that I possess. One that I haven't used in ages. One that just might be useful.

Hella smiles and, having healed just enough, slowly takes a step forward. Fenrir steps up next to her and leans forward.

"Alright, Hella." I crack my knuckles, then raise my left hand. "Time to end this."

"I heartily agree," Hella snaps. She nods at Fenrir. "Care to do the honors?"

Fenrir barks, then bounds forward. A grim smile breaks across my face, and I point my left palm at Fenrir.

"Skill: Monster Trainer."

CHAPTER TWENTY-NINE

ShadowDancer: No . . . He didn't just . . .]

[ViperQueen: HE DID!!!]

[DarkCynic: Don't get too excited just yet, guys. The odds of success are only 50% if the tamer is the same level as the creature. They're both Level 99, so . . . it could still go either way.]

[GoldenShield: Don't be such a Debbie Downer!]

[RazorEdge: Yeah! This is our last hope!]

Energy crackles from my palm and pulses across Fenrir's body. Hella screams and rises, but she sways after a moment and steps back onto the stairs. She's still weak and doesn't want to attack me while I'm holding her own weapon. That said, her eyes grow wild as I continue to try to steal away her only remaining ally.

[Fenrir is resisting your efforts to tame him.]

"I imagine that he is." I grit my teeth as energy crackles between our two bodies. "I don't really care if he lobbies a complaint with the supreme court."

Hella cackles and raises her hands as Fenrir growls. He can't move forward at all, but he can still glare at me, growling fiercely.

[Fenrir is resisting your efforts to tame him.]

Hella smiles as lightning crackles from fingertip to fingertip. With a flare, she blasts me with lightning. I raise her sword and find myself pleasantly surprised as the lightning simply curves and is sucked in by the black stone. Wonderful! Not quite what I expected, but really, it's even better in a lot of ways. Hella's face darkens, and she takes another step back. She's getting really nervous now, that's for sure.

[IceQueen: Hella looks like she's sweating bullets!]

[ChaosRider: Yeah! This is SO COOL!!! We're praying for you, Jason!]

[FireStorm: You can do it!!!]

Fenrir snarls softly and forces himself forward, fighting against the crackling energy.

[Taming attempt will fail in 00:00:05.]

I grit my teeth as the timer begins to count down.

[00:00:04]

"You're doomed, Jason!" Hella laughs. She seems to be relaxing as the timer slowly drains and the odds of my success lower. "You'll die like the dog you are!"

[00:00:03]

"I wouldn't insult dogs so much," I counter. "My own have saved me dozens of times, and right now, your only hope is that yours remains loyal. He might not like to learn that you think so little of him."

I see Fenrir's eyes widen slightly. I don't know how much

he can understand of my speech, but I'm sure that he can at least get a little bit of it—he *is* basically one of the gods, after all. I can't remember exactly, but I think he's, like, a son of Loki or something.

[00:00:02]

"Fenrir is loyal to me," Hella sneers. "He would never go with the likes of you. I own him. I own everything. And soon, you'll be so dead that you'll—"

[00:00:01]

[Fenrir has been tamed!]

My chat *explodes* with cheers, and I let the crackling beam of energy die down. Fenrir blinks a few times, then looks up at Hella. Hella, for her part, stares down at him rather dumbfounded. Slowly, Fenrir walks over to me and bows down, placing his enormous head upon the ground.

"Master." His lips don't move, but his voice trembles through the air. "You've . . . you've freed me."

"I do my best." I smile and pat him on the nose. "You're a good boy, aren't you?"

Fenrir begins to pant, and his tongue lolls out of his mouth. I open up my pocket dimension, and Bjorn, Astrid, Balder, and Gabe all come out. They start sniffing each other, and Fenrir slowly rises back up.

"I will serve you however you believe to be best." He nods firmly. "I can't express my joy at having those cruel shackles fall away."

"Well, I'm certainly glad to have you." I smile, then gesture up at Hella. "I know it's a lot, but would it be too insensitive to ask you to turn against your old master?"

Fenrir's eyes become hard, and he slowly turns around to face Hella. She flinches and backs up the stairs even faster, and he snarls.

"No, Master. It would not."

Hella screams, then turns and runs. Fenrir opens up his mouth and lets out a powerful howl, and a great torrent of wind blasts through the cavern. In that instant, a great many things happen. Every single evil monster is picked up and dashed against the walls, leaving only the armies of Earth and the few monsters who rebelled against Hella. The winds concentrate upon the throne, and Fenrir howls all the louder.

Cracks spread across the stairs, and the whole structure begins to crumble. Stone upon stone comes tumbling down, and Hella shrieks as she loses her footing and falls into the midst of it all. A great plume of dust and rubble explodes up into the air as it all crashes together, and I let out a long breath. "Wonderful!" Slowly, I take a step toward the pile, but Fenrir stops me.

"Don't ask me why, Master, but climb up onto my back."

I nod, then run to his right shoulder. His fur is long and thick, and I'm easily able to climb up onto his back, where I perch at the base of his neck. There's a long and painful pause, and then, slowly, the pile of rubble starts to shift.

With a mighty blast of lightning and fire, Hella comes roaring out of the pile, fury written across her face. She snarls and launches a great torrent of energy at us. Fenrir spins and catches the bulk of it with his side, then spins again as Hella flashes over our heads and flies for the portal. I don't know exactly *how* she's flying, other than simply that she's using some sort of magic, but she's fast. Fenrir bounds after her, and together, we all three go crashing through it.

The rift portal opens into Times Square, the very place where all this started—at least for me. Hella comes crashing to the ground, then holds out her hands. Two jeticopters spin to start shooting at her, and she fires thick bolts of lightning into their engines. Several nearby warriors rush to engage, and with a flick of her hand, she breaks their necks cleanly. Fenrir pounces forward and smacks her with a massive paw. She's thrown into the side of a building, and stone cracks under the impact. She groans and sinks to her knees, then draws in a deep breath.

"If I can't win, I'll take this world with me as I die."

With that, she jumps upward and flashes into the sky. Fenrir snarls, then speaks quickly.

"She's going to commit suicide by plunging into the core of the planet. The blast will destabilize the surface of the world. Earthquakes, volcanoes, tsunamis—it'll be bad. Almost every-one on the planet, if not everyone altogether, will die."

"Then we've just got to stop her." I draw in a deep breath and stand up. "Is there any way you can get her back down?"

"No, but I can get you up."

"That'll have to work."

I run up his neck and jump off his head, using his skull as a springboard. As I enter the air, Fenrir tilts his head back and opens up his mouth. For that moment, I'm suspended over his gaping maw, over teeth as long as my torso and a gullet that could swallow me whole.

And then he howls.

It's like being shot from a cannon, like when Balder bounces me with his shock waves. I'm launched upward like a rocket, sailing higher and higher into the sky, piercing the clouds. Ahead of me, I see a black speck that grows steadily larger. I prepare Hella's obsidian sword and grit my teeth as I come rushing up.

She doesn't see me coming. I flash right past her and slash her from her left ankle all the way up past her right eye. Black blood fills the air, and she pauses in flight. I reach the pinnacle of my own flight a second later and pivot downward to see Hella, arms spread wide, falling down toward the ground. I follow, spreading my arms and legs to control my descent.

The two of us smash into Central Park hard enough to leave massive craters and send rubble hundreds of feet into the air. I land about ten feet away from her and slowly rise to my feet to find the angry goddess struggling to stand up, dripping a great deal of blood. She snarls softly as I step toward her.

"Foolish boy." She cracks her knuckles and flings a bolt of lightning at me. I raise the sword and catch it, letting it fizzle away into nothingness. "I"—she throws another bolt—"am"—another bolt—"inevitable!"

She raises her hands, and an impossibly thick bolt of lightning falls down from the sky. I raise the sword and brace it with the flat of my palm.

BLAM!

The bolt hits with extraordinary force, and lightning arcs around me, forming a dome of sorts. It hurts—don't get me wrong—but I weather it well enough. As the blast dies away, Hella leaps at me, screaming wildly.

She throws a punch at my face, which I narrowly dodge. As I spin out of the way, I slash her across the stomach, then continue around and slash her across her chest. She gasps in pain, then snarls and makes a grasping motion. Black smoke pours out of the ground and wraps around my arms and legs, holding me tight, and she makes a lunging motion at the sword. I headbutt her in the face to keep her away, then flex my muscles and snap the black bonds. Hella gasps, then snarls and attacks once more.

I slash upward at her, but this time it's her turn to dodge. She catches hold of my wrist as it passes, twists sharply, and knocks the blade from my hand. It falls into her own palm, and she slashes at me as hard as she can. I only narrowly duck out of the way, then retreat several steps. A large rock on the ground catches my eye, and as Hella charges at me, I bend down, grab it, and fling it at her as hard as I can. It explodes into gravel against her face, and she blinks as she shakes it away. By the time she can see again, I'm already throwing a powerful punch into her chest.

The impact sends out a small shock wave, and she's slammed backward into the side of the crater. She groans and slowly staggers upright, and I run up and kick her in the side of the head, knocking her down once more. The sword falls from her grasp, and I reclaim it once more.

Before I can stab her, another smoky tendril erupts from the ground and wraps around my wrist. I'm not expecting it, so it yanks me off-balance, and Hella strikes an instant later with a kick in the chest. I'm lifted off my feet and thrown backward onto the ground, and I lose my grip on the sword yet again. As I recover and jump back up, a tendril snaps back into Hella's hand and the sword is returned to her once more.

"You're a good warrior, Jason," Hella snarls. "I'll make sure you have a nice *low* place in the afterlife."

I can only shrug. "It can't be much lower than yours."

Hella grips her sword and charges forward, only for something long and gray to flash through my vision.

It's Fenrir's tail.

[ShadowDancer: YEAH, Fenrir! You're the new MVP!]

[FireStorm: That was totally worth waiting for!]

[DarkCynic: Do it again!!!]

Hella gasps as the tail slams her into the ground. Before she can move, Fenrir spins around and bites down, pinning her between his teeth. She flails about as he lifts her up into the air, but he only bites down harder. Something cracks, and black blood begins to dribble down across the soil. It hisses, and I see several trees nearby wilt, but I don't have time to worry about those consequences. Slowly, I pick up her sword and walk toward her, gripping the hilt tightly in my hand.

"Hella." I speak softly. "Do you know how many people you've killed since you came to Earth?"

"Not a clue," she spits. "I don't count the deaths of humans any more than you would count the deaths of ants."

"And how many people have you killed on other worlds?" I press. "How many, Hella? How many innocent lives have been lost because of you?"

"I don't know," Hella sneers. "And I don't rightly care."

"You're not sorry for any of it?"

"I would do it all over again in a heartbeat." Hella draws

in a deep breath, and lightning begins to crackle in her eyes. "I *will* do it again. You might think you've won, Jason, but all you've managed to do is—"

I tune her out and lift the sword. "This is for you," I whisper softly. "This is for all the people we've lost. For all the people who have been lost on other worlds. This is for all the people who *would* have been lost." Hella catches my eye, and her own face twists into a countenance of hatred and defiance.

And with that, I bring the sword down.

Her head hits the ground with a *thump*, and the lightning dies away in her eyes. Fenrir slowly spits the body out onto the soil, then bounds away to one of the lakes to wash his mouth out. I sigh as I look down at the pitiful corpse.

"And to think," I mutter softly, "that all of this death and destruction was so that *you* could be worshipped as a goddess. All that death . . . and you'll be eaten by worms just like any of us."

I slowly walk away, leaving her body in the dirt. Fenrir walks back over to me, and together, we leave Central Park.

[DarkCynic: Was . . . was that it?]

[ViperQueen: I think it was!!!]

[FireStorm: Does that mean that the war is over???]

[GrendleH8tr: Yeah. Yes, everyone, the war is finally over. Hella is dead. The Earth is safe.]

[IceQueen: And it's all because of Jason Lee.]

[RazorEdge: Long live Jason Lee!!!]

[GrendleH8tr: Amen to that.]

CHAPTER THIRTY

I climb up on Fenrir's back, and we slowly make our way to the club that Mr. Wang owns. When we arrive, he lets me down to the ground, and I turn and look at the city.

New York, at this exact moment, looks like something from a post-apocalyptic movie. It's in a sorry state, but . . . as the sun slowly starts to set, I see lights flickering to life across the entire area. Power is coming back. Businesses are opening again. It looks simply lovely. A boombox starts to play from high above me, and I look up to see people in apartment buildings looking out through their windows. They're smiling, waving. A few people come out and start dancing in the street while a small jazz band struts out of a club with saxophones and trumpets. It's really quite the display, and I expect that it will only grow more and more intense.

"There's the man of the hour!" Mr. Wang walks out of the building, arms wide. "Jason Lee! You have no idea what I . . .

what the world . . . what . . ." A tear trickles down his face. "We all owe you one. We owe you two. Pfft, far as I'm concerned, if you want to run for world dictator or something, I'll vote for you."

I laugh and hold out my hand. He shakes it, and I pull him into an embrace.

"I couldn't have done it without you," I whisper in his ear. We pull apart, and I take a long deep breath. "That's the long and the short of it. Without your connections, without the ability to shoot me into random dungeons, without . . ." I find my hands trembling, and I turn to look at Fenrir. "Without my dear friends, who fought alongside me the entire time, it all would have been for naught."

Fenrir bows his head, and Mr. Wang waves at him.

"Well, don't just stand there! We're putting on the best party you've ever seen! You're heavy, but I'm sure I can pay off the building inspector just once if you'd like to come join."

Fenrir laughs, then shakes his head. "I know we haven't known each other long, but it was a joy fighting at your side, Jason." He leans forward and gives me an enormous lick, then steps back. "If you don't mind, I'm going to go ahead and leave. I imagine that I will become somewhat of a curiosity if I stick around populated areas, and after thousands of years of war . . . I'd rather go up to the northern wilderness for a few years."

"Of course." I smile. "If you ever need anything, you know how to find me."

Fenrir bows his head, then turns and bounds away. I watch him go, then turn back toward the club. Mr. Wang escorts me inside, and we ride up to the top floor.

There, the whole place has already been turned back into a proper club. Glasses are lined up on the bar, half a dozen grills have been set up on the helipad, and several drones carrying pizzas come flashing through a broken window as I walk inside. It's not the classiest food in the whole world, but honestly, it looks *just* like what I'd like to sit down and enjoy.

"You sure set this up fast," I comment as Mr. Wang and I step off the elevator.

"Ah, not really. I started putting it together as soon as you went off to fight Hella."

"Really?" I laugh. "You were that confident?"

"Meh. I figured that the odds were sitting somewhere at fifty-fifty," Mr. Wang answers. "If you won, I wanted a party ready. If you lost, I wasn't *losing* anything by setting this up, you know? Plus, it kept people busy instead of panicking, which I figured was a bonus."

"Well, I'm not complaining in the slightest." I shake my head and walk over to a table where a massive meat lovers pizza has just been set out. "I'll be right here. Let me know when I need to punch something else."

Mr. Wang laughs, and he walks off to meet with some other warriors just walking back into the headquarters. I help myself to a large slice of pizza, then lean back in my chair. It's not long before John and Ali join me—though, Ali slips over and takes a slice of vegan pizza from a different table first. None of us says anything for quite some time. Finally, John sighs, and he glances over at me.

"What are you going to do now?"

I shake my head and laugh. "I don't know. I came to New

York on vacation, and I have to say that it's been the craziest one I could have dreamed of. I suppose I'll just head home and see if there's anything left of the small town I came from. I still have the money from Mr. Wang, so I ought to have enough to help rebuild things, if necessary." I nod to him. "What about you?"

"I'm heading back up to my sister in Jersey," John answers. "She's doing alright—I just talked to her on the phone—but she's pretty shaken up. My house here in the city was obliterated, and it was just a rental anyway, so I don't really have anything keeping me tied down. I'll spend some time with her, then go from there."

"Ali?" I turn slightly. "What about you?"

Ali shrugs. She has to finish chewing before she can answer, but I already have a pretty good idea what she's going to say. "Honestly, my goal hasn't changed much. There are a *lot* of people who were displaced when the dungeons arrived, and it's a sure bet that others will do everything in their power to take advantage of the situation. I aim to plant my feet and stop as many of them as I can."

"A noble goal." John holds up a bottle of Pumped! in a silent toast.

"Well, I figure that Jason here fought his way through hell and back in those dungeons, trying to save our hindquarters." Ali shrugs. "The least I can do is keep up the fight back here on Earth."

"Now I sound pathetic." I snort. "I'm just heading home to take it easy."

"Jason, if you went and lay out in a hammock for the rest

of your life and required butlers to wait on you every moment of the day, it wouldn't be enough to repay the debt that we've incurred." Ali laughs. "You've earned your rest. Go home and get some sleep, and then, in a year or two, if you're still feeling like you need to do something, go join the Marines. With your superpowers, I'm sure you'll be the star of the show."

"Not a bad idea." John raises his glass again. "There wouldn't be a terrorist anywhere on the globe that would dare to stick their head out of the bomb factory."

"Well, I certainly appreciate your confidence in me." I shake my head in disbelief. "It's been a wild ride, that's for sure. I'm just so thankful for—"

A sharp ding echoes through the room, the sound of a knife on a glass, and the room falls silent. All eyes turn toward Mr. Wang, who's just mounted a small podium.

"Greetings." Mr. Wang's voice is firm, though it also holds traces of sorrow and joy. "I had intended this address to just be for the ears of those in this club, but thanks to the livestreams, as well as a recommendation from the president of the United States and a few other sovereigns, I have been asked to deliver a few remarks to the entire world." He draws in a deep breath. "So . . . here we go."

You could hear a pin drop as he moves into his speech. I'm among those captivated by his words, hanging onto every sentence.

"When the dungeons first appeared, about three weeks ago, I knew that the world had changed forever. I knew that the systems of money were changing, the systems of government, of entertainment, of commerce. What I couldn't have imagined was how our perception of people would change." He pauses for a moment, looking out across all of us. "When this all started, I saw dollar signs everywhere. As the war got going, I started to see more than that." A smile flickers across his face. "I saw pesos, euros, yen, pounds . . ." The room bursts out laughing, and Mr. Wang shakes his head.

"My point with this is that, as things continued, as the war intensified, I suddenly began to see lives as something more. None of us is immortal. None of us lasts forever." He holds out a hand, and his sister slowly walks up to join him. "*People* are what matter. There are billions of people on this planet, and every single one of them is a life. Every single one of them is a story written in a hundred different books, the books that make up the hearts and minds of those others we know, those we love and those we hate, those that obey us and those who tell *us* what to do. I've gained a whole new appreciation for it all, and . . . as so many of us do, I owe it all to a single man."

Something swells up in my heart, and I catch sight of several television cameras, which I'm just now noticing, swiveling in my direction. Mr. Wang motions for me to stand, and I slowly rise. The entire world is watching me, far more than have ever tuned into my stream. So . . . no pressure.

"Nothing I say could possibly put into words what Jason Lee has been through, the sacrifices he's made." Mr. Wang's voice is soft. "Nothing I say could adequately express my joy and delight at knowing that I had the brief pleasure of having him in my life. Thus, from the whole human race, Jason . . . Thank you. It isn't enough, but I do hope you'll accept it."

The room falls eerily silent, and all eyes focus on me. I draw in a deep breath and slowly put my hands behind my back.

"I . . . I don't like being up in front of crowds." I blush slightly. "What I *will* say is that I couldn't have done it without so many people. I had so many running support for me. Ali, John, Mr. Wang . . . the ones who jury-rigged the tech that shot me out into space . . . the cab driver who brought me back from the Statue of Liberty. There are so, so many, and"—my voice quivers—"I'm only sorry that I couldn't save more lives."

With that, I sit back down and the cameras pan back over to Mr. Wang. I notice Elrith standing next to him now. Mr. Wang clears his throat.

"We will now move into the more technical side of things. As you all know, the dungeons have been closed down. There still *are* dungeons that exist, but without Hella's power holding them together, they will begin to disperse and won't affect the Earth again, excepting the odd incursion, which, in years past, provided the foundation for our myths and legends." Mr. Wang's face begins to turn slightly red. "Warriors will notice their interfaces beginning to close down. All powers will fade, and, within an hour or two, you should be ordinary humans once more. In conjunction with that, the livestream feature that so many of you have grown to know and love will fade as well. I wish we could keep it—I do—but it was all being powered by Hella. The magical field has stuck around for a little bit, but it will soon fade."

A thought strikes me, and I quickly rise and slip out of the room. I'm near the back, and no one tries to stop me. I run down the hall and into the auditorium, the same one where we watched Hella's broadcast. There, I open up my pocket dimension and call out, "Bjorn! Astrid! Everyone!"

There's a thunderous rumble, and all my pets come bounding out. The portal begins to flicker and destabilize, and soon, it collapses upon itself. I bend down, and my pets press in around me.

"Ah, there we go! You're okay."

Master . . . Bjorn's voice sounds sad. *Master, your powers are fading.*

"I know," I whisper softly. "I just heard. That's why I got you out."

Bjorn and Astrid glance at each other. *Well . . . once they're gone, we won't be able to communicate with you anymore. We won't understand your speech, at least generally speaking, and you won't hear our thoughts.*

Horror shoots through me, and I sigh. Now *this* is the most heartbreaking thing of all. Slowly, I pull them in for a hug, and we spend a moment together.

"Well," I say quietly, "you've been the best friends that a guy could ask for. When my powers fade, I certainly won't ask you to stay with me. You're welcome to, of course, if you can bear me, but I won't hold it against you if you want to go live with Fenrir or something."

As I pull back, I look into the warm, loving eyes of Bjorn, then over to Astrid and Balder and Gabe. I look up to Lightfax, and to Burnie, who's perched on her head. I look to Blub, floating in the air nearby, and to Elrith, who's just slipped into the room as well. I look to Rat . . . Rata . . . Well, I can't remember his name, but it actually looks like he managed to slip away at some point. Oh, well. In any case, they all look back at me, but none of them says a word.

"They really do love you." Elrith walks up next to me. "If you'll allow, I'll take the ones who want it and will rehome them. I know some secluded places on Earth, and I might even be able to take them to some other realms with people of their kind."

"If they want to, I won't stop them." I nod as I stand up. "They've been through just as much as I have—more, really. Whatever they want, they can have."

Elrith bows, then speaks a long string of Elvish. Slowly, I turn around and start to walk away, back toward the club.

Back to figure out what to do next with my life.

The next several hours pass slowly. The world parties, New York lights up like the Fourth of July—no, really, there are a gazillion fireworks that go off overhead—and I join in the fun. I dance, I laugh, and, when the morning finally comes, I fall into bed and get the best sleep that I've ever had. When I wake up once again, I find everyone gone, but . . . there's a letter on my bedside table. On top of it is a set of keys. I slowly pick it up and frown as I read it.

Jason, this is for you. Parking stall ChaosRider7. Treat it well, and don't make me buy you another one. I'll catch you around. Don't worry, Jason . . . your adventures aren't done yet, not by a long shot—at least, if you're willing.

I laugh and stand up, then slowly make my way down and into the club. There, I have a bit of breakfast and find Ali and John. We say goodbye, and they show me sets of keys that *they* found upon waking up—along with very similar ominous-sounding notes. I take my time getting ready, then slowly make my way downstairs to the parking garage.

Somehow, I'm unsurprised to find a brand new . . . Well, I'm not a car guy, so I don't know the make or model or anything, but it's a *nice* car. Bright red, lots of curves, and one of those roofs that you can put down when the weather is good. I climb inside, fire it up, and slowly pull out into the streets of New York.

It takes me almost two hours to get out of the city. Traffic is already terrible as the world gets back to normal. Finally, though, I exit the metropolitan area and shoot down toward the mountains of Pennsylvania, where I'll then journey across to the plains of the Midwest. All around me are thick trees, marred here and there by claw marks or burn patterns across the trunks. I sigh deeply, then feel a smile flicker across my face.

Darting through the trees, keeping pace with the car, is a white wolf. Just beside him is his wife, and behind them comes their son. On the other side of the road, I glimpse a white horse, mane flowing in the wind, whipping between the trunks as if she were out on the open grasses. From above, a tiny level-two Phoenix swoops down and lands on my dashboard, then glances over at me. He doesn't say anything, and I reach out and caress the back of his head.

"Alright, you guys!" I call out loudly. "Let's see just how fast you can go! Horsepower against dungeon power?"

Lightfax is gone in a flash, shooting faster down the road, and Bjorn and his family speed up as well. I laugh and press down on the gas pedal, racing along the winding road. With that, as I move further away from the city, the last bits of my HUD begin to flicker and vanish.

[ChaosRider: I'm getting a notification that you're about to sign off for good. Bye, Jason! It's been great traveling with you!]

[RazorEdge: Yeah! I wouldn't have watched anyone else!]

[ViperQueen: Many thanks! Best wishes moving forward!]

[FireStorm: We love you!!!]

[GoldenShield: Drive safe! Wouldn't do for you to die in a car crash after surviving all of that.]

[LunarEclipse: Make sure to write!]

[DarkCynic: I have to admit, I would have done it all differently, but maybe that's for the best.]

[ShadowDancer: IT'S BEEN EPIC!!! GO ENJOY YOURSELF!!!]

[IceQueen: Dude . . . you're the best.]

[Originalgoth: Until we meet again.]

[ChaosRider: WAIT, WHAT?????????]

[Originalgoth: I'm just kidding. This is actually GrendleH8tr. Changed my tag, thought I'd mess with you. Go have fun! You've earned it.]

[Transmissions Ended.]

[All Powers Reset.]

[Disconnecting Livestream.]

ABOUT THE AUTHOR

Kaz Hunter is the author of the Apocalypse Reincarnation, System Bound, and Rise of the Strongest Sovereign series. A graduate of Texas A&M University (go, Aggies!), he started writing on Wuxiaworld and Webnovel. He has since moved on.

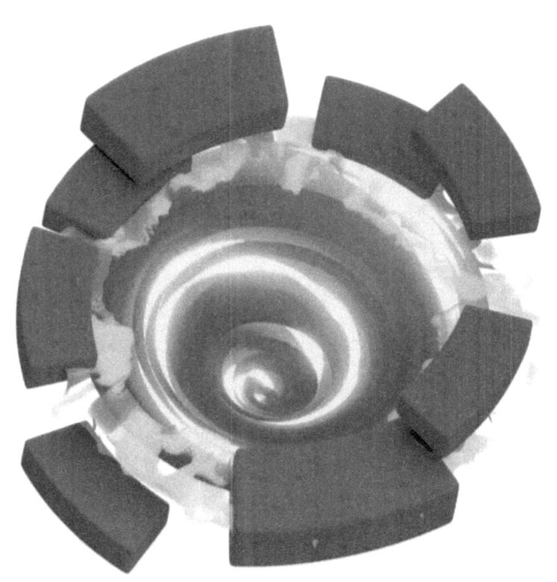

RESPAWN YOUR CURIOSITY

follow us on our socials

 podiumentertainment.com

 @podiumentertainment

 /podiumentertainment

 @podium_ent

 @podiumentertainment

9 781039 454651